Jerry Roth

Ghost from a Yard Sale

by

Jerry Roth

Published by Aberration Press Books 2025. Copyright © 2025 by Jerry Roth

This novel is entirely a work of fiction. The names, characters, and incidents portrayed in it are the work of the author's imagination. Any resemblance to actual persons, living or dead, events, or localities is entirely coincidental. They often claim designations used by companies to distinguish their products as trademarks.

All brand names and product names used in this book and on its cover are trade names, service marks, trademarks, and registered trademarks of their respective owners. I do not associate the publishers and the book with any product or vendor mentioned in this book. None of the companies referenced within the book have endorsed the book.

Hotel California – Written by Don Felder and Don Henley and Glenn Frey - Owned by Eagles, Ltd. Copyright (1976).

Lyin' Eyes – Written by Don Henley and Glenn Frey – Owned by the surviving heirs and estates of Don Henley and Glenn Frey. Copyright (1975).

First edition ISBN: 978-1-7369804-5-3

Photo of St. Pious – Perry County Historical and Cultural Arts Society

Editing by Elle Turpitt & Ellie Killiam. Cover by Matt Seff Barnes and artwork by Jerry Roth

<u>**Early praise for Ghost from a Yard Sale**</u>

*"**Combining small-town paranormal mystery with a dose of splatterpunk** ...* Roth does a sterling job of navigating the paranormally strange narrative with Harper's deteriorating mindset. A horror novel that evokes memories of films like Poltergeist and The Haunting and books like Needful Things." -**Independent Book Review**

*"**A horror outing that delivers, thanks to its memorable settings and robust cast.*** Roth's action-laden horror tale sets terrifying encounters in various memorable locales, including Moxie Manor. Strange and terrible incidents ... paranormal sightings, murders, assaults, disappearances abound in the narrative." -**Kirkus Reviews**

*"**Ghost From a Yard Sale is Roth's most ambitious horror work to date*** ...* buried histories that slowly crawl to the surface, ghosts, ravenous tree monsters ... Roth manages to knot all the loose ends together in a creepy, dramatic denouement that readers probably won't see coming ... not without a sizeable mangled body count." -**Perry County Tribune**

For Tricia. You have been the unwavering light through every chapter I write. I am endlessly grateful that I've walked this path with you.

In 2020, we moved into an old church called St. Pious also known as *Moxie Manor*, nestled in the forgotten corners of Moxahala, Ohio. The idea was simple—immerse myself in a chilling new environment to spark inspiration for my next horror novel. What I got was far more than I ever bargained for.

To breathe authenticity into the story, I dove into the local legends and whispered lore passed down through generations. Because the church gave us a disjointed feeling with every step inside, my goal was to match that sensation with each transition from one character to the next like a ghost wandering between the veil. Every photo of *the church* featured in the book is real. The scenes I wrote were stitched together from fragments of truth, eerie inspiration, and the darker corners of my imagination.

A note to the curious among us
Things in this story are not meant to be seen at first glance.
Ink fades, shadows linger, and secrets settle beneath the surface.
If something feels ... off, it probably is. Trust your instincts—and pay attention to the small details. Grab a magnifying glass and you might find more than you bargained for.

. . . Welcome to Moxie Manor

"Some houses are born bad."

—*Shirley Jackson*

"The scariest ghost is the one you invite in."

—*Unknown*

Chapter One

WELL-LOVED

*B*reathless, Harper Finch opened the door to find her dead daughter's nightgown ripped apart. Seeing the border collie in the act was like stumbling upon a crime scene. Her plan had been to dress her infant in a nightgown, cap, and socks. None of that happened. The injustice stirred her anger.

Her eyes twitched as they followed the puppy, playing rough with something so heartbreaking to look at, let alone watch it torn to shreds. Her spine pressed against the wall. The outrage demanded justice—punishment. Each bite of cloth was a reminder of the life she was supposed to have. An urge to scream began in Harper's belly.

"Why did you do that? Stop it! Just … stop!"

Harper's voice, choked and twisted, emerged from her throat as a raw, jagged sound, utterly unfamiliar. She glared at Twix, her husband's "thoughtful gift" as the dog destroyed the delicate nightgown. The garment was supposed to be her daughter's, cradling her tiny body. Instead, there was no child. Just a dog ripping and tearing at the cloth as if it were nothing but a chew-toy. Her breath came in shudders, anger and heartbreak biting at her. Each jerk made her feel as if *she* were between his teeth.

"You fucking mutt! It's not for you!"

She screamed until her voice splintered. Her hands balled into fists, knuckles white with the urge to grab and snatch that precious fabric back from jaws that didn't deserve it. Rage, hot and electric, flared through her veins, tightening her throat, making her body tremble. She couldn't remember the last time she'd fought against anything so powerful, so primal and wild. This wasn't just anger; it was a deep grief mixed with fury, burning through her like fire.

"That was hers, you piece of shit! Do you understand me? That was hers! Not yours. Not some plaything!"

But Twix didn't understand. He couldn't. He looked up at her with big, clueless eyes, his mouth still holding pieces of what should have been her daughter's first outfit. The betrayal of something so cherished, something that should have meant safety and love, ripped apart by this clueless animal. The unfairness of it, the injustice of it, clawed at her heart until she was hollow inside, as if he'd torn her heart to pieces too, leaving it scattered across the floor along with the shredded fabric.

"Do you know what you're doing to me? Do you have any idea?"

Her voice cracked as a sob shook her whole body. She couldn't see through the flood of tears, but she didn't care. The anger and despair were too much to contain, the pain too sharp to swallow. She dropped to her knees, reaching out to gather the tattered, ruined cloth as if that would somehow bring it back, somehow make it whole again, make her whole again.

"You're just a stupid, thoughtless animal! You don't know what you've taken from me, do you? You destroyed it!"

She cried, hands clutching the scraps, feeling the soft fabric. She had imagined dressing her daughter in it a thousand times, guessing the way her little face would look peeking out, her tiny fingers reaching up, grabbing hold of her hand. But now that image was gone, like the dress. She couldn't escape it. The realization hit her over and over, each time a fresh stab of pain: her daughter was gone, and severed pieces were all she had left.

Harper looked down at Twix, who had the nerve to wag his tail, as if everything were fine, as if this had meant nothing, as if he hadn't just destroyed one of the few things she had left of her child. Her face filled with blood. Her chest heaved with the effort to breathe, to steady herself, to resist the urge to scream until there was nothing left of her.

"You can't replace her," she whispered to herself. "I will never love you."

She pulled the remains of the gown to her chest, rocking back and forth, tears streaming down her face.

There was no evidence that the puppy cared if she was in the room, let alone plotted the dress's destruction. It was the carnal thrill of the fabric between his teeth, and Harper winced with every scrape of his canines across the delicate material.

Steadying herself first on her knees, then on wobbly feet, Harper shuffled toward the gnawing pup with renewed purpose. For the first time since she'd caught him in the act, he acknowledged her presence. His jaw slowed, head tilting in a wary motion at her approach. Eyes locked onto eyes as she bent down, hands reaching for a leash and slipping the latch onto its collar.

A hint of guilt curled up next to satisfaction at the minor victory. And as she twirled her hand, the slack in the leash dwindled; the distance between the rivals vanished. The hand tangled within the leash jerked too hard for a puppy, but miles away from her intention. The dog's yelp mirrored the guilt. The guilt she pushed deep into the regretful part of her brain.

"Bad dog!" There were no bad dogs, only bad owners, according to the experts. Nothing could convince her of that.

She led the scrambling collie from the room and down a dark corridor, the baby clothes she'd been folding left behind. Her curly brown hair bounced with each step, and her shadow, cast by the moonlight from the windows, mimicked her every move.

For over a century, the red brick walls of the church had stretched three stories high. When they'd first toured the place, the sheer enormity had jolted her senses. She couldn't imagine owning such a cavernous structure as a home.

Breathing was something she took for granted until she spent time inside the walls of the former Catholic church. Inhaling became a conscious effort. The aroma was pungent in the way graveyard soil might smell, as if past lives had left their mark on the skin of the interior. The odor pushed inward with every step Harper took. Memories from the house's past mingled with the stench and floated into her nostrils.

She swept the thought away and focused on the labyrinth that was her new home. With a few twists and turns, she found the right door leading outside.

Cold air slapped her face, harsh and frigid. Even Twix yelped as they left the warmth inside. The cobblestone walkway wound toward the driveway before vanishing around a bend, and Harper saw a trace of her usual self. As Twix scampered and sniffed the ground, her mood lightened, and the dog's poor behavior faded into that part of her mind where minor annoyances went.

"Potty, Twix?" The dog sniffed, hunting for the perfect spot. He tugged on the leash, and she let him lead, the motion grounding her. The haunting returned. Thoughts she couldn't share with anyone, least of all her husband, Caspar. They attacked her sanity like an infection turning on its host.

Twix's black and white fur flickered in and out of sight as moonlight filtered through the trees. After a pause, he found his spot, sniffing one last time before squatting. Harper turned away, hoping never to grow accustomed to the sight. As Harper glanced back at the towering structure that was now her home with the bell tower staring down.

A familiar chill settled in her bones. Each shadow, stretched thin under the moonlight, made the church appear less like a home and more like an ancient sentinel watching over her. Dark windows, some still bearing stained glass, shimmered. A gust of wind whipped around the building, carrying a faint echo of something she couldn't quite place—a whisper lost to the night.

Harper glanced across the street at the house opposite, a generous term for the dilapidated farmhouse, with its chipping white paint and sagging porch roof. But it was the windows that haunted her, black and lifeless, like the eyes of a watching monster.

Twix gave a sudden tug, followed by a low, uneasy yelp. Glancing down, she found him rigid, his ears pulled back. When she looked up again, her heart skipped. On the decayed farmhouse's porch, between two columns, stood a child. Harper blinked, a chill running down her spine. She'd seen no one enter or leave the house since they'd moved in.

The figure was slight, framed against the peeling wood, a girl in a white nightgown that fluttered in the breeze. Harper's mouth went dry as she took in the scene. There was no wind, no reason for the gown to stir. And yet, it moved, as if pulled by an unseen force.

The child clutched a pink teddy bear with snowflakes within her thin arms, its head flopped to one side over her forearm from the force of her grip. Harper's thoughts spun as she looked at the child, who stood motionless. Harper blinked hard, rubbing her eyes, questioning her own vision. But as her sight cleared, the girl remained a solid form two hundred feet away.

"Are YOU okay?" The roar of a passing truck swallowed her voice. Twix pricked his ears but stayed fixed on the silent figure. A flicker of movement caught Harper's attention as the girl shifted, gliding down from the porch steps. She moved with an eerie grace, each step light and deliberate, as if she could cross a field of eggs without cracking a single shell.

The girl's white nightgown drifted around her as she descended the stone path toward the highway, her gaze locked onto Harper. In the pale moonlight, Harper SAW her face more clearly. Round, with cherubic cheeks and spirals of brown curls framing her jaw, an uncanny reflection of herself as a child.

A pang of unease lodged in Harper's chest, sharpening her breath. Why would the child seek the road so desperately? Her thoughts tangled in unanswered questions. But beneath her worry, a more chilling realization formed—the girl looked like her, or a daughter that would never be.

Ignoring the strange resemblance, Harper took a step forward, leading Twix closer to the road. The girl mirrored her, each small limb moving with purpose. They moved toward one another across the divide, headlights flickering past on the highway between them.

"Can I help you?" Harper called out, but the girl's expression didn't shift; there was only a steady longing, with no trace of fear or hesitation. The girl's feet stepped onto the road as if drawn forward by some invisible force. Harper's gaze snapped to an oncoming truck in the distance, its engine growling as it barreled down the slope. A driver who wouldn't see them until it was too late.

"Stay there!" Harper's shout cut through the night, but the girl either didn't hear or didn't care, her slim figure still moved forward.

Twix, agitated, yanked hard on his leash. Harper fumbled, her fingers slipping as he broke free and dashed after the girl into the street. Time thickened around her, slowing her thoughts as her body surged forward, the sense of imminent disaster pulling her into motion.

The leash flapped behind Twix, his legs a blur as he bolted toward the girl. Headlights loomed from the darkness. The roar of the engine grew louder. Panic jolted Harper as she saw that not one, but two figures were now in the truck's path. Without hesitation, she plunged down the steep embankment, sliding toward the flat stretch of asphalt below.

Twix and the girl were moving to each other like characters in a heartfelt reunion. The possibility of a vehicle crushing into the child on the road flashed in her mind, fueling her with desperate energy. As her feet hit the road, Harper saw with chilling clarity that she, too, would soon be on the truck's path.

She sprinted, closing the gap just in time to reach Twix before he crossed into the center lane. In one swift motion, she grabbed his leash and wrapped it around her hand, yanking him close as she extended her arms toward the girl, ready to pull her to safety. But the girl's expression stayed fixed on her goal, oblivious to the danger, even as the truck's headlights surged over the hill, bathing them in blinding light. *We're not going to make it,* Harper thought, the realization heavy and sharp.

She tugged Twix closer, then lunged for the child just as the truck's hulking frame thundered past. A sharp clip of the side mirror against her shoulder awakened a pain in her. The impact spun her off balance. Stinging pain rippled across her skin, but she landed on the asphalt, unharmed. The truck's taillights receded into the night, never slowing.

Twix sniffed at the ground, his excitement of the chase already forgotten. Harper scrambled to her feet, her gaze darting in search of the girl. But she was gone. There was nowhere she could have hidden—no bushes, no trees close enough to cover her escape. Harper's eyes drifted to the soft mud along the roadside, where tiny footprints marked the soil.

Twix lowered his nose to the prints, then lifted his head to look back at Harper. "Where did she go, boy?" As if answering, Twix turned to gaze at the old farmhouse, and Harper followed his lead. She saw the front door boarded shut, its weathered wood long untouched.

They stood there together, staring at the empty house, the weight of the silence settling around them.

Harper spotted a vein in Caspar Finch's neck bulge. She still couldn't understand why they were hauling an arcade machine up the church steps, or why Caspar recruited *her* to help.

"You make good money. Can't you sell a few more books and hire someone to save our backs?"

"It would be nice if I could," he admitted.

"What do you mean?"

"Nothing. You write a book, and we'll talk." He slapped on a cheerful smile. "It's not that heavy." Caspar smirked, which only made her imagine the hulking 80s arcade machine sliding backward and flattening her against the stairs. "And make sure not to give one of my books to the people we bought the house from. The last time you did that I got a bad review for our troubles. At least until you know they're not Goodreads assassins."

"Only if this is the last arcade I have to move, right?" Harper asked, exasperation creeping into her voice. Caspar ignored her.

They wrestled it up the last step into the loft. As soon as they reached the flat surface, the machine's back wheels kicked in, and it glided to its new home.

"We got you now, Pac-Man!" Caspar shouted, still catching his breath. Harper hung back as he nudged the machine into place.

"You know." Still adjusting it. "Pac-Man was the first ghostbuster—way before Bill Murray and Dan Aykroyd."

He grinned as if struck by brilliance, then stared down over the open loft to the living space below.

His readers would be surprised to know he was a geek at heart. It had been his love for Star Wars and role-playing games that won her heart. Why°he wrote horror instead of fantasy eluded her.

"This place is incredible." Harper glanced around at the manor's sprawling interior.

"I'd say so." The arcade machine held Caspar's gaze. You know how many people got married here?" She shook her head. "Half the town sat under this roof or got hitched here." He wiped sweaty hair from his forehead.

"The real question is, how many corpses were brought in for funerals?"

Caspar's gaze drifted from the arcade machine's flashing lights. "I never thought about that." Pac-Man's iconic *Wakka Wakka* filled the silence. With a bemused shake of his head, he turned back to the screen.

"Caspar, can we talk for a minute?" Harper asked.

"Huh? Is it the puppy?" He sounded impatient. She shook her head.

"No. Well, yes. But it's ... something else." The image of the girl filled her mind, and a chill spread over her. "Come with me a sec?"

Caspar sighed, but she ignored his irritation and led him downstairs to the center of the house. The living room, bordered by the loft above, made her feel trapped, as though she were in a pit. Despite the soaring cathedral ceiling and exposed wooden beams, there was a sensation of claustrophobia.

"What is it?" Caspar's tone had sharpened, pulled away from his 80s escape. She brushed off his annoyance and pointed to the massive window facing the highway.

With a slight flourish, Harper drew back the curtains, revealing the farmhouse across the road. The old place sat framed in the window like a haunting photograph.

"It's that." She gestured like a game show host presenting a prize. "That house."

Caspar stared through the glass, waiting as if the answer would come to him. It didn't.

"Did someone die there? Is that why we're here?" Harper asked.

"I'm not sure yet."

"I need to know about that house." Harper's gaze held a resolve.

"It's … just a vacant home," his tone flat. She sensed guardedness, something buried under his casual words.

"What's the history? What happened there?" Her voice was steady, but as she looked at him, unease prickled through the room like a gathering storm. His expression shifted from tense to calm, like he was forcing himself to act casual.

"No," Harper cut in, raising a hand to stop him. "Don't treat ME like I don't belong here. I'm your wife, Caspar—not some stranger." Guilt flickered in his eyes.

"It's not that I think of you that way." He rubbed his face with deliberate slowness. "I just … want to protect you."

"From what?"

He glanced out the window, toward the decaying farmhouse. "A little over a year ago. That's when it happened." Harper opened her mouth to ask what, but he continued. "A family lived there—the place looked just like that. Run-down, standing. But they got by. The father did odd jobs, the mother grew vegetables. Modest, but they managed."

"What happened to them?" she prompted, unable to keep the urgency out of her voice. Caspar looked at her for a long moment.

"They disappeared."

"I don't understand. What do you mean 'disappeared'?"

"One day they were there, and the next, *poof*." Caspar made a vague, magician-like gesture. Harper's thoughts stumbled to a halt.

"What did the authorities find?" She turned her gaze back to the farmhouse, the windows looking like watchful eyes, the door a dark, open mouth. Caspar moved beside her, wrapping his arms around her. His embrace was a smothering weight.

"Was there a little girl who lived there?" she whispered with a voice muffled against his chest. "Missing children are the center of all the books you write." Caspar tensed with a face as pale as she'd ever seen it.

"What made you ask that?" His voice was low, his usual warmth replaced by a wary edge. He rubbed his stubble, an unconscious gesture he used when trying to calm himself.

"Answer me first." She watched his expression.

"There was a girl. Riley Spears." His gaze darted toward the farmhouse, then back to her, searching for signs in her face. "How did you know?"

"I must have heard it somewhere," she lied. She wasn't one to hide things from him, but now the truth was too strange to share. She avoided his gaze, feeling the weight of her own deception. "Why didn't you tell me?" she asked, her voice thick with hurt. "People vanished where we are now living, and you kept it from me?"

He sighed. "Would you have agreed to move here if I'd told you?"

"Who knows now? I don't want to live under a ceiling so high I feel small, or across from a house that hides God-knows-what!" She gestured toward the looming farmhouse beyond the window. "How am I supposed to sleep at night, knowing something so dark—"

"Mysterious," he corrected.

"—happened right there?" Her last word echoed in the manor's expanse. Twix's pitiful yelp echoed from another room, breaking the silence.

"Saved by the dog." Caspar forced a smile. "Your pup's awake."

"This conversation's far from over." She watched him retreat toward his office and thoughts of his next book. Alone in the stillness, Twix's cries pulled her from her brooding. But something flickered at the edge of her vision, a slight shift near the farmhouse.

A shape stood on the slanted porch, motionless under the thin moonlight. Harper's feet moved from their own accord, carrying her to the window. Her rational mind dismissed it as a shadow, a trick of the light. But something in her refused to believe it.

"I'm coming, Twix." She tore her gaze away. When she looked back, the figure had blurred, fading into darkness. The urgency that captured her slid away. A strange calm settled over her. She moved toward the dog's insistent whining, but her mind lingered at the window, where shadows whispered secrets just beyond her understanding.

Chapter Two

Junk Drawer Special

*E*choing in her mind, Harper couldn't shake the feeling that Caspar was lying to her about the abandoned house and the owners that vanished. She'd learned that writers were a secretive bunch, and although she had no reason to mistrust him, her mind tingled from the possibilities.

Twix sat in the passenger seat like a suitor on his best behavior rather than a dog along for the ride. She should've put him in a crate, but the long night of taking him out for bathroom breaks had worn her resolve. Who was training who? She watched as he steadied himself with his paws—until a pothole jolted him off balance, sending him sprawling across the seat like a drunken sailor. Despite her irritation, she couldn't help but laugh.

"It's you and me for a while, Twix." She glanced over. Twix turned his head, looking up at her as if he was clear about everything she said. When she pressed the window button, the glass slid down, and his ears flapped in the wind as he faced forward, eyes squinting in bliss. His fur rippled in the breeze, and she sighed. "At least one of us should be happy."

Twix ignored her, mesmerized by the rushing wind and the blur of scenery racing past. Her initial fondness faded as she watched him, giving way to a bitter realization. *Twix is a replacement for your baby.* The thought stung as its truth settled over her with a heavy weight. It wasn't a sudden flash of understanding, like in movies WHEN characters see the truth. She'd known Caspar's intention the moment he brought home the collie; part of her had even wanted it. She'd thought the helpless puppy could fill the void of not carrying her own child to full term.

Growing up, she'd never had a pet—her parents thought THEY were too messy—but she'd always wanted something to love, something that needed her. Now, Twix was here, all paws and fur, but he wasn't the child she'd hoped for. The rawness of that unfulfilled desire lingered, nagging at her like a wound that wouldn't heal. The tears that formed in the corner of her eyes were salty, warm, and unexpected.

Not wanting Twix to notice, she reached for the radio and twisted the dial until a familiar voice poured through the speakers. Hotel California by the Eagles filled the car, echoing in the darkness, pooling in her chest. The song was perfect, mirroring her own tangled emotions too well. She hummed along, the haunting melody amplifying her sadness, fueling a lingering self-pity. She and Twix were opposites. He, delighted by the wind and freedom. And she, feeling like she was disappearing, like the missing girl across the street.

Her vision blurred as tears spilled over. She blinked hard, trying to focus on the road, but the ache wouldn't let go. Ahead, a bright yellow poster board caught her eye. *Yard Sale*, it read in handwritten letters. The sign was a small mercy, an excuse to pull over before her grief took her somewhere worse.

She eased off the gas and steered toward the roadside, her hands trembling as she wiped her eyes. For now, this distraction would be enough.

Through the windshield, Harper took in the sprawling yard sale, where folding tables stood in all directions on the lawn. The tables looked haphazard, but she noticed the method and saw their arrangement in a winding maze. Clever—everyone had to walk through the whole setup, like a curated exhibit.

Rubbing away the last traces of her tears, she saw Twix craning his neck out the car window, bewildered by the sudden lack of wind in his fur.

"Let's stretch our legs, boy." She clipped on his leash. Twix hesitated, casting one last wistful glance at the open window before hopping down and falling into step behind her.

The swarm of people darting from table to table captivated Twix. Harper smiled at his wide-eyed wonder. "It's quite the show, huh? All this fuss over other people's leftovers." She gave his leash a gentle tug and guided him into the commotion.

Harper wasn't a regular at yard sales; they were more of a whim, like impulse buys at a checkout line. She'd always thought of them as a classic Midwest trap, colored signs luring in travelers with promises of hidden treasure. Springtime was prime season for these sales, and there wasn't a street corner without a neon sign pointing the way to "attic gold" and forgotten trinkets.

The other customers, however, didn't like casual browsers. They moved with purpose, scanning each item with the calculating gaze of a treasure hunter. In the era of eBay and Facebook Marketplace, everyone was hoping to stumble upon a miracle or hidden gem (like an original copy of the Declaration of Independence) that would make them an instant millionaire. But for most, Harper suspected, it was the thrill of the hunt that kept them coming back.

She sidestepped an older couple in surgical masks rummaging through a bin of dusty picture frames, a lingering reminder of the 2020s pandemic. As she maneuvered around them, a younger man barreled into her, his eyes glued to his phone. Harper pulled Twix out of the way just as the man's foot landed where the dog had been.

"Excuse you," she said to get his attention.

"Excuse me," he replied, still scrolling.

"It's Friday. Shouldn't you be at work?" Her comment went unanswered as he stopped to photograph a table of tarnished war memorabilia, talking into his phone, "Here they are ... are they rare?"

She led Twix deeper into the maze of tables, past rows of clothing, dishes, and assorted odds and ends. Something on a nearby table caught her eye—a small, worn baby video monitor. Harper stopped, transfixed.

"Are you alright, dear?" An older woman's voice broke through the static. Harper glanced up, realizing she hadn't moved. Twix had seized the pause as an opportunity to gnaw on her shoelaces, growling with each tug.

"Need help with something?" the woman persisted, smiling as she watched Harper's gaze drift back to the small screen of the device.

"Oh, no ... I'm fine, thank you." Harper fought off the obsession over the small screen in front of her.

The last word came through the fog in Harper's mind, bringing her back from a distant place. She blinked, her gaze lifting to meet the woman's cheerful expression.

"Your dog's having a field day with your boots." The woman chuckled, nodding toward Twix.

"Stop it." Harper tugged her foot away. "You little maniac."

"I'm Carol." A hand extended over the table, crowded with miscellaneous items, feeling guarded in Harper's haze. She took it, feeling her focus sharpen as her vision drifted back to the item that had caught her attention.

"Harper Finch." She met Carol's steady gaze.

"You're not from around here, are you?" Carol asked, still holding Harper's hand for an instant too long.

"How'd you guess?" Harper raised an eyebrow, glancing back at the strange item on the table.

Carol's laugh was sharp and loud, surprising Harper enough to make her take a half-step back. "It's in the way you stand, like you're just passing through. Most folks around here blend into the scenery—you *are* the scenery." Carol rearranged clothes on the table.

"Or maybe I moved back here?" Harper suggested, letting her gaze drop back to the object.

Carol shook her head with a knowing grin. "People born in the Appalachians don't just leave. When things get tough, we dig in—like ticks, you might say." She laughed again, louder, and the sound jolted Harper out of her trance.

Harper's eyes fixed on the device half-buried beneath a pile of old clothes. Carol's words became a murmur in the background.

"Is that for sale?" she pointed.

Carol followed her finger to the baby monitor, pulling it out from beneath a tangle of shirts. Its plastic casing had yellowed with age, and the small monitor had a screen that sat scratched and foggy.

"Are you serious?" Carol asked, puzzled. "Of course it's for sale. Everything here is." She looked at Harper with renewed interest.

"Does it still work?" Harper's voice seeped with desperation. Her gaze never left the device.

"I plugged it in once—it lit up. Five bucks?" Carol asked, eyebrows raised.

"Deal." Harper fished a crumpled bill from her pocket and pressed it into Carol's hand. She clutched the monitor as if it were something rare and precious. Even Twix stopped gnawing and sat up, cocking his head at the unusual item.

"Where'd you get this?" Harper asked, her eyes never left the device.

"A rummage sale, maybe? Sometimes stuff from foreclosed houses ends up in church sales." Carol's gaze dropped to Harper's flat stomach before rising again. "If you don't mind me asking…" She paused. "Why would you want an old baby monitor?"

Harper hesitated, glancing down at Twix. "This one can't be trusted yet." She gestured to the dog.

"So, you said you just moved here?" Carol asked.

Harper nodded. "Moxahala."

"Oh, Moxie, huh? Nice little place." Her smile fading.

"We're in the old church—the one that used to be called St. Pius."

At this, Carol's expression shifted, and she made the sign of the cross in the air. "Well, good luck to you." A faint smile returning to her face. She took a step back from the table, her gaze lingering on Harper, a beat too long.

With the baby monitor against her, Harper turned and walked away, a faint chill trailing after Carol's words.

Chapter Three

Too Good to Be True

Surrounded by silence, Caspar Finch saw the church as a world of shadows, with its vaulted ceilings stretching high above. Drawing his gaze up toward where the echoes of past sermons might still linger. Caspar's footsteps rebounded, each one magnified in the cavernous space, as if he were an intruder. His fingers brushed the cold, rough surface of the stone walls, still scented with incense and aged wood, a ghostly reminder of the building's past. He° glanced up at the loft, where narrow arches cast jagged shadows across the open space below, making him feel insignificant—like something was always watching from the dark. He reached his writing room, a space that still carried the weight of its past. The locals had named his church-turned-home "Moxie Manor," a knick name for the town and a label that suited the seductive curves of its doorways and the stained-glass windows peering down.

No matter how many awards he stacked on the shelves or books he placed on display, the bones of the old church showed through, like a stain that couldn't be covered°up no matter how many coats of paint.

Caspar's writing room, tucked into what had once been a confessional, exhaled the church's ancient history. Light filtered through a narrow stained-glass window, casting fractured reds and greens across the wooden floor, like patches of old blood. The air was heavy with secrets°, pressing down on him as if to say, 'You are not alone.' Even in°the stillness, Caspar could sense a presence, a silent congregation of memories crowding around him, watching, waiting.

He'd convinced himself that filling the room with enough accolades would make him believe he was a talented author. The°more books he published, the more signings he held, and the more fans he gathered. But it never killed the imposter syndrome. After each novel, doubt crept back, nestling close like an unwanted lover.

This had been his routine for over a decade, and it had worked. Mostly. But this time, something was different. Moxie Manor, with its red brick exterior and imposing architecture, wasn't like the rest of his former homes°. He stared at the paneled wainscoting, which had stood for over a century, and imagined that it had grown from the ground itself. As if ancient roots held it there, wise and unyielding.

Even though Caspar had walked away from religion years before, churches still pierced him. He'd visited many over the years, and each time he stepped inside, there was a lingering sense of reverence, an echo of his old beliefs. His parents and most of his family remained devout, often asking him why he'd abandoned his faith. He'd brush it off as the contradiction between religion and his work. As a Christian, how could he justify conjuring demons and killers, only to send them out into the world through his writing, like unleashing a virus into his readers' minds.

But the real reason for leaving his faith ran deeper, though he struggled to put it into words. Every new home and each book he published had, in a way, buried his motivations further, like soil heaped over something best left undiscovered. The truth, whatever it was, lay too deep now, impossible to unearth.

Caspar stacked his books on the shelves of his writing room, fortifying his ego with each one, much like the bricklayers who'd raised the church a century before. This move was different. Despite all the stories he'd crafted over the years to hide the truth, the end was within sight. In the small town of Moxahala, Ohio, the past he'd tried to outrun had been waiting for him.

Whatever power the church once held had faded. His mind wandered to *Pet Sematary,* a favorite of his, and how that ancient burial ground went sour. A place that had echoed goodness for years was a conduit to something darker. As he stepped through the red front doors and beneath the cathedral ceiling, he sensed a strange awareness, as though watched by unseen eyes.

The stained-glass windows lining the interior walls were a witness to everything he did. Whatever the church had absorbed over the decades had stuck to its skin, lingering like the charred scent of burned toast. And as the walls pressed in, a fresh fear rose in him. The darkness radiating from the structure bombarded him.

Leaving his unpacked books for another time, Caspar sank into the chair behind his desk, letting the house's energy wash over him. There was malice there, reaching out, but there was something more below the surface, something testing its boundaries, probing to see if he was an enemy or an accomplice. He wasn't sure of the answer himself.

The blank screen of his monitor glared back at him, the blinking cursor a constant reminder of his own procrastination. All that empty white—an ocean he'd have to fill. Even after writing many books, the old insecurities coiled around him, slipping their way back like shadows creeping into the light.

Although finding the story was his job, Caspar hadn't yet begun his investigation. He did not know where it might lead, but his new home was inspiration enough. He positioned his hands on the keyboard, fingers poised, just as his typing teacher had taught back in school. But before he could start, his phone rang.

The shrill sound echoed off the walls, making him jump. He rolled his chair back, eyeing the phone as it lit up with "Unknown" on the small screen. *Where's your head? Turn off the phone.* Rule number one for a writer.

As his career grew, so had the demands on his time. His once-simple contact list had ballooned from a handful of friends and family up to hundreds of names. Though it was time to find an assistant to manage the calls and emails, he clung to his last bit of independence. A decision he regretted now as he debated whether to answer.

"This is Caspar," he tried to sound optimistic. All he heard in response was a raspy inhale. "Hello?" He frowned. A pause, then more breathing. "Alright, I'm hanging up if—"

"I know the secret to your books." The voice was gruff, distorted, like it spoke through a voice changer. "And how you choose your homes." Caspar's heart skipped at the words.

"Who is this?" Silence stretched, thick and unnerving. "Answer me!" he shouted, but only a click echoed in response. The line went dead, leaving him holding the phone, his hand trembling.

Caspar sat there, feeling a hum in the room. Whether it CAME from the house itself or just his imagination, he couldn't tell. But somehow things were going to be different inside his new home. *Why did I buy this place?* He knew the answer—and the call WAS a scary signal that others might know, too.

Chapter Four

Creepy Collectible

Unerved, the wooden steps creaked under Harper's weight, and the railing wobbled with each shift. *Someone needs to fix these before I break my neck.*

At the bottom, the brick walls of the cellar showed their age. Some rows of bricks hunched inward where a century of shifting earth had pressed against them. The years of freezing and thawing left the space with a musty, tomb-like odor. Harper shivered, pushing the unsettling thought aside before it took root in her mind.

Twix sniffed the uneven floor, where the bricks swelled up in some places and dipped down in others. He paused, glancing up at her with uncertain eyes.

"It's not that bad, shithead," she tried to reassure herself as much as him. "It just looks scary at night." Twix let out a worried yelp as if to disagree. *You'll be fine, you little troublemaker.* Her eyes drifted to the dog crate in the corner left there by the movers. With the condition of the stairs, she was thankful she hadn't attempted to carry it down herself.

She scanned the cellar, expecting to see something watching her. Every time her gaze found nothing, but the feeling of prying eyes only grew stronger. Twix, standing in the middle of the room, sniffed the air and tilted his head, as if sensing it too.

"Do we want to be down here?" she asked aloud. Twix cocked his head, as if in agreement. "Me neither."

The cellar was already oppressive, as though the walls themselves were closing in. The air grew thick in her lungs, and eyes upon her multiplied, surrounding her like a swarm. Harper's resolve waned, done with the basement for the moment or forever.

Harper patted her leg for Twix, already stepping backward toward the staircase. *Something wants me to stay down here.* The thought was absurd. And yet, under the heavy stillness of the cellar, it was all too real. Her foot found the bottom step just as Twix obeyed her command. An urgent need to escape rose within her, a feeling as instinctive as backing away from a spider.

Then it became a certainty: *Something was moving toward her.*

"Twix!" she shouted, spinning on the rickety staircase. Her sudden pivot made the stairs shift underfoot, as if she were in a carnival funhouse meant to disorient its visitors. Twix's claws clattered on the bricks behind her, but a new sound rose above his steps, a faint dragging noise. Her frantic mind scrambled to make sense of it: thick fabric, canvas, scraping along the floor.

Through the open stairs, she could still see into the cellar, but she kept her gaze fixed on her feet, too afraid to look down. "Twix?" She stumbled upward. Her voice was inaudible.

The wooden steps groaned beneath her weight, and her foot slipped on the worn edge of a step. She slid, her whole body going rigid as she fought to regain balance, the sensation like something pulling her down. The dragging sound echoed, getting closer, though it was still distant enough to spur her forward. Then she saw Twix bounding up toward her, his presence giving her the strength to stand.

The urge to sprint vanished as a fresh fear struck her; what if the staircase collapsed under her hurried steps, trapping her below? She took a deep breath, moving upward in slow, deliberate strides. The dragging grew louder. Twix darted past her and shot through the doorway, vanishing in an instant. "Traitor." She didn't risk glancing down to see what was following.

The grinding noise intensified, a frantic rhythm that clawed at the walls. She kept her gaze fixed on the top of the stairs, legs pumping faster as she neared the doorway.

She crossed the threshold and swung the door shut, pressing her ear against it, straining to hear. Her heart thundered as she listened, her gaze flickering across the quiet laundry room. Twix sat at her feet, his presence grounding her, but his sudden bark shattered the silence, making her jump. "Shut up." She listened again.

After a long while, she exhaled the breath she'd been holding. "Are we being idiots, Twix?" she murmured, glancing down. When she saw the dog's tail tucked between his legs, a silent answer deepened her unease.

The narrow library passage pressed in on Harper as she made her way to the spare room. She noticed Twix moving beside her, his cautious steps mimicked humans in their hesitation, as if he, too, expected an unseen hand to reach for him. She saw humanity reflected in his gestures.

As Harper walked through the library, each step triggered a new sound. A faint creak overhead, the whisper of a draft sneaking through hidden cracks in the stone. She thought she could hear murmurs, the remnants of long-forgotten prayers still echoing in the walls. It was as if the church were breathing, alive in the dark, watching her every move with a cold, patient gaze.

As she passed each wall outlet, the LED nightlights blinked on when her form blocked the sensors, only to flicker back off once she moved past. Everything in the house was a strange hybrid—part historical relic, part modern intrusion. Harper had protested, but Caspar insisted on adding tech: Wi-Fi dimmers, an app-controlled thermostat, and nightlights in the outlet plates.

Thanks to Caspar, it gave the unsettling impression that the walls were alive, and Harper hated it.

Reaching the end of the hallway, she opened the door to her refuge: the spare room. The old, rounded door frame reminded her of something from a Tolkien novel, more suited for a Hobbit than a human.

She held the door open as Twix scrambled inside, then cast one last look down the shadowed hall, making sure she was alone. The darkness pooled behind. She couldn't shake the dread of having to cross that corridor again, like the bridge from *Three Billy Goats Gruff*.

Harper flicked the light switch. The lights bathed the small room in brightness. Harper sank into a chair in the corner, letting out a long breath.

"This was supposed to be my craft room." She dug into her pocket and pulled out a handful of dog treats like a magic trick. She tossed them in the air, watching Twix chase each one. "Guess that's not happening now, thanks to *you*," She saw him hunt down every treat.

Harper pulled the baby monitor from the yard sale out of her bag, holding it up to the light. The device, which looked like a tiny, weathered phone, had seen better days. "Let's hope you work." She found an empty outlet and plugged it in.

A green glow lit up the monitor, accompanied by a steady hum. For a moment, the sound reminded her of UFOs in those Saturday morning movies she'd watched as a kid. The hum grew louder, morphing into a high-pitched squeal, like feedback from a microphone too close to a speaker. Twix stopped his scavenging, stared at the device, and let out a soft growl.

Harper back peddled from the monitor, holding the screen up as she stepped away. The squeal faded with each step, leaving only the low hum as she studied it in silence.

Harper gazed at Twix, fascinated by the baby monitor. She adjusted the camera to face him, then picked up the display, looking at the dog on the tiny screen.

"If you tear up my stuff, I'll see it." She smirked. Twix tilted his head, and his movement mirrored on the screen, as if he were watching her back through the device. Just as she moved to turn it off, a tingling sensation warmed her fingers, spreading up her wrist and into her arm.

Startled, she took a careful step back, forgetting she still held the monitor. A fierce heat filled her chest, and she dropped the screen to the floor. It landed upright, and Twix remained centered on the display.

Even as the heat faded from her chest, the tingling intensified in her hands, as if the baby monitor might explode. She backed away until her legs bumped against the guest bed. Easing down onto the mattress, she kept her eyes fixed on the small screen.

Without warning, a light appeared in the middle of the monitor—and at the room's core itself. It floated in mid-air, surrounded by jagged, crayon-like lines, as if sketched by a child. The light on the screen was a step ahead of the actual light, like the monitor was projecting rather than capturing the scene.

Harper leaned forward, curiosity overtaking her fear, as the aura doubled in size. Twix lowered his head, whining, sensing something Harper couldn't. She covered her mouth as the jagged edges of the light smoothed, forming the rough outline of a face.

The aura took on the shape of a girl. But just as it solidified, the image flickered, pulsing as if struggling to materialize. The child's outline glowed, and for a moment, the window behind her vanished, then reappeared, flickering in and out like a faulty connection. She was no longer just watching an image, and Harper's heart raced.

Something was trying to break through.

Twix buried his head under his paws, trembling as an invisible breeze rustled papers across the room, even though the windows were closed tight. Harper's heart thudded; she recalled the church's stained-glass windows depicting angels with faces she recognized.

Transfixed by the ghostly girl taking shape, Harper regarded the scene with a mix of awe and horror at the girl's strobing form.

"What's your name?" Harper asked, her voice tentative. The girl's face, suspended in mid-air, turned toward her, lips moving in silent response, like the fuzzy static of an old television. "I can't understand you." Harper's heart raced as the child's form drifted closer.

Twix whimpered, backing toward the door. Every instinct told Harper to retreat, but she stood rooted to the spot, her muscles tensed, fists clenched to steady herself.

"Are you here to warn me of something?" she asked, above a whisper. "Will you hurt me?" The apparition continued to glide forward, her expression as cold and unmoving as carved stone. Just as she neared Harper, the ghost stopped at the monitor on the floor.

The girl nodded, reaching toward the baby monitor with hands that were only half-formed. She patted the device, her movements both haunting and deliberate. Harper watched, her mind racing as realization dawned.

"This monitor ... it belonged to you, didn't it?" The child's expression didn't change. "Your things must have been donated after..." An idea took hold. "Gathering your things might..." She trailed off as the girl raised her ghostly fingers to her face, miming the motion of taking a photograph, her half-formed hands framing her face.

The light within the girl faded, and her form grew translucent. "Your things can bring you back. Is that it?" Harper asked, her voice edged with desperation.

The hum that had filled the room dropped a notch, making the girl's image harder to see.

"Wait! Are you Riley?" Harper called, just as the girl gave a faint smile and blinked out of sight.

The hum vanished, leaving only shadows in the room. Twix, who had huddled by the door, stared at the place where the apparition had stood. Harper met his gaze, finding no comfort in the surrounding dimness.

Chapter Five

A Collector's Dream

Ruin on his heels, the moon sat high in the Moxahala sky as Caspar passed out of the red double doors of his church. Despite the comforts of its modern interior, the exterior still bore the unmistakable marks of age.

Every step revealed the church's red brick walls, the skin of an old dragon. The clay-tiled roof, uneven from a century of settling, folded upon itself like scales, giving it an eerie sense of movement.

When he'd first visited the converted home, the realtor mentioned its Spanish style and how the original priest had made a pilgrimage to Spain, falling in love with the architecture. When construction began in 1908, the Catholic church's foreign style had shocked the small town of Moxahala, as if a cult had turned up to take over the local population.

As Caspar looked up, the clouds were a vivid shade of pink as they passed in front of a purple moon.

Below the horizon, the stained-glass windows of Moxie Manor looked out over the dark woods beyond, where tall sycamores stretched like ghostly figures, their twisted shapes casting grotesque shadows.

Caspar edged down the slope toward the woods, the wind picking up out of nowhere and pushing against his face. Under sunlight, it might have been refreshing, but in the cold glow of the purple moon, the breeze carried a warning. The trees, looming even taller as he approached, appeared to watch him, their white trunks like the skeletal remains of gnarled beasts.

He paused on the downslope of the hill, turning back to the house. "This has to be a dream."

"What if the world you know is a dream?" a voice asked.

Caspar whipped around to nobody standing there.

"Who said that?" Only silence answering him. He glanced back at the house, fear knotting in his gut, his rational thoughts swirling. A primitive part of him prayed it wasn't the house speaking.

"There's more ALIVE in there than in all the woods."

Caspar turned to the voice and stared at a small border collie squatting on four legs beside him.

"Twix?" The dog nodded, and Caspar clenched his eyes shut, as if it would cause his vision to disappear.

"Are you really here?" he hoped his words would make the dog vanish.

"The question is are *you* really here, Caspar?" the dog replied. Caspar opened his eyes wide, his heart pounding, as he saw the dog's mouth twist into an unsettling grin, a ferocious, unnatural smile, like the Big Bad Wolf from a fairy tale. Twix swatted the ground with his paw and sat. Caspar slid down to sit beside him, the cold earth chilling him through his pants.

Man and dog sat side by side, Caspar towering over the pup. Twix lifted his head, as if he might lick Caspar's face, but he spoke again.

"You got yourself into it this time." Twix lifted his snout higher. Caspar noticed a green tint shimmering in the dog's eyes, though there was nothing green around to reflect it. "The church draws evil to its things and things to its evil." The dog's hungry smile returned.

"How are you speaking to me?" Caspar asked. The black-and-white collie scratched his neck, a gesture so dog-like that Caspar questioned if he'd heard anything at all. "Are you ... part of the house?"

Twix tilted his head. "You're a horror writer—look at the woods." He motioned to the dark tree line. "Does that sight look holy to you?"

"How do you know I'm a writer?"

"Isn't that why you bought the church?" Twix's gaze was sharp. "It's your macguffin."

"What?" Caspar frowned, startled by the word coming from his dog's mouth.

"The object that drives the plot."

"I know what a macguffin is." Caspar's voice was terse. Twix looked away, as if taken aback by his tone.

"This church is your macguffin, and soon Harper will find hers," Twix continued, fixing Caspar with a piercing stare. "Be careful where your obsessions lead you. You won't like what you find."

A distant noise from the woods caught their attention.

"What was that?" Caspar asked.

Twix's eyes didn't leave the trees. "Moxahala used to be a coal mining town. Old coal shafts run beneath the entire area, even under this church. Years ago, a group of miners became trapped when the support beams collapsed, and rescuers abandoned the site. To this day, people say you can still hear their screams when the wind blows exactly right."

Caspar shivered, feeling the weight of the words. "So, they were just ... left down there?"

Twix nodded. "Some even claim they've seen faces in the woods. People who wander in after dark swore eyes watched them."

Caspar swallowed, glancing back at the church. "What happened to the people here?"

"The groundskeeper came one morning and found them all gone—the priests, the nuns, anyone who worked with the church. They vanished without a trace."

"They were never found?" Caspar gazed at a sky that had turned a bright shade of red.

Twix tilted his head, then shook it. "People have been disappearing here for years. But you already know that, don't you, Caspar?"

Caspar looked away, unsettled. "Am I creating this reality with my writing? I think I've lost control," Caspar admitted.

Twix gave a low chuckle. "You know what ruins a story? Too much exposition." he gave a low growl.

"Where have they gone ... the missing people?"

Caspar turned back to Twix and together they looked toward the woods. Shadows that were a part of the trees broke free from their prison. Huge humanoid figures crawled from the opening. The outside of their skin took on a slimy appearance as the purple moon highlighted their undulations.

Next to crawling blackness, creatures°stepped forward and kept pace. The mass of creeping intruders picked up speed.

"What are they?"

No answer as the beasts rushed toward the pair bathed in the moonlight. "We should go." They never had the chance as a swarm of claws covered them.

Chapter Six

Everything's Negotiable

*E*yes still adjusting, the ethereal sensation of the dream clung to Caspar as he sat up in bed, waiting for it to fade the way dreams did. But the memory of talking to Twix was as vivid as anything real. Shifting, there was dampness on his clothes, as if from the grass he'd sat on, and he questioned which reality to trust.

A flicker of memory brought him back to the present; his publicist was due to arrive early that morning, and no amount of time ever prepared him for Eliza. Part publicist, part mystic, she was a whirlwind on two feet.

He heard doors slamming and footsteps echoing through the halls of Moxie Manor. Her arrival was closer to a poltergeist.

"Oh, Caspar." Eliza's voice reverberated off the high cathedral ceiling beams, "you have outdone yourself with this place!" She swept into the room and wrapped him in a grand embrace, leaning close like a star on the red carpet.

She pressed against him, adjusting her dress as she pulled away with an exaggerated spin, taking in the space. "The stained glass, the architecture—"

Her gaze found his, gleaming with admiration. "I swear I could write a novel here myself if I had the time."

"How are you, Eliza? And where's—" Before he finished, a gigantic figure lumbered down the hallway toward them.

"As usual, he found his own pace," Eliza said without a glance. Scott Sedge extended his hand, gripping Caspar's.

"Good to see you, Sedge." Caspar had once compared the private investigator to Clint Eastwood. No amusement came from Sedge, so he never mentioned it again.

Caspar led them through the maze of hallways to his writing room. "How do you not get lost in here?" Sedge asked, settling into an old mission chair with a heavy sigh.

"You get used to it." Caspar took his seat behind the desk. Eliza wandered around, still entranced by the room.

"This place is magnificent. Too bad you'll have to leave it behind." She threw him a sidelong smirk. "They don't make places like this anymore."

"I'm glad you approve. How about I make this my permanent residence?"

"You never stay in one place that long."

"Ready to get down to business?" The abrupt shift in tone brought an awkward silence. "Sorry." he glanced at his folded hands. "The first meeting always feels heavy."

"Let the Crematorium Club meeting commence," Sedge joked, but the humor fell flat. Eliza, who had been pacing, found a seat, and the three sat in silence until she finally spoke.

"Your fans are catching on. Honestly, I think this will be the last book we can do in secrecy."

"She's right." Sedge pulled out his phone and showing them a screen. "Someone created a website tracking your purchases and house sales. They're trying to predict your next book's storyline."

"You're joking."

"People are frothing at the mouth for more," Eliza replied. "That's a good thing, right?"

"I have an empire to protect and every misstep we make throws away my readership," he raised his voice. "The numbers were down from the first book and *Forever Midnight* fell off a cliff."

"I wouldn't say it was that bad," Eliza massaged.

"Bullshit! We need to throw everything into this book. And how we do that is for you to find my story! I can't afford another decline in sales!" Eliza found her feet more interesting. "Are we clear?" Caspar eyed his employees. They nodded in the uncomfortable shadow of Caspar's anger.

Chapter Seven

NAME YOUR PRICE

*T*he abandoned school sat on a slope so steep that Harper doubted her car would make it to the top. With every bump up the hill, she expected the wheels to slide backward. *How did a bus full of kids ever make it up here?* She exhaled in relief as her back tires finally hit the level surface of the parking lot.

She stepped out of her car, letting the school's worn exterior wash over her. Long windows and arched doorways stretched across the façade, where paint curled and cracked like dry skin. Retired schoolhouses dotted Ohio, but this was the first she'd seen with a yard sale tucked inside.

A pungent scent hit her. Damp wood, moldy paper, and layers of lead paint prickled her nose. As she followed the crowd through the halls, the musty smell mingling with the sight of worn walls and faded lockers brought back her own high school memories. She placed a hand to her nose and pushed the thoughts aside where they belonged.

As she stepped through the double doors into the gymnasium, her eyes widened at the appeal the sales held. Though the basketball floor still shone and the clocks on the walls remained locked behind steel cages, hundreds of booths packed the gym. Crammed together like tables in a sci-fi autopsy lab.

"Maybe you *are* a yard bird after all," a familiar voice said nearby. Harper glanced to her left and saw Carol and two other older women watching her, amused. "It's awe-inspiring, isn't it?" Carol asked.

Harper nodded, remembering how Carol had walked away when she mentioned her home. She'd wanted to ask more questions if she got the chance.

"I think I'm out of my depth here," Harper admitted.

"This is Madge and Edna." Carol nodded to the gray-haired ladies at her side. Harper registered their names before they slipped out of her mind, though she thought they looked like veterans of the rummage-sale world. Yard-sale warriors.

"Inspect everything." Madge rattled a box of batteries. "If it takes batteries, always check if your treasures work."

"Run your finger over any glass to feel for chips," Edna added. "And always carry a magnifying glass to find things smaller than the eyes can detect." Edna placed the magnifying glass up to her eyes like Sherlock Holmes.

"Always negotiate. Sellers expect it." Carol grinned. "And next time, don't dress like you came out of a magazine." She looked Harper up and down, amused.

"I'm dressed wrong for a yard sale?" Harper glanced at her outfit, puzzled.

Carol ignored the question and exchanged smirks with her friends. "Look modest, not shabby. Sellers won't budge if they think you've got money. Leave watches, jewelry, and makeup at home. And always bring small bills—nothing over a five."

"Be fair with your offers," Madge said. "Don't be disrespectful, but don't be afraid to walk away, either. If the seller won't negotiate, put the item back where they can see. They're more likely to reconsider."

Harper's head spun with the flood of advice. Carol leaned closer. "Do you know what you're looking for?"

"No. I'm clueless as hell," Harper admitted.

"You'll be fine, then." Carol gave her an encouraging pat. "If you need us, just holler." And with that, she and her friends melted into the crowd, leaving Harper to navigate the bustling sale on her own.

Harper scanned the busy sale, watching as eager shoppers hurried in every direction. What had started as curious whispers when she arrived had turned into excited chatter. She caught snippets of conversations from the energetic crowd.

Standing in the middle of the old gymnasium, she was unsure of what she was even there to buy. When the ghostly girl had patted the baby monitor, it had made sense to look for more items—like piecing together a puzzle. But now, surrounded by discarded school gym equipment and blue-haired women intent on bargains. She thought it was foolish.

Spirituality wasn't in her nature, and mysticism was even further down the list of things she believed in. What she could see, and touch, grounded her like a balloon tethered to the earth by skepticism. But the moment she'd seen the girl crossing the road, that tether had snapped, and a part of her—anchored by fear and doubt—had drifted free.

She took a breath, trying to calm the anxiety in her stomach. Something was waiting in the room. Something that could explain the girl's appearance. She didn't expect an answer in words. It was a truth locked somewhere deep within her, waiting for a release.

Drawing on the intuition she'd seen in books and movies, Harper closed her eyes and stretched her arms out, like antennae. The surrounding voices faded as she focused on her inner stillness. Standing there, she imagined herself as a human planchette, giving herself over to something beyond her understanding.

With her eyes still closed, she took a tentative step. Part of her expected to collide with another shopper, yet a gentle pull guided her forward, as if she were a balloon following close behind a tugging child. Her pulse quickened when the pull intensified, drawing her toward the center of the maze of tables.

When the sensation stopped, she opened her eyes, and the sounds of the sale returned, buzzing all around her. A strange pride swelled in her chest; she had quieted her mind and followed an instinct she didn't know she had. *Was it because of the girl?* The implications were overwhelming, but she'd have to face them.

Booths surrounded her in a loose circle. Instead of examining each one, she let her feet drift.

When doubts crept in, Harper stopped at a seller's stand and let her gaze fall over the items on display. The assortment was random: folded clothes, dusty vintage electronics, stacks of faded books. It was as if someone had emptied an old man's bedroom onto the table. She thought of the girl and asked herself which possessions she might have left behind in a collection like this.

"Tchotchkes," a voice warned. Harper looked up, surprised to see the booth's vendor hadn't spoken. "Am I right?" Carol said from behind her.

"I ... don't know what you mean." Harper remained focused on finding something that might have belonged to the girl across from her house.

"Yiddish. It means worthless." Carol flashed her yellow teeth. Harper thought of asking where the other "yard birds" had gone as Carol hovered like a vulture. Taking a deep breath, she extended her hand over the scattered items, letting her intuition guide her once more. Her fingers trembled as they hovered over a Polaroid camera and paused.

Just as she touched the instant camera, another wrinkled hand appeared. She looked up, meeting the gaze of a weathered man with his pants pulled up far too high.

"I think I got here first."

"The hell you did!" Carol slapped his hand away. He recoiled, glaring, before shuffling off to another booth. Harper watched him go, still unsure of her next move, her hand resting on the camera.

"Are you interested in that?" the seller asked, breaking Harper's concentration.

"I think so." Harper lifted the camera for a closer look. The body was white, with a rainbow band that ran down the middle like a racing stripe.

"It's a vintage OneStep," the seller explained. "I bought it for a project but never used it."

"It looks pretty beat up to me," Carol chimed in, giving Harper a conspiratorial wink. The seller bristled.

"How much do you want for it?" Harper asked, a little too hungry. She sensed Carol cringing beside her.

"I've got a bunch of unused black and white film for it. I will throw that in for free. Hard to find these days. Unless you buy online." The seller paused, considering his price. "Three hundred."

"You're out of your mind," Carol scoffed. "One fifty, tops."

"I'll take it." Harper ignored their bartering. Carol's shoulders slumped.

"The second mouse gets the cheese." Carol shook her head before moving to another booth. Harper clutched the camera and the stack of film the seller handed to her. Though there was a strange connection to the camera, she wasn't sure what it meant or what to do with it.

Then something told her to turn the camera over, and she obeyed. Carved into the bottom were two letters: R.S. It belonged to Riley Spears. She ran her fingers over the etchings, picturing the girl holding the very camera and snapping photos.

Chapter Eight

CURBSIDE SPECIAL

Old habits resurfaced as Scott Sedge rubbed the scar on his head. A constant reminder from his days on the force that no one was ever quite what they seemed. He was now working on Caspar Finch's fourth novel, yet the author remained an enigma. Sedge had no doubts that Caspar was brilliant, but his instincts as a former homicide detective urged him to dig deeper. Only Haley, his wife, kept him from following that urge. His years as a detective had taken a toll on her in ways he preferred not to admit.

However hard an officer tried; they always end up bringing the job home. Working for Finch had been Sedge's way of making it up to her—and why he resisted pulling on threads from the author's past.

He'd looked evil in the face more than once, but that didn't mean he'd always seen it coming. Horror writers, he told himself, had to dive into the darkness to drag out a story. Still, the trapped rat in the BACK of his mind kept scratching.

The bar and grill in Moxahala—emphasis on "bar"—looked just as he'd expected. Paneled walls, dim lighting hiding the greasy tables, and the faces of patrons nursing drinks before noon. A jukebox played a mournful tune, masking the silence as the regulars dulled their senses with alcohol.

Sedge scanned the room and spotted a woman sitting alone in a corner booth, sipping what looked like a Coca-Cola. Stalking cases led to men, but book-obsessed fans were a different breed. Since most readers were women, Sedge suspected Caspar's stalker was too, despite the deep voice Caspar claimed to have heard. Voice modulators were easy to find if you looked hard enough. He followed his gut and approached the booth.

Recognition was the goal as he positioned himself in front of her. Sedge had learned early that the eyes told the true story. The mouth might say one thing, the body another, but as The Eagles put it, *You can't hide your lyin' eyes.* He waited until she glanced at him. Her long pause said everything, and he was sure he'd found the fan.

Though Sedge was well into middle age, he still moved with a younger man's confidence, sliding into the booth like a dancer finding his mark. The gaunt woman with dirty-blonde hair reacted to the uninvited company.

"You're not Caspar Finch."

"Good start. Reality hasn't left you." He gestured to the waiter for the same drink she had. "Coke, right?" She nodded. Sedge was long past his alcohol phase and glad of it.

"You're not special." He took the glass as it arrived. "Everyone wants something from an author. There've been dozens like you over the years. What they're after has nothing to do with the writer—just their own fixation. So, what do *you* want?" He leaned forward, fixing her with a sharp gaze.

"Save lives." She fixed her eyes on her drink. Sedge hadn't expected an answer, especially not one like that. It matched nothing he'd heard from others he'd confronted on Caspar's behalf.

"What's your name?" he asked. She stiffened, and he added, "I can think of five ways to find out if you make me."

"Gloria," she said.

"Why are you contacting Caspar Finch?"

"To stop the murders. His murders." She sat up straighter, meeting his gaze with a steady look. She believed what she was saying. Was Gloria unhinged? It was possible, but she wasn't lying.

"You understand he writes about the crimes after they happen—not before?"

Gloria dismissed his question with a shake of her head, taking a sip of her cola.

"He was born in the same town I was." She watched him. "Corning, Ohio." Sedge remained unmoved.

"So?" he asked, impatience creeping into his tone as he watched a hint of panic cross her face.

"It was his novel *Forever Midnight* that tipped me off. He mentioned Corning, and if I hadn't been born there, I wouldn't have noticed the signs."

"Which signs?" he pressed, his voice low and edged with irritation. Gloria leaned back until her head touched the booth's cushion, her face betraying a flash of fear. Realizing he'd pushed too hard, Sedge raised his hands and palms up. "Sorry. Go on."

She hesitated, then reached into her purse, pulled out a five-dollar bill, and dropped it beside her drink. "There's an abandoned house in Corning." She stood to leave. "Next to the firehouse. You'll find answers there—if you want them."

"Wait—" he began, startled. The conversation hadn't gone as he'd planned. He hadn't even reached the part where he'd warn her to stay away from Caspar or mentioned how she'd end up behind bars if she didn't. Gloria was already walking away, leaving Sedge staring at an empty booth, his questions unanswered.

Prying the wood off the back door took some effort. Sedge paused several times to check the neighboring houses and the fire station before continuing. Despite the plywood sheets covering the windows, the house didn't look abandoned at all.

Sedge slipped his pry bar into the doorjamb and, with a final push, broke the door free. He scanned the area one last time, then stepped inside, clicking on his Maglite. The home's interior bloomed into view.

"It's a damn time capsule." Everything was untouched, as if the owners had walked out one day and never returned. A fine layer of dust covered every surface, but nothing was out of place.

What unsettled him was the lack of information. His search online had turned up nothing—someone had gone to great lengths to erase this house's history from public records. *Okay, give me a challenge.* He could always call in favors at the Columbus Police Department for answers, BUT he hadn't even considered it. The dead end had sparked something he hadn't experienced in years: the thrill of the chase.

As he moved through the rooms, he took in the stale, dusty air and walked on the brittle carpet. It crunched beneath his feet. Mold crept up the walls, twisting like a monster strangling its prey.

In the beam of his flashlight, the first clue revealed itself: pale squares on the walls, marking where picture frames had once hung. *Too fast.* He reminded himself. *Slow down.* Someone had removed every sign of life from this house. The empty spaces where family photos should have been.

"What are you hiding?" A whistle blew outside, loud enough to startle him. The town's old railroad tracks ran nearby—a reminder of Corning's coal-mining past. *Forever Midnight,* Caspar Finch's book title, flashed in his mind as he checked his watch. The hands pointed to midnight. *Not creepy at all.*

He continued from room to room, finding nothing personal. The drawers were empty, and not a single photo lay on the dressers. After checking two bedrooms, he was certain one had belonged to a couple and the other to a child, a little girl, though he couldn't say why. To his astonishment, the parents' room had all the markings of a fire. Black ash spread out along the walls and ceiling, but no personal items remained from the devastation.

Then he opened the door to the last bedroom and dropped his flashlight. Unlike the other rooms, modest furnishings and decorated, this room was empty.

"What the hell?" He swept his light around, finding nothing, not even curtains on the windows. It was as if something sucked everything out of the room, leaving only bare walls. *Whoever emptied this room left no clues at all.*

In frustration, Sedge rattled his flashlight, the beam bouncing off the walls. The flickering light caught something on the floor. *Broken glass?*

He crouched in the center, focusing the flashlight on the glinting object. Bending down, he found a small metal charm. A piece from a child's bracelet, shaped like a girl's head. Its silvery face wept, or that was just his impression of the tiny, haunting figure. He clenched the charm tightly in his fist, feeling a chill settle in his bones.

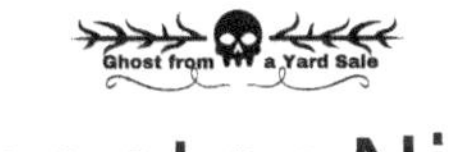

Chapter Nine

BUYER BEWARE

Drenched in sweat, Caspar sat up in bed. Had a sound awakened him? The sensation faded as his eyes adjusted to the darkness. Shadows softened the usual sharp angles of the room, distorting them into strange curves.

Before he even turned, he sensed Harper beside him. The warmth of her skin under the covers, mingled with the faint scent of her lotion, stirred something in him, as it always did when he saw her resting. He watched her naked back rise and fall with each steady breath, like the ticking of a clock. He expected to see Twix curled at the foot of the bed, but it was empty.

Sliding one foot then the other to the hardwood floor, he embraced the chill beneath him. As he stood, he noticed Twix by the open door, watching him. The dog's eyes glowed in the dim light, a reminder of his ancestral instincts. Caspar staggered toward him, and Twix's ears perked up as he approached. With one last glance at Harper, he motioned for Twix to follow him out of the bedroom.

"Was it you who woke me? Or did something wake us both?"

"I showed up when you did." Twix trotted alongside Caspar as they moved through the grand living room of the old church. Moonlight filtered through the row of tall windows at the entrance, casting faint patterns across the floor. Caspar listened to the soft patter of Twix's nails on the wood.

The light from the outlet's switch plates cast a glow. Twix paused with his gaze fixed upon a shadow above one outlet.

"Caspar?" the dog murmured, uncertain.

Caspar turned to where Twix was looking and saw a shadow taking shape on the wall. At first, it was just a vague form, but it soon twisted and morphed, becoming a gnarled, grotesque creature, like something out of a fairy tale. He thought the light switch cover might cast a shadow, but he couldn't understand how.

"What is that?" Twix gave no reply. As they stared, the shadow shifted again, transforming from a troll-like figure into the outline of a little girl with pigtails. A teddy bear dangled from her swinging arm.

"Who are you?" With ears pointed upward, Twix watched as if waiting for an answer.

The head of the shadow-girl turned, the jaw rounding as her form shimmered, like the static on a TV screen. Her face sharpened, and Caspar imagined unseen hands squeezing the shape into a grotesque distortion. Then her mouth fell open, and a row of long teeth grew, each one with the sharpness of a scalpel. Menacing and real.

"Shouldn't we move?" Twix urged, watching as the girl's chest heaved, expanding to fill the wall. Caspar stumbled backward, pulling his gaze from the monstrous shadow that stretched taller and wider across the wall but narrowed near the outlet below.

Leaving the girl's form behind, he bolted toward the back of the house, with Twix close behind. Glancing back, he saw the shadow vanish, only to reappear above the next outlet in the row. With lighted outlets lining the hallway, both ahead and behind, Caspar broke into a sprint he hadn't attempted since his teens.

The phantom figure jumped from outlet to outlet, trailing them. Twix yelped a mix of panic and warning, craning his neck to check if the creature was still giving chase.

They burst into the library hallway, and Caspar hesitated. To the right was Harper's craft room, to the left, *his* writing room.

"Which way?" he said, half to himself, half to Twix. The dog bolted left, and Caspar followed without a second thought. As he reached the office, he noticed more outlets lighting up, casting the creature's murky form along the walls.

"Hurry," Twix urged, already waiting by the office door. The shadow closed in fast. Caspar yanked the door open, let Twix dart inside, and slammed it shut just as the shadow reached them. Silence fell. No thud, no screech of frustration. Only his own ragged breathing.

"I think we're safe." He glanced around his office. "No outlet lights in here." Twix nodded, but his wary eyes stayed fixed on the door.

"This is the part in the story where the heroes think they're safe."

"Heroes?" Caspar asked, glancing at the dog. Twix nodded.

"And then, just when they let their guard down—"

A flash lit up the office, drawing both their gazes to the security monitor on Caspar's desk. The screen filled with the face of the girl, her empty eyes taking up every inch of the display.

"What do you want from me?" Caspar shouted, backing against the door. Twix whimpered, tucking his head beneath his paws. The girl's face pressed closer, and her head pushed through the screen as her body twisted out, sliding onto the floor like something oozing from a can.

Without warning, the shadow crawled toward them, snapping its mouth open to reveal those gleaming, razor-sharp teeth.

"Get back! You're not real!" Caspar shouted. The creatures moved fast, jaw stretching impossibly wide. In an instant, it lunged, engulfing him in a mouthful of darkness.

Caspar looked up from his grapefruit at Harper, absorbed in her newspaper. Twix sat on his haunches, watching him. *Would the dog speak if she weren't in the room?* The nightmare still lingered in his mind, feeling more real than any ordinary dream.

"Hey, Twix. Morning, boy." He waited to see if the dog would respond. Harper didn't look up, and Twix only tilted his head, holding Caspar's gaze just long enough to stir his unease. Around them, workers bustled, installing automated displays, Wi-Fi lights, and voice-activated locks.

"How long will they be here?" he asked Harper.

"Today, I think," she spoke from behind the paper. "The installers said adding tech to this old house is like major surgery."

Caspar nodded, though she didn't see. "I'm going to write."

Harper set her newspaper down and finally looked at him. "I wanted to let you know—Mara's coming today." Caspar's face went from pale to deep crimson.

"Already?" Harper gave a slow nod. "We just moved in!" he snapped.

"She's my sister, Caspar. I need her here."

In one swift motion, Caspar swiped his breakfast off the table. Plates and cups sat awkwardly in his arms.

"What I need is time."

"Mara won't be a bother. We'll stay out of your way. I promise. Please." Caspar's anger flared, but his eyes caught onto Twix, who sat perfectly still, unfazed by the outburst.

"I swear it won't be like before." Harper clasped her hands in a pleading gesture.

Caspar let out a frustrated sigh, gave a curt shrug, and walked out of the room without another word.

Chapter Ten

HIDDEN TREASURE

Reluctantly stepping forward, Mara passed through the red doors of Moxie Manor, her gaze drifting up to the expansive space overhead. Harper watched her sister's expression of wonder, glancing at Mara's tense posture.

"This place *has* to be haunted, right?"

Harper noticed Mara still dressed as she had when she was a teenager. Tight clothes to accentuate her thin frame, revealing more of herself than Harper was happy doing. *Some things never change.*

"You'll have to decide for yourself." Harper smiled. "It feels strange here during the day, like it's ... hibernating," she admitted.

"Are you sure I WANT to be in here after dark?"

"I wouldn't if I were you." Harper laughed, exchanging uneasy glances. The library's narrow, shadowed walls gave them a sense of confinement as they walked down the hall to Harper's spare bedroom.

At the rounded doorway, Mara hesitated before ducking into the dim room. Harper flicked on the lights.

"Quaint. But I bet your husband wasn't thrilled about my arrival."

"You two just have a complicated relationship." Harper caught the roll of Mara's eyes. "Moving on, it's better if I show you. It won't happen again, and I can just tell myself I'm crazy."

Mara folded her arms over her chest, settling in. Harper opened a drawer and pulled out a Polaroid camera, handling it as though it might crumble. Twix scrambled into the room and sat close to Mara.

"Don't worry, he's friendly." Harper laughed, aiming the camera at Twix and Mara. The camera's charging circuit gave a high-pitched whine before she clicked the button. As the film slid out, Mara shrieked.

"Don't you dare take my picture!" She made a half-hearted attempt to snatch the print.

"I forgot you hate having your picture taken." Harper tossed the photo onto the bed. "My mistake. Won't happen again," she added, raising her hands in surrender. The sisters stood in silence, looking down at Twix until the tension eased.

"I hope this camera gets me closer to real answers."

Mara frowned. "This doesn't sound like you, Harper." She watched as Harper lifted a baby monitor and set it down, clicking it on. The hum filled the room, just as it had the night before.

"Move back," Harper warned, nodding toward the floor. A warm glow rose from the surface, creeping up Mara's legs. She jumped away from the light show as it took over the room.

"What the hell is this?" Mara whispered, inching back.

Harper moved closer, holding the Polaroid camera up. The outline of a young girl grew clearer as the baby monitor amplified her form.

"Was this yours?" Harper asked, shaking the camera slightly. The girl's shadowy figure bobbed in response, her head bowing faster, the glow intensifying. Twix pressed himself against the wall, unable to retreat any further.

"Her lips are moving—what's she saying?" Mara asked, reaching toward the figure. A small bolt of electricity shot from the apparition, zapping her hand.

"Shit!" Mara yelped and pulled back.

"How do I use the camera?" Harper shouted as the girl flickered then dissolved. "Damn." She stared at the empty spot where the girl had been.

Mara shook her hand, her expression shifting to one of excitement. "I don't know what just happened, but whatever this is—I'm in!"

Harper watched a smile spread across her sister's face. She wasn't sure which unsettled her more: the ghost or the joy it brought her sister.

"How did this all start?" Mara asked.

Harper moved to the window, sliding the curtain aside. "There." She nodded at the vacant house across the street. "The girl came from there."

Mara stared out at the empty house, shadowed in the distance. "You really want to go over there?"

"Will you go with me?"

Mara glanced at her and nodded. "I'm always with you." They both stared at the shadowed house, watching for any signs of life.

"I'm afraid of what we might find. What if she's looking for REVENGE for what happened to her?" Mara asked.

"We've got each other." Harper offered a fragile smile.

The chill of the night seeped through Harper's clothes as she and Mara crossed Route 13, feeling the weight of the divide between the church and the abandoned house. Glancing back, they saw Moxie Manor perched high on the hill, its stained-glass yellow windows glowing like jaundiced eyes. The row of windows circling the top floor looked sinister in the darkness, and a shadowy figure filled one of them.

"Do you see that?" Harper froze. Her eyes fixed on the darkened window.

"What?" Mara looked around.

"Someone's staring out from the left window." Harper pointed. "Right there."

Mara squinted, then nodded. "Probably Caspar."

"No, he's in his office. That figure just moved. You saw that, right?"

"It's just a trick of the light." Mara looked up at the shadow. "And this isn't the conversation I want to have right before we walk into a dark, deserted house looking for a ghost."

"You're right." Harper tore her gaze away from the manor, but the shadow lingered in her mind.

As they approached the embankment leading to the house, lightning cracked through the sky, illuminating the house's peeling paint and cracked façade. Darkness fell again, followed by a rolling rumble of thunder.

"Is this a good idea?"

"Since when are you afraid of anything?" Harper teased. Mara opened her mouth to respond but stopped as they reached the porch. From a distance, the house looked sturdy, with a wraparound porch and round wood columns. Up close, they saw algae slicking the wood and boards split from water and age, some sagging beneath the weight of time.

"Should we knock?"

"You're so funny." Harper smirked, pulling a crowbar from her waist-band and wedging it into the door frame. "Mother's little helper."

"Full-on cat burglar." Mara chuckled as lightning flashed, and Harper leaned her weight into the tool. The old wood gave way with a splintering crack, and the door swung inward with an eerie creak, as if inviting them inside.

Moonlight seeped through broken windows, casting shadows that closed in from all sides. Though the house was empty, a few pieces of worn furniture remained: a splintered table here, a water-damaged chair there, like silent sentinels left behind to guard the home. In the living room, a metallic sound rattled through the walls.

"It's just rain on the metal roof." Rainwater trickled through the ceiling, landing around them with soft splashes.

"Where should we start?" Harper asked, noticing her sister's tense expression. Mara tilted her head toward the staircase.

They shuffled over the creaking floor, each step bouncing on weak, weathered planks. As they placed their feet on the staircase, the boards groaned beneath them, echoing through the hollow house.

"Is this going to hold us?" Mara asked but got no answer as they hurried up to the second floor. Rain fell harder, and the metal sang a chorus with the rising drops. From a bag hanging on her shoulder, Harper pulled out the Polaroid camera, careful to avoid raindrops as she held it out in front of her.

Harper clicked the camera, and a small flash lit up the hallway. A second, larger flash of lightning burst outside, mirroring the camera's glow. She grabbed the film as it slid from the camera and stashed it in her bag. Twice more, she photographed different spots upstairs while Mara led the way into a room at the end of the hall.

A broken dresser leaned against the wall, and a lone mattress lay on the floor. Harper aimed her camera at the mattress, snapped a shot, then turned to capture the center of the room. She gasped as she noticed a dark stain in front of her.

"Is that blood?" Harper asked.

Both sisters circled the large, dark stain. Harper aimed the camera at the ominous mark and clicked, letting the Polaroid's light expose it. The stain wasn't the bright crimson of fresh blood but a deep, dried brown—a relic of a disturbing event long forgotten, now unearthed by them.

Without hesitation, Mara reached toward the stain.

"Don't touch it!" Harper warned, but Mara pressed her hand onto the spot. Lightning flashed, flooding the room with a harsh, blinding light. As Harper's eyes adjusted, another flash of lightning illuminated the windows, followed by a thunderclap that rattled the walls.

Mara, still with her hand on the stain, looked up at her sister, her mouth opened as if to speak. Mara's body slid backward, away from the dark mark.

"Harper?" she whispered, before vanishing into a dark corner of the room. She clawed her way back toward her sister, fear in her wide eyes.

"What's happening?" Harper asked. Panic was alive in her voice. Before she could react, something lifted Mara into the air, hovering above the center of the room. The lightning pulsed, flashing like a strobe light, as if charged with a life of its own. Harper raised her camera, snapped another photo, and stared at the image that developed in her hands. A shadowy figure held Mara in mid-air.

"Run!" Mara screamed from above, but Harper could only shake her head in horror. One moment, Mara floated near the ceiling and the next, Harper saw her crash to the floor with a bone-jarring thud.

Harper lunged forward, reaching for her sister's hand, but before she could grab hold, the dark figure dragged Mara away, scraping her across the splintered wood floor.

"No! Stop!" Harper's heart pounding as she raced after her sister. She could hear the dragging sounds, already out in the hallway.

Harper ran to the door and saw Mara sliding down the staircase, her head thudding against each step as she disappeared around the spiral bend. Harper reached the top of the stairs just as Mara disappeared.

"H-help…" Mara's voice was a whisper. Desperate, Harper launched herself down the stairs, taking them three at a time, but her foot smashed through a rotten step. Her leg plunged through the wood, splinters cutting into her skin as she teetered between the steps.

She caught herself panting and relief washed over her. She hadn't fallen all the way through. The wood scratched at her leg, but she pulled herself free, her mind racing with one thought. *I have to get to Mara.*

Harper pulled herself free from the broken step, moving more cautiously down the rest of the staircase. Soft cries echoed off the walls, and flashes of lightning illuminated the house. As she rounded the corner, she froze. Mara levitated a foot off the ground, held by the dark figure, which slammed her against one wall, then another. Mara collapsed to the floor, staring at the ceiling.

Before Harper could react, the shadow lifted Mara's legs, dragging her across the floor toward a dark cellar doorway.

"Don't let it take me," Mara whimpered, grabbing the door jamb as she teetered over the basement's dark threshold, her lower half already lost in shadow.

"Hold on!" Harper shouted, running to her. The shadow pulled harder, but with a mix of fear and determination, Mara wrenched herself free from its grip and scrambled out of the doorway.

As Mara stood, the shadow shifted toward them once more.

"We have to go!" Harper yelled.

They bolted for the front door, bursting into the storm outside. Rain pelted them, and lightning crashed nearby, but they didn't stop until they reached the safety of the church and shut themselves in Harper's spare bedroom.

"What the hell just happened?" Mara gasped, catching her breath. "Was that the little girl?"

Harper, still shaken, sank onto the bed and pulled one of the instant photos from her bag. The shot showed the brown stain in the upstairs bedroom, but there was something else lying across the floor. It was the faint image of a child, her lifeless eyes staring at the camera. A red line stretched across her stomach, just below her ribs.

"This can't be..." Harper whispered, her hands trembling.

"What?" Mara leaned closer as Harper turned the photo around.

"This Polaroid ... it captured the moment of the girl's death. But I didn't see her in the room."

Mara swallowed, glancing back at the darkened window. "Then who was the shadow?"

Harper shook her head, staring down at the Polaroid camera in her hands as though it might spring to life.

Chapter Eleven

TRADES ACCEPTED

*I*ndecision gnawed at him as he waited for Gloria Mazel to open her front door, Sedge rehearsed the conversation he was about to have. Each scenario was more nerve-wracking than the last. When she appeared, sleep softened her expression, but that faded the instant she peered through the screen door. Sedge saw the shift, recognized the fear in Caspar Finch's superfan.

"How do you know where I live?" Sedge stood silent on the porch, refusing to answer. They were like two gunfighters locked in a showdown, only in the middle of a quiet suburban street. Gloria sighed and motioned him inside. "Well, come in."

He saw books stacked everywhere, on shelves, tables, even the floor. The living room looked infected, as though the books were multiplying, consuming the space.

"Sorry about the mess." Gloria cleared a stack from one of the couch cushions. "Wasn't expecting guests." Sedge sat without waiting for an invitation, wondering if she'd ever had company. "Found more than you bargained for?"

"What makes you think I found anything at all?" Sedge asked, feeling uncomfortable in his skin. Gloria gave him a sleepy, knowing smile.

"You wouldn't be back if you hadn't. I'm not *that* interesting." She sank into a worn armchair, the only furniture not covered with books.

She eyed him. "I didn't recognize you the last time we met. You look different on TV." Her smile sharpened. "I devour everything crime related. Your story WAS fascinating, Scott Sedge." She drew out his name for emphasis.

"I came here—"

"To ask me questions? Like, how you find peace after killing your wife?" The room spun around him. "Even if it was self-defense, how do you live a normal life afterward?"

"You can't."

"Is that why you quit the Columbus Police Department?" Gloria leaned forward. "It must be hard to have others' respect when a homicide detective doesn't know his own wife is a serial killer."

"I didn't come here to talk about that." Sedge shook off the memories.

"Then WHAT *did* you come here for?" she asked, her eyes narrowing.

"Who owned the house in Corning? What happened in there?" Sedge saw her fading, withdrawing from his questions. "Caspar Finch is just an author. What does this all have to do with him?"

"I didn't start seeing her until Caspar moved to Moxahala."

"Her?" Sedge's voice dropped to a whisper, and Gloria nodded.

"Everyone around here knows about St. Pius Church. It's a beacon. It draws ... malevolence. Evil attracts evil." Gloria shoved aside a column of stacked books, sending it tumbling. "Have you noticed any changes in Caspar?"

Sedge didn't move for a long time. "After his last book, I wondered what happens to him when he taps into the darkness of each story. What would that do to a writer? Could it twist a mind, encountering so much blackness?"

"My bet is that the church and Caspar are the same now," she offered.

"What happened at Moxie Manor—St. Pius?" Sedge asked, observing her as she weighed her response. When she began, Sedge held his stomach as he sank into her words describing the dark history of the church.

Chapter Twelve

FORGOTTEN THINGS

Nervous energy crawled under his skin, as the sound of slow, creaking death woke Caspar. It rose from the darkness like the wail of an angry woman. The house was prone to creaks, and he was fine with the odd noises during the day, but night made all the difference. *A house needs to settle,* his father once told him, after a loud creak startled him as a child. But tonight, as the familiar unease settled over him, Caspar's heart wanted to explode.

Beneath the heavy duvet, Caspar made himself small, pulling his body tight to occupy as little space as possible. *Disappear.* The thought churned in his mind as he glanced to find Harper but found the bed empty except for Twix watching him.

"Did you hear that?" Caspar whispered to the dog.

"I sure did," the border collie replied.

Caspar's father might have been right about creaks and groans. But ever since they'd moved into the old church, the hour between three and four held a power over him that nothing in the light of day could explain. The grandfather clock, a relic left by the former owner, often woke him with its third chime, marking the start of what Caspar called the wicked hour.

WICKED HOUR

He pulled the duvet over his head. The soft fabric brushed his cheeks, comforting him, forming a barrier he imagined as impenetrable as steel. Nothing could get through if he stayed hidden. Caspar slowed his breathing, drawing in small, quiet breaths to help calm his nerves. If I can hear it, it can hear me.

He made up the rules as he went, but that didn't change how real they were in his mind. Moving around in the dark wasn't a death sentence, though it wasn't risky—*unless* you entered the wicked hour. Letting his feet dangle over the bed was out of the question, a rule he would never break. And keeping the covers tucked in around him was essential. Even in the daytime, he obsessed over this detail.

"What should we do now?" Twix asked, watching him with wide, glowing eyes.

"We have to tuck the covers between the mattress and the frame." Caspar worked around the bed, pressing the fabric down. "All it takes is one opening, and it'll find its way in." Twix's expression shifted to a look of worry.

"It's waiting for us to make a mistake?" the dog asked.

Caspar nodded gravely. The duvet was so close to his mouth that each breath he took pulled it in. "Inside the wicked hour, time twists."

"What is that?"

"An hour feels like three on the best of nights. This one will be worse."

Then came the scratching.

"It's starting."

"Why does it always start with scratching?" Twix whispered.

"Shh."

"Is something on the other side?" Twix crept closer to him.

Caspar clinched his jaw to keep from peeking over his cloth barrier but pushed it aside, letting the mystery claw at his mind. The scratch grew louder, climbing in intensity as if whatever it was, scrambled up from somewhere deep, clawing its way closer. His heart raced as he imagined each desperate snag of claws pulling the creature nearer. There was a ravenous intent in each sound, a hunger he could feel through the covers.

In the dark, Caspar's eyes darted, seeing only shadows and the soft glow of Twix's eyes. But his mind formed an image, imagining the creature clawing toward him. His childhood fear resurfaced; he imagined a spider, its movements frantic and relentless. Moxie Manor had more than its share of unseen eyes, slipping from the smallest cracks, like creatures materializing from another world into their own.

The comparison was easy to latch onto, even if it was wrong. It wasn't a spider, but what else could he imagine? He kept picturing it as a spider, its legs churning as it closed in on him. A sound rose like the creature crossed a great expanse to reach them, meaning it was already in the room.

"It's just a trick," he said to calm himself. In daylight, the lie might have worked.

A heavy thud struck the bottom of the bed, jolting Caspar as every muscle locked up, his body rigid with fear. The pounding stopped, but a slow scraping followed, as though something rubbed against the underside, inching its way out.

"I'm scared, Caspar." Twix's eyes glowed in the dark.

"Me, too."

The scratching stopped, and somehow that was worse. He heard its breathing now, raspy and unnatural, coming from just beyond the fabric barrier. Caspar reached for his ears, desperate to block out the sound. But as his hand shot up, he yanked a corner of the cover loose.

Idiot. He froze, horrified. In his haste, he'd created an opening, six inches, a foot at most, but it was enough. A door.

Caspar and Twix stared, paralyzed, at the gap near the foot of the bed. The faintest sliver of light revealed the outline, the fabric gaping like a mouth, waiting for something to crawl through.

The rasping breaths shifted, moving closer to his ear before heading toward the opening at the bottom, as if it sensed the breach. Caspar was a trapped mouse, paralyzed as he watched the darkness around the gap.

The bed dipped, and he could see the dim impression of fingers pressing down on the fabric as it crept closer to the opening. In a surge of panic, Caspar lunged forward, his hands stretching for the cover. He yanked the fabric down, sealing the opening as best he could. But as he did, pale fingers appeared just beyond the gap, pressing against the cloth.

In a frenzy, he jammed the cover down between the mattress and the bed frame, sealing them in once more. Only then did he realize he'd pulled himself out from under the safety of the blanket.

With the creature circling the bed, Caspar pushed back with his feet, sliding under the covers again and dragging Twix with him. As he tucked the blanket tight around them, the thing sniffed, thwarted but still relentless, prowling around the bed, searching for another way in.

Twix was close to hyperventilating, pulling in air more shallowly than he released it. The game of pretending was over. The creature was there, each waiting to see what the other would do next. He dared to hope for anything, not sure what that would get him.

Caspar lay motionless, his arms trembling. He doubted they'd make it to the other side of the hour. Then, the wet breathing that had hovered near his head faded. It hadn't left. He could still sense it, but now it was distant, retreating. As if it were returning to wherever it had come from.

The room fell silent, and Caspar's eyes darted back and forth in the darkness, his senses straining to detect any change.

"Is it safe to pull the blanket down?" he whispered. Twix didn't answer. Caspar's fingers twitched as he touched the edge of the fabric, ready to lower it. That's when he heard it—a soft, dragging noise. His mind filled in the gaps: the creature rubbed two objects together. He remembered his father teaching him to start a fire while camping, rotating a stick over wood to create friction. But something about this sound was different.

With a desperate heave, Caspar pulled the blanket from his face and onto his lap. Scattered wooden splinters littered the floor at the foot of the bed, a disturbing reminder that something had been there. He leaned over the edge, careful not to let his leg dangle, and looked closer. Faint grooves marked the floorboards, blending in with the wood grain so well that he questioned if they had always been there or if they'd appeared tonight.

"Is this what they call foreshadowing?"

Caspar froze as ghostly white hands appeared from beneath the bed, followed by the pale face of a woman. Her icy fingers gripped his leg and yanked hard. Caspar screamed, feeling himself sliding from the bed and into the darkness.

In the next instant, he jolted awake to find Harper shaking him. "Caspar, you're having a nightmare."

Harper sat beside him, and Twix was gone. Caspar's heart still pounded as he glanced down, expecting to see the woman's hands clinging to his legs. But there was nothing there.

Chapter Thirteen

UNDER A LAYER OF DUST

Keenly aware of the tension, the silence made the air as thick as cotton in Harper's throat. The dining room sat at the heart of Moxie Manor, its cathedral ceiling soaring high above them. They were in the belly of the old church. Stained-glass windows circled them from above, passing judgment on those who had never attended a single mass there.

Harper watched Sedge and Caspar sitting together at one end of the dining room table, while Mara sat across from her at the other. Caspar was the writer, and Sedge, his employee, yet an invisible line divided the men from the women. Harper didn't like feeling the distance between them that night. She glanced at her sister as they all settled into their meals.

Caspar was always uneasy after learning the history of the homes he purchased. This time, though, there was something different, more intense about his behavior. He spoke about the nightmares. Even if Harper hadn't experienced the dreams herself, she connected the dots. None of the homes they'd lived in over the years held the oppressive atmosphere as the church. Every breath taken within its walls came with a residue from the past, like soot after a fire. The church's dark history clung to the place and seeped into her lungs.

"Thanks for dinner. It was great, as always." Sedge speared the last of his chicken with his fork.

"It's become a ritual, hasn't it?" Caspar looked at Harper for reassurance, and she offered a weak smile. "I know you've had no time, Sedge, but is there a story here—something about our church?"

Sedge put down his fork and tilted his glass of wine, taking a long drink before he answered. Harper watched him drown himself with alcohol. "I don't drink anymore," he said. "Haven't in years." He went in for another sip.

"But tonight's an exception?" Harper asked after catching the danger in his tone.

Sedge nodded, and the weight of his response made everyone fall silent.

"I'm not much of a reader—no offense." He studied Caspar, who shrugged. "But as a kid, I couldn't stay away from movies. Sometimes I'd play hooky from school, sneak into the local theater, and sit high on the empty balcony, watching every film they played. All those haunted house stories taught me one thing: if someone tells you to leave a place, you better listen°"

"You think my sister should move out?" Mara asked.

Sedge didn't acknowledge her, and Harper saw Mara shoot an annoyed look her way.

"I've seen my share of ugliness. The world can be a dark place, and people disappear more often than you might think. It's easy for us to justify why it happens. A little girl's unhappy and runs away. A husband's miserable at home and starts a new life somewhere else. But sometimes there are no reasons, just empty spaces where people used to be."

"What are you getting at?" Caspar asked, his eyes narrowing.

"More people have vanished from this church than from the entire surrounding towns combined," Sedge replied. "The original clergy were the first reported missing. All of them vanished at once. Years later, a member of the church staff walked into the woods, never to be seen again."

Harper glanced at Sedge, then turned to see her husband leaning down to whisper into Twix's ear. She could've sworn the dog had nodded back. *Ridiculous.*

"When the church shut down, the first private owner moved in, but the disappearances continued. Sarah Deville, the wife of a wealthy man, got swallowed up by this house."

"Swallowed?" Mara blurted out, but Sedge ignored her question. Mara folded her hands and slumped into her seat.

"They never discovered the cause." Sedge paused for effect. "Then, years later, something terrifying happened here."

"What?" Harper asked, her voice cracking with anxiety.

"They called it a curse. 'Hex' was the word everyone used." Sedge's gaze fixed on Harper. "One night, a letter appeared at the front door of every woman's house in the area."

"What kind of letter?" Caspar asked, leaning forward.

"Have you ever heard of a chain letter?" Sedge asked.

Caspar nodded. "I've heard of them. But how would chain letters have to do with this church?"

"Superstitions are passed down like anything else—from one generation to the next," Sedge began. "When a new family arrived in town, the welcome wagon would bake bread, keeping part of the dough to start a new batch, and give the rest to the newcomers. This cycle of sharing brought good fortune. But then, someone turned it into something darker—the letters."

"Who created them?" Harper asked.

"No one knows," Sedge admitted. "Some people swore it was Sarah Deville herself, reaching out from beyond the grave. When the letters arrived, addressed to the women in the community, the husbands became enraged—jealous that a stranger would write to their wives. In their anger, they tore open the letters, only to find them blank. But for the intended readers, the letters contained something ... deeply unsettling."

"And what did they say?" Caspar asked, on the edge of his seat.

"Darkness. Secrets those women had tried to bury. The idea behind these chain letters was that each recipient had to copy the message onto ten *new* letters, then send them out. If they failed to follow the exact instructions, the curse would fall on them."

The room was so quiet that every small sound—a creaking chair, a rustling sleeve—magnified, adding to the discomfort.

"What's the catch?" Harper asked, her eyes fixed on Sedge.

"The catch was that they couldn't make a single mistake. Not one missed period, not one repeated word, not even a single misspelling. If they failed, the curse was forever. Many of the husbands, in jealousy or fear, would tear the letters to shreds or burn them. And this condemned their wives to a death sentence."

"What happened to the ones who couldn't complete the chain letters?" Caspar asked, his voice above a whisper.

"One night, not long after Moxahala received the letters, people reported seeing shapes in the woods among the sycamore trees. They described the shapes as creatures; figures with hands close human but were wrong. The skin looked twisted, as though sculpted from a material that shouldn't belong on a person. It's the woods, people cried. Withered flesh, molded into human form."

Sedge tilted his cup and drained the last of his wine. "Like a fever dream, witnesses saw their animals howling and sometimes staring at the moon for hours. While others claimed to see women and their servants stumbling from their homes, as though in a trance. Some moved of their own accord, but not all. Others dug their fingers into the ground as stronger hands dragged them into the darkness. Screams echoed from distant properties, cutting through the night. Little girls cried out for their mothers, who drifted toward the woods in a dreamlike state. One by one, the voices died away, as if extinguished like a candle. Whether they walked willingly or dragged, they all vanished beyond the sycamore and ashtrees, swallowed by the night."

Caspar edged closer to Sedge.

"One woman who escaped said the creatures' faces were leathery and black as coal."

"They were the coal miners. They came for revenge."

"Maybe."

"How did it end?" Harper asked, her voice thin.

"A church bell rang. From this very church. The bell of Moxie Manor tolled for all to hear, shattering the spell. The creatures retreated, and the women dragged toward the woods slowly awakened. Some found themselves just inches from the tree line." Sedge fell silent, his words hanging in the air. Everyone watched him and the weight of the story settled over them like a shroud.

"Wow. That's ... quite a story," Caspar said.

"There are dozens just like it. This place draws evil."

"Who told you all this?"

"Her name is Gloria Mazel. A local superfan ... of yours." Caspar's eyes widened.

"She's either the most diligent investigator I've ever met or a certified wacko," Sedge added. "I haven't decided yet." He turned to look at Caspar and Harper. "Both of you were born in Corning, Ohio, right?" They nodded. "Did either of you ever live near a fire station?"

Harper glanced at her sister before Caspar answered, "No."

"Damn. Thought I had something." Sedge paused, then continued, "Gloria has threatened to go to the authorities, you know. She claims you've DONE something wicked in the houses you write about." He chuckled, but his eyes remained serious. They exchanged uneasy glances.

"What about Sarah Deville?" Caspar asked. "Did they ever find her?"

Sedge's face darkened. "They did, her body was discovered buried within these walls. "He fell silent, and all eyes turned toward the darkened corners of the room, as if expecting something to reach out from the shadows.

Caspar took the temperature of the room and stood up. "I may never sleep in this house again." Everyone around the table laughed. "I have writing to do. Goodnight." He made his way to his office with the thought of someone buried in the walls lingering.

Slipping into the library hallway that led to his writing room, Caspar heard a sound behind him. A voice spoke before he turned.

"Hey, stranger." Caspar's first thought was Harper, saying goodnight, but when he turned, the shadows hid their form.

"Mara? That you?"

Mara slid her arms around his shoulders, letting her fingers caress his hair, and settling on the back of Caspar's neck. Before he reacted, her lips pressed hard against him.

As if a wasp landed on his skin, Caspar pulled away.

"What are you doing?"

"Didn't you tell Harper about us?"

"There is no us. Not anymore."

Mara slid her palm across his cheek. He flinched, yanking her hand away.

"I don't want Harper to ever know. And if you care about your sister, you'd want the same."

"I'm not one to give up so easily."

"If you want TO be welcomed into our home, you will." Caspar walked into his office without another look back.

Chapter Fourteen

Unwanted Item

Yellow light filtered through the trees, as the early morning sun cast shadows along the road. Harper pulled into the parking lot, feeling a strange tingling—an intuition that today, she might find something extraordinary.

She and Mara sat in the car, Harper behind the wheel and Mara stretched out in the passenger seat, both watching the locals file into the church rummage sale. Some wore clothes that came straight from a yard sale themselves, while others looked fashionable for the occasion.

"You can't throw a rock without hitting a church around here. But how you two bought one is beyond me," Mara said. "Why are you so obsessed with this ghost girl?"

Harper looked straight ahead with her gaze fixed on the front doors of the old building. "If you're not talking to me, I'm not sticking around." Mara looked out her window. "This whole thing is hazardous to my health. Is this about making things right?"

"You think I'm trying to replace my daughter? I'm not." Harper turned to her sister. "Every item belonging to the girl makes her more real, more solid." Mara remained quiet. "I was pregnant. I don't care what the doctors told me." Tears filled Harper's eyes.

"I know."

"You never believed me. Neither did Caspar. One day I was having a baby and the next ... she was just gone."

"No matter how many things you find, Riley will never be real," Mara changed the subject.

"How would you know?" Harper snapped.

"The fucking girl ... ghost or whatever tried to kill ME. What if we open something we can't close?" Mara asked. Just then, the church doors swung open, and the crowd rushed inside.

"We need to go." Ignoring her sister's warning, Harper got out of the car. She glanced back to see Mara fall in line behind her, reluctant but following. With each step, Harper's urgency to find something tied to the girl tightened in her chest. *What if someone gets to it first?*

She quickened her pace, brushing elbows with Carol as she reached the tables.

"Glad you made it! This sale always has the best deals." Carol kept pace with Harper.

"I brought some backup this time." Harper gestured to Mara, lagging.

Carol turned to glance at Mara, then back to Harper. "Are you okay?" she asked. "Yard sales can become an obsession, and—"

"I got it under control." Harper gave a nervous smile.

Carol looked confused but smiled back. "Glad you found your passion."

"Thanks." Harper scanned the tables with laser focus. The rows of tables stretched before her, cluttered with potential treasures. During her first sale, the noise had been overwhelming, too much to bear. Absorbed in the chatter, she formed a protective shield against it.

Sliding the Polaroid camera from her bag, she rubbed its plastic surface, like Aladdin rubbing a magic lamp. "Where should we aim for first?" she asked, lifting the viewfinder to her eyes. Mara didn't respond.

Through the viewfinder, the rows of tables took on muted shades of white and gray, their colors fading as if the camera filtered out anything irrelevant to her quest. Even Mara, standing just in the periphery, vanished from sight. The camera altered her perception and sent a shiver down her spine. Harper scanned the rows with deliberate slowness, exhilaration building with every pulsing vibration that ran from the camera into her hands and up her arms, covering her skin in goosebumps.

With the world muted and other shoppers fading away, Harper was on the verge of uncovering something no one else could see.

The first difference in the scenery was a faint red glow. Harper snapped a picture and listened to the camera's mechanical moan as the film slid out. She grasped the corner and waited for the image to develop. Though the film was in full color, everything appeared in charcoal shades, except for a soft, crimson aura hovering over a distant table.

"Over there." Harper pointed toward the back of the hall. "That way." They hurried past other shoppers, stopping near the closest display. She squeezed her eyes shut, letting herself absorb the moment. Holding the camera between her palms like a basketball player preparing for a free throw, she raised it high above her head and stretched until her shoulders strained.

The familiar, faint vibration returned to her fingers. She pushed past her unease, falling into the sensation as if she were diving into a pool. Immersed in this otherworldly awareness that no one else sensed the wind brush against her face and chest. A breeze that hadn't been there a moment before.

She hesitated, then opened her eyes, steeling herself for whatever she might see. The shoppers had disappeared, though their distant chatter lingered. Around her stood a circle of doors, like funhouse mirrors, all painted red. Except one. The lone black door stood out.

Harper took a step toward it, keeping the camera raised like an antenna. As the door flickered, she lowered the camera to eye level and pressed the button. A flash of light bathed the black door, spreading over its surface like liquid before it dissolved, as if melting away.

When her vision cleared, color returned. Mara stood nearby, and a table crowded with objects was only a foot away. The rummage sale buzzed with life again, shoppers bustling around as before. Piles of items, large and small, covered every inch of the table.

"How do I know which item to choose?" Harper asked, her voice low. Mara remained silent, and they both stared at the worn items, giving no hint of their significance. Harper lingered, oblivious to the vendor's curious gaze.

She thought of checking the photo she'd taken while in her trance, expecting to see the black door aligned in her path. But the image showed the table before her, rendered in black and white. At the center of the picture, in the middle of the table, a glimmer of red stood out like a campfire.

It was a motel keychain with a silver key hanging below. Embossed on the front was the number "73" and, above it, the words *Recharge Inn.*

"It's the key," she said half to herself, half to Mara. Harper's eyes darted from the photo to the table, landing on the motel keychain, still the same vivid red but the photo remained black and white. She couldn't explain how the camera worked, how the world had fallen away, or how these objects carried power.

Harper WAS one step closer to bringing the girl back from the dead.

Chapter Fifteen

Attic Find

On the edge of sleep, Scott Sedge dreamed of ancient stained-glass windows; their silent colors whispered his name. A single night inside Moxie Manor, and it made sense why no one in town dared speak of the church after dark. He couldn't shake the feeling that it was watching him. The deeper he dug into the manor's history, the more he uncovered secrets that were best left buried.

Now, Sedge stood off to the side—head down, eyes averted—as Caspar finished a phone call. He let his gaze drift over the uneven lines of the plastered walls, thinking how much they resembled reptilian scales. With each visit, a feeling of contamination crept deeper into his mind.

The cracks held a century of dust - paint made from long-forbidden. The church was rotting, but in Sedge's imagination, it was a slow decay, like a vampire feeding on the souls of its inhabitants to stay alive. Moxie Manor had a thirst for life, warding off its inevitable collapse.

"Do you know the weight of a book?" Caspar's voice startled him from behind, cutting into his thoughts. Sedge hadn't heard him approach and blinked at the question, surprised.

"A pound?" he ventured, knowing there was no right answer.

Caspar's gaze settled on him, intense and unwavering. "The choice of what to put in or leave out of a novel keeps me up at night," he said. "That's why I hired *you*—to ease the burden. But this time…" Caspar's words trailed off as he sank into a nearby chair, his tone thick with disappointment.

"With all due respect." Sedge sensed a tension in the air but pressed on, "you find these houses. You never tell me how or what draws you to places marked by tragedy. But you find them." He settled back in a chair across from his employer, watching Caspar's reaction. "My job is to uncover recent deaths, deaths that you always helped me find."

"And this time, you've failed," Caspar said, the accusation sharp as a blade.

"Things aren't working out as they have before." Sedge struggled to keep his composure. "There have been no recent murders in this house."

"Pardon my French, but that's bullshit," Caspar shot back, his voice rising. A jolt of energy ran through Sedge's frame.

"Breathe in. You can taste the evil in here," Caspar continued. "It oozes from the beams, stirs under our footsteps." Sedge gave a reluctant nod, feeling the oppressive atmosphere seep into his skin. "If you can sense it in minutes, what do you think it's doing to me?"

Sedge looked at him, seeing a strange flicker dart across Caspar's face. "What is it doing to you?" he asked, but Caspar only returned his stare, his expression guarded. They sat in silence until it was clear Caspar would not answer.

"There are … disappearances," Sedge said, "like I mentioned before. But as for deaths … they're all in the past."

"That can't be."

"Did I mention Sarah Deville? The woman swallowed up by this house?"

"Yes." Caspar leaned forward.

"What I didn't tell you was that her husband, Nathaniel Deville, had three wives, all of whom died under mysterious circumstances here. Sarah was his first wife. The second was Lauren, a good woman who went mad within these walls. She became stepmother to Nathaniel's son, Jesse. Loved him like her own."

Caspar's eyes narrowed. "What happened?"

"I'll have to show you." Sedge led the way out of the study. Caspar followed, watching Sedge. Although well into middle age, Caspar's frame remained youthful, and Sedge could handle himself—if it ever came to that.

"Where are we going?" Caspar asked, glancing back.

"To the attic." Sedge caught the hint of fear in Caspar's voice. "I tracked down a descendant of a servant who once worked here." Reaching the foot of the staircase leading to the attic, Sedge continued, "According to her, Lauren dragged Jesse between three and four in the morning up this very staircase. I can imagine his slight frame resisting her the entire way." Sedge looked down and saw his own hands as if he stood in the Moxie Manor from long ago.

"Though Jesse wasn't small for his age, her grip was relentless as she continued her course through the church. Witnesses said he let out a scream, begging her to stop, but she ignored his cries. Lauren reached the staircase to the fourth-floor turret room, a place off-limits to Jesse, as a servant later recounted.

"At one point, when she loosened her grip to readjust, Jesse kicked free from her hand, but his effort was feeble. Lauren seized his ankles again, tightening her hold with a furious glare. Her mouth contorted, nostrils flaring with rage. She dared Jesse to resist again.

"With renewed force, Lauren dragged Jesse up the stairs, as if pulling a wheelbarrow. His back—and his head—thudded against the steps as he tried, in vain to escape."

"This is the staircase they used?" Caspar asked. Sedge answered with a nod. "When they reached the top, she pulled out a key hidden in her dress, unlocked the turret room, pushed Jesse inside, and locked the door from within." Sedge opened the now-unlocked turret door.

"I didn't even know this passage was here." They stepped inside and studied the space. The turret was hexagonal, six walls in total. There was some significance to the number, though Sedge said nothing.

Burned-down candles circled the room, and symbols covered every inch from wall to ceiling. The thought of how long it must have taken to create the symbols by hand made Sedge uneasy.

"Lauren forced Jesse to look up," Sedge continued, pointing to the hatch in the ceiling that led to the widow's walk around the bell tower—the highest point of the church. Sedge released the latch and watched the hatch door swing down on its hinge. He barely hesitated before climbing the steel rungs and following the same path up into the open air.

Like the turret, the walkway had six sides, except here a wrought-iron fence lined the perimeter, keeping visitors from plummeting four stories to the brick courtyard. Iron spikes jutted toward the sky, decorative in purpose but menacing in their appearance.

"Lauren dragged Jesse through then bell tower, out onto the widow's walk. Witnesses below heard the boy's terrified screams—'Leave me alone! Why are you doing this?' She seized him, lifting him in her arms like a bag of potatoes, causing him to panic and grab the wrought-iron railing, clinging to it with all his strength. It was then that he put everything together. She was going to throw him over the edge."

Caspar leaned over the iron railing, peering down at the stone path far below as Sedge continued. "Jesse may have been young, but he was big for his age, and she struggled to lift him high enough to clear the fence. One of the iron spikes dug into his cheek, piercing his left eye. Blood streamed down his face, spilling like water from a spigot.

The boy's screams drew a crowd around the church. Lauren, with a surge of strength, pushed him over the fence. He dangled, holding onto the iron rods, begging her to stop. She hesitated, then backed away. Witnesses said she nodded to herself, climbed onto the fence, and, after meeting her son's eyes one last time, leaped from the widow's walk to the unforgiving stone below." Sedge gestured downward.

Straightening up, Caspar looked across the street at the crumbling farmhouse. Sedge, however, watched him. "Such a horrible story." Caspar turned to his investigator. "What a delicious detail to add to my novel."

Sedge broke his gaze from the house, a slight smile playing at his lips.

"I was hoping to tempt you away from here. There's a goldmine of heartbreak in these stories—perfect material for a novel. Use them and leave this place before it leaves a mark on you."

"No!" Caspar's voice was firm.

Sedge's smile faded. "If you stay, this church will take its toll. It's already working on you. You dined on an empty plate last night. Can't you feel it?" Sedge gripped Caspar's shoulders.

"Ridiculous." Caspar shook him off. "I can't leave. This is where my work ends."

As he shrugged, Sedge saw a flicker of desperation in his expression.

"I can't leave," Caspar repeated, then hesitated, a gleam of hope brightening his face. "But you could stay." Sedge tensed, surprised. "Yes! Be my guest here—help me unravel this story and protect me." Caspar glanced at the abandoned house across the road. "You have no one waiting for you back home." He was blunt as always.. "What I mean is ... you're needed here. Now."

Sedge's gaze shifted to the ground, wrestling with the sting of Caspar's words. Then, after a pause, he nodded. "Alright. But the moment you find your story, we leave. Agreed?"

Caspar grinned, bouncing. "Yes!"

"Promise me." Sedge held his gaze.

"I promise." Caspar's grin widened.

"You know I have expensive tastes." Sedge laughed. "Where am I staying?"

"The servant's quarters, of course," Caspar said in a playful tone. "They're in the back of the house. You'll have your own bathroom, a small kitchen, and a separate entrance. All the privacy you could ask for."

"Will I get a chocolate on my pillow?" Sedge asked, smirking.

"I'll place it there myself." They shared a laugh, despite the uncertainty looming over their future.

Chapter Sixteen

Timeless Piece

Under the dim light, the motel keychain—a vivid, unnatural shade of red—sat in Harper's clenched fist. It vibrated like a tuning fork. The harder she squeezed, the more her hand trembled from its relentless shudder.

Mara had been a good sport, following her from one yard sale to the next. Harper glanced at her sister in the passenger seat. Mara still looked as young as she had when they were teenagers. *You've still got me there, sis,* Harper thought with a wry smile.

"Let me see the key," Mara demanded. Harper dangled the keychain over the console, then snatched it back just as Mara's hand reached out.

"Look with your eyes, not your hands," Harper teased, but there was an edge to her voice, too.

With the faded sign of the *Recharge Inn* filling the windshield and room 73 etched on the key tag, they exchanged a final, apprehensive glance.

"Some things you can't undo." Mara's face went pale. "We'll never unsee that girl—she's burned into our minds. But I think there might be worse things if we keep up this ... scavenger hunt."

The motel was a crumbling two-story structure with railings and stairs painted an unsettling shade of pink. Each step up the salmon-colored stairs made Harper think of entering a hungry mouth.

From the top of the stairs, the town of Moxahala stretched out below, a stunning view, but one that underlined the motel's isolation. This was the sort of place where someone could disappear without a trace, leaving only the wary motel manager and a single guest as witnesses.

As they reached the second-floor walkway, Harper focused on the numbers above each door, moving past one faded number after another, with a pink railing to her left and the parking lot a blur below. The keychain vibrated in her palm, as if urging her forward.

In the heat of the chase, she'd forgotten her sister, but when she turned, Mara was there, lagging but caught up. She struggled to match Harper's pace, but it was her expression that stopped Harper in her tracks. Mara's face shifted in terror.

"What's wrong?" Harper asked, taking a closer step. Mara nodded toward the door in front of them. The tarnished brass numbers read: *73.*

"We're standing on the edge, treading in dark water," Mara said. "If we swim past this point ... everything's going to change."

"What do you mean?" Harper asked. Whether they found a clue or nothing at all, she sensed the danger ahead, a shadowy threshold they were about to cross.

Harper opened her hand and looked down at the keychain, the shade of red on it bright and raw, pooling in her palm like fresh blood.

"I'm sure management changed the locks ages ago. This key is just a souvenir from a yard sale." Harper wavered as the key slid into the lock of door 73. The sisters exchanged one last glance before Harper turned the knob and pushed the door open.

They stepped inside, moving through the doorway like travelers crossing into a different realm. Yet the escape from the ugly pink exterior was no escape at all—Room 73 had its own clashing palette. The walls wore a shocking bright blue that could only have come from the 1980s, and the trim, a hot pink was an assault to their senses..

"When the hell are we? It's like a time warp," Harper's voice half-mocked. But there was no humor in the garish room. Mirrors lined every wall, amplifying the intense colors, and furniture in pastel geometric patterns filled the space. The headboard and armchair frames were white lacquered wood, influenced by art deco.

"How has this place never been updated in decades?" Mara asked, frowning. "It's like it's been preserved."

"Maybe they just bring in backup pieces from storage."

"That's just dumb," Mara scoffed. "This is a tiny, rundown motel in the middle of nowhere."

They moved further into the room, each detail more surreal than the last, as if they had stepped into a time capsule showroom. Mara looked around, unwilling to touch anything.

"So, now what?" Mara asked, unable to hide her unease.

"Look around. There has to be something here—a clue that led us to this room."

While Mara scanned the room with her eyes, Harper searched every corner, starting with the bed and moving to the bathroom. Yet nothing about the room held any mystery.

"There's nothing here," Mara warned. "Maybe the key was just a random find."

"You saw the Polaroid." Harper pulled the picture from her bag and held it up. "Look."

Mara gave a reluctant nod. Harper's determination weakened, but she shook her head, not willing to give up. She glanced at the Polaroid camera in her bag, and the camera had worked before. *Lift the camera, fall into the trance, find the clue.* But something else called to her this time, just as the key had when it first started vibrating.

"Wait." Harper raised a finger to her lips. Mara fell silent, watching as Harper put the key into her bag and set it on the floor. "The key's too close. The key's signal blocks everything else."

Harper extended her hands outward like antennae, closing her eyes. She could still sense the key, but the feeling was fainter, allowing her to search for other vibrations in the room.

"What do you feel?"

"Shhh." Harper made a small "O" with her finger, focusing on each faint vibration in the air. *"I'm a radar,"* she told herself, drifting around the 80s relic of a room, her finger sweeping in SLOW, deliberate arcs like a metal detector.

The vibrations ebbed and flowed with each careful step, her finger trembling as she searched. Time stretched and pulled, her energy fading like a sparkler burning out. She was close, but the clock was ticking.

With a last turn around the room, Harper's finger jerked—just a slight movement, but enough to signal something. It wasn't about direction; it was also about height. *Up and down.*

Crouching, the vibrations intensified as her finger moved faster.

"You found something," Mara said.

Harper wanted to tell her sister to be quiet, but she was too deep in her faraway place, too immersed in the trance to break it with words.

Her finger kept circling, her body moving until her momentum ran out, and everything stopped. She found herself on the floor, facing a wall. Blinking away the blur of keeping her eyes squeezed shut, her vision cleared, and she spotted a vent in front of her.

Once the dreamy fog lifted, Harper moved to her bag, pulling out an item from inside. Each step back to the vent was careful, like a soldier crossing a field of landmines. She slid down to sit on the carpet, crossing her legs.

A Swiss army knife lay in her outstretched hands, like an offering. Caspar had given it to her years ago, though she'd never imagined needing it, much less using it. *What use will I ever have for this?* She'd thought then. Now, she pulled out the screwdriver attachment and looked from the ordinary air vent cover to her tool. Both waited.

"Don't open that," Mara warned and clutched her chest with her arms. A voice that sounded like Mara's echoed in her mind, urging her to stop. But the fear had no power over her now.

Her trembling fingers lifted the screwdriver to the vent's screws. The heads of the screws had chipped paint on them, a hint that she wasn't the first person to unscrew them. Somehow, the thought reassured her; she was on the right track.

With steady determination, she unscrewed three of the bolts, her hand shaking again as she worked on the last one.

"Just wait! Give me a second. We can leave without opening this. Can't you see we're right on the edge of something?"

"I can." Harper turned back to her task. The last screw clattered to the carpet, and the vent cover fell open. Harper reached into the dark opening with the same trust a lion tamer might have when placing a hand inside an enormous cat's mouth.

"Harper?" Mara's voice trembled as Harper's arm disappeared up to the elbow. Her hand found soft clumps of a cotton texture that she was sure was dust bunnies. Her fingers brushed something solid, and she wrapped her hand around it, pulling out a dusty object.

"How did you get in here?" Harper said and wiped away the grime to reveal a portable cassette player.

"It's only a Walkman."

"There's something else in there too." Harper plunged her hand back into the vent, holding her breath. When she pulled it out, a small metal box came with it. The box looked like the kind used to store recipes or yard sale cash. With it perched in her palm, she reached for the lid.

"What are you doing in here?" a shrill voice snapped from behind. A woman, about Harper's height but imposing, stood in the doorway, a chain of keys jangling at her hip. "You're not supposed to be here! I'm calling the cops!" The woman's tone was full of accusation as she stared at the items in Harper's hands.

Harper gathered the dusty objects and slung her bag over her shoulder.

"What do you have there? Are you stealing something?" the woman demanded, blocking their exit.

We're done for, Harper thought as the cleaner slid her chain of hundreds of keys into a pocket and fumbled in her apron for something just out of sight.

In a flash, Mara grabbed a brass lamp from the nightstand, something that looked more suited to an 80s Pizza Hut than a motel room and slammed it down on the cleaning woman's head. The woman's phone clattered to the floor as she crumpled, blood seeping from a wound on her scalp. Mara stepped over her without hesitation.

"You left me no choice." She looked toward Harper. "None at all."

"Did she?"

"We have to go."

Harper hesitated, frozen in shock. Mara's hand fell to her side as the reality of the scene hit her, breaking the spell. Careful not to step into the growing pool of blood, Harper turned and hurried out the door, her sister following close behind.

A nightmarish thought clung to Harper's mind and wouldn't let go—they might have killed someone, and there was no turning back. By the time the sisters reached the spare bedroom in Moxie Manor, Harper had devolved into something wild, muttering syllables instead of full words.

"It's fine. We're okay."

Harper shook her head, clutching the items from the vent tighter to her chest.

"You killed her." Harper's eyes went wide.

"We don't know that."

"Did you see her body? The way it fell … lifeless, like a doll? And all that blood?"

Mara nodded; her expression was uneasy. "We'll call and check on her later. Hurting her wasn't my plan. I just reacted. I'm sure she's fine."

"I guess…" Harper's pained expression softened, her breathing slowed.

"What did you find in there?"

"It's…" Harper looked down at the items for the first time, then set them on the floor between them. Even under layers of grime, the metal box gleamed. She lifted its lid, peering inside the pitch-black interior. Tipping it over, she jolted as small objects spilled out onto the floor.

"Holy shit." Mara inched back while Harper pressed a hand to her mouth to stifle a scream. Scattered before them lay a strand of hair, a tooth, and a fingernail.

"A fingernail. It's ripped from the root. Does this … belong to the girl?"

"I think so." They stared at the gruesome items in silence. The fingernail was small and yellowed, a grim reminder of the time spent hidden away.

"These are trophies." She hovered her hand over the disturbing items, as if warming herself by an invisible fire.

"What are you doing?"

"Can't you feel that?" A strange energy thrummed just under her palm, like a faint pulse. "It's reaching out to me. Trying to … communicate." Harper dipped her hand lower, letting it catch the subtle force like dangling a hand outside of a moving car window. "These are more pieces to the puzzle." She arranged the baby monitor in the center of the room and flicking it on. The screen glowed with a bluish, straight from a horror movie, but she ignored the dread it stirred in her. Mara watched her sister's movements as if witnessing a ritual.

Harper picked up the tiny remnants of the girl and scattered them around the other objects. As she did, an aura shimmered above the floor, shifting the atmosphere in the room.

Wiping the dust from the cassette player, Harper held it close to the monitor. Finding the PLAY button, she pressed it, hoping the batteries would still work. The player whined, and the wheels turned, though no sound emerged.

"There's nothing..."

"It needs headphones, dummy," Mara said. Harper nodded when she saw the problem. She dashed to the desk, grabbed a small speaker from her laptop setup, and plugged it into the cassette player. As she connected the speaker to the headphone jack, sound filled the room. She staggered back, as though she'd lit a firecracker.

The aura hovering above the floor pulsed in time with The Eagles and their song Hotel California blaring from the speaker.

The apparition made of static grew, as if it were an inflatable toy gaining girth in mid-air. The shapeless form trembled in the room—lines jutting out and in with the tempo of the song. The jerking motion settled on the rhythm of the drums. Escalating, the movements turned the floating presence into a violent light show. The music continued as an abstract swirl of light and sound grew with each lyric until Harper had to shield her eyes from the jarring spectacle before her. Beneath it all, the vibrations from the objects under the ghost intensified, making the floor thump like the beat of a bass drum. When Harper looked again, the ghostly girl appeared more solid than before—still translucent, but less ethereal, with a faint out-line of flesh.

The child mimed reaching for something. Her ghostly arms stretched out and, as they came back, she held a pristine version of the cassette player lying on the floor nearby. The headphones she held looked un-touched by time, a stark contrast to the worn set they'd found.

"This is working," Harper whispered.

The girl clipped the player onto her waist, raised the headphones, and slipped them over her ears. As soon as she hit PLAY, her eyes glowed red, and a wide smile spread across her face. She lifted a finger with a missing nail and pointed at Mara.

Harper glanced between the ghostly girl and her sister, catching the fear etched across Mara's face.

"Go to her. She's calling you," Harper urged. Mara took a step back, her head shaking.

"I don't want to." She backed away further from the child.

"You must," Harper insisted. Mara's eyes met her sister's, pleading, but Harper's resolve didn't waver.

"Okay," Mara said in a resigned tone. "I'll do what you want."

With a trembling hand, Mara reached toward the girl, her steps slow and hesitant. Harper watched as the child's smile stretched even wider, satisfaction gleaming in her ghostly eyes, and Mara moved closer, her own hand finally outstretched.

A small, ghostly hand gripped a larger one, pulling Mara close. Harp-er watched in horror as the girl lifted her sister two feet off the ground, her red eyes glowing brighter as both hands clamped around Mara's throat.

Harper instinctively stepped back, one foot lifting to retreat, but she wouldn't leave her sister.

Mara wasn't choking, wasn't even breathing as far as Harper could tell. Mara's life was being drained from her by the girl in utter silence.

"Leave her alone, damn you!" Harper yelled. The apparition didn't break focus, its eyes fixed and relentless. Somewhere else in the house, a scream erupted. It took Harper a moment to realize the sound wasn't human; Twix was howling. Whatever force had awoken in this tiny room of the enormous church had set the dog into a frenzied alarm, filling the silence left by her sister's strangled voice.

Desperate, Harper lunged for the baby monitor and the precious objects arranged around it. Without warning, the girl released her grip, and Mara's limp form dropped to the floor like a rag doll, limbs falling at lifeless angles.

Don Henley's raspy voice played on as the ghostly child, floating on a phantom breeze, turned her head toward Harper. The innocent face twisted, contorting into a mask of pure hatred. *Hotel California* soared toward the final chorus.

Twix had stopped howling, but Harper saw him bare his teeth at the scene unfolding around them.

She lifted her gaze to meet the intruder. "What do you want from us? We're only trying to help you." The child's expression twisted from human anger into something demonic, her features contorting with rage.

One moment, the girl floated; the next, she shot forward as if propelled by invisible rails. Whatever fury fueled her now also fed her speed. The music swelled as the chorus hit, the instruments reaching their peak, underscoring the growing terror in the room.

Leading with her head, the child's eyes narrowed to glowing red slits, her mouth open wide as if ready to consume everything in her path. Harper glanced at her sister, still lying motionless on the floor. The apparition transformed before her eyes, shifting from a translucent figure to a more solid, horrifying presence as it glided ever closer.

Harper was certain the ghost had taken something from her sister and intended to do the same to her. Whether it was the objects that had summoned the spirit, or the child herself, had drawn her into the nightmare. Harper pressed her lips together, wishing she had never opened the door and inviting it into their lives. The ghost closed the gap, and Harper accepted her fate, feeling the weight of her sister's loss settle on her.

One last thought flashed through Harper's mind as the intruder's chilly hand wrapped around her neck. The power cord of the baby monitor was just beneath her toes. Her throat tightened as the grip closed off her windpipe, blocking any hope of breath. Slipping the top of her foot under the cord, she wiggled it upward, hooking it with her toes. The pressure on her neck increased, nails biting into her skin as she struggled.

The cord slipped. With her vision fading, Harper made one last desperate attempt, looping the cord once more with her foot and yanking it away. Her leg burned from the effort, but the tension released when the ghostly hands around her neck loosened.

As her vision cleared, she saw the monitor go dark and the child's expression twisted into fury.

"Riley," Harper said through a sore throat. "Your name is Riley." For an instant, the girl's expression softened, surprise flickering across her face, replaced by anger again, fiercer than before. The ghost faded, her once-solid form dissolving back into transparency until only her glowing red eyes remained, two piercing lights that lingered like afterimages from staring into the sun.

Chapter Seventeen

What Remains

Reality slipping in, Sedge found himself ensnared by a waking dream, blurring the line between sleep and a twisted reality. He lay in bed, staring at the wooden beams crisscrossing the ceiling. The rafters spanned the entire church, and he wondered if they were decorative or if each timber played a role in holding the old structure together.

The servants' quarters lacked the warmth and inviting atmosphere found in the rest of the manor. A pious, sparse lifestyle was intentional for a priest's residence.

Only the moonlight gave him any sense of calm, streaming through the windows in a soft, silvery glow. It washed away some of his fear, soothing the discomfort of sleeping in a house that was too large and too full of unsettling history. Yet, as his weariness pulled him deeper, Moxie Manor closed in around him.

Footsteps woke Sedge from his slumber. Though the room was dark, his eyes had adjusted, and that's when he saw her—standing in the doorway, just out of the moon's light, watching him from the shadows before vanishing into the hallway beyond.

Still heavy with sleep, Sedge moved toward the door, stopping at the spot where the woman had stood. His heart was still pounding from the shock of an unfamiliar presence in opening. His mind urged him forward even as his body resisted. He expected his own voice to tell him to get back in bed. Then, with a burst of resolve, he took a step, willing his body to follow the night visitor.

Moonlight streamed through the top windows, casting squares of light across the woman's path. Each time she passed through a patch of light, her body dissolved, fading like melting snow, only to reappear on the other side. The sight was eerily mesmerizing. Sedge quickened his pace, but so did she, always staying just out of reach. She rounded a corner, vanishing again.

"Faster." He broke into a run.

Rounding the corner, he found himself at the start of a long, shadowed walkway, the former center aisle of the church. He thought of all the brides who must have walked down it, stepping into a new life, then of the funerals, the caskets that had lain there. Standing in the dark, he couldn't help but feel like he was in a place haunted by endings. He started down the aisle, moving as quietly as he could, but his footsteps echoed in unison with a second, ghostly set that followed his every move.

Sedge froze. A chill ran down his spine, raising the hairs on his arms, as if someone were trailing their fingers along his skin. He glanced around but saw no one. *You're scaring yourself. There's nobody here.*

He took another step. The echo followed. Only this time, the steps didn't sound like they were beside him, but ... above.

He looked up and saw the woman walking along the rafters, mirroring his movements below, only upside down. Her pale frame glided along the wooden beams; her head aimed straight toward him.

Panic surged, and he bolted. Her steps matched his, keeping pace overhead as he sprinted for the front doors. Sneaking a peek once more, he needed to see her, to know she wasn't too close. She had vanished.

No matter. The doors were straight ahead. Reaching them, he fumbled for the deadbolt, twisting it hard before shoving the heavy, red double doors open.

The damp night air hit his face, but his relief was short-lived. There she was, standing in the open yard, her form unmoving, watching him. Her dress, plain and fit for chores, billowed in a wind that wasn't there. Sedge saw through her now, her outline faint against the yard beyond. He opened his mouth, wanting to speak, but she raised a finger to her lips. The motion sent an icy shiver down his spine, like a scene from a horror film—a figure shushing him before revealing a hideous form.

Floating a few inches above the ground, she studied him.

"Do I know you? Are you ... Lauren?" Sedge asked, voice a whisper. A faint smile twisted at the corners of her mouth, pulling her cheeks and jaw taut. Her dull eyes glared with anger; her nostrils flared, and yellowed teeth appeared between cracked lips. But the broken left side of her face gave her mystery away.

The intact part of her face contorted into a mask of pure malice, so horrifying that Sedge stumbled back. When the woman registered his fear, she paused, and her expression smoothed, returning to an eerie calm. She beckoned him forward, gliding toward the edge of the property.

He shook his head. The words slipping from his mouth, *I can't. Please don't make me.* But as the apparition moved further as the moment SLIPPED away. With a deep breath and trembling resolve, he stepped forward, following her.

They gazed out at the moonlit woods beyond. The woman from another era raised an arm, her hand pointing toward the row of sycamore trees bordering the land. Sedge followed her gesture, eyes drifting to the shadowed tree line.

"What's in there?" he asked, his voice thick with fear. The phantom remained motionless; her arm outstretched. At his question, she tilted her head, as if puzzled by his hesitation. A detective's instinct tugged at him, compelling him to seek whatever lay beyond, even as unease pooled in his chest. He took a tentative step forward.

"You're not the first to search for answers in the woods," a small voice broke through the silence. Sedge spun in every direction but found only the woman still pointing. "The answers have always been in the house. But if you don't look enough, the woods are where you'll end up," the voice continued. He spun once more, this time glancing downward to find a dog—Caspar's border collie.

"You're talking to me." Sedge's eyes widened.

"And you're listening." Twix gazed toward the moon. "Do you know what the word 'detective' means? To uncover the truth."

"Is this really happening?" Sedge asked. Twix lifted his snout toward the woman, then back to him.

"All things are possible until they're not. Everyone has a purpose, even the things in this house. Isn't it your job to uncover that purpose?"

Sedge, caught in a daze, gave the dog a slow, uncertain nod.

For the first time since they'd reached the back of the property, the woman lowered her hand, casting a glance toward the dog, baring her yellow teeth. Sedge sensed her reaction was one of anger, as if she were only now aware of Twix's presence. She pointed to the woods again, her gesture urgent, not an invitation but a warning.

"No." He shook his head. Defiance sparked in his features.

"The best way to capture a moment is to pay attention," Twix said. "You'll see each other now."

The woman lowered her hand once more, biting down on her tongue, which twisted from her mouth like a serpent. Then she rushed at Sedge in a blur of darkness.

Sedge shut his eyes. When he opened them, he was no longer outside. Twix was gone.

"What are you doing in here?" a man's voice invaded the silence. Sedge glanced around and saw he was standing in a bedroom. "Answer me," the voice demanded. Turning, he found Caspar clutching his blankets, his expression a mixture of fear and confusion. When Sedge looked down, he saw with horror that he held a butcher's cleaver—and was naked.

"What's your plan to do with that?" Caspar asked, his voice sounding distant and unreal, as if in a dream.

"Do with what?" Sedge spotted the cleaver gripped in his hand. He dropped it, recoiling as if bitten. Holding his hand close to his chest, he struggled to make sense of his surroundings, a deep chill settling over him.

Each time Sedge blinked, the world shifted, making him question whether he was awake, asleep, or trapped in something far worse. Caspar didn't bother with cream or sugar; he poured hot, black coffee into a cup and handed it to Sedge.

"That was messed up." Caspar tilted the cup to his mouth.

"Yeah," Sedge agreed, taking a sip.

"Why the hell were you naked in my bedroom?" Caspar asked, raising an eyebrow. "And with a weapon, no less. I don't know what Harper would have done if she'd walked in on that."

Sedge's expression shifted, cycling through emotions as he searched for an explanation. "I was following Lauren."

"The woman that took a long fall from the widows' walk?"

"She wanted to lead me into the woods." They both glanced toward the line of trees just visible beyond the windows. "And ... Twix spoke to me."

Caspar dropped his coffee cup, hot liquid splashing across the table.

"He talks to me … too." They stared at each other for a long moment, not eager to be the first to dig into the implications. Caspar broke the silence. "Between a horror writer and a detective, we should be able to figure this out. But please … don't show up naked anymore."

Sedge chuckled, and Caspar couldn't help but join in, reaching for a towel to mop up the spilled coffee. But a sudden, loud bang on the door shattered their moment.

"Expecting company?"

"At seven in the morning?" They exchanged anxious glances.

"Want me to get it?" Sedge offered, but Caspar shook his head, moving to the double doors himself. Before he could open them, Eliza barged in, her expression fierce.

"Why haven't you answered your damn phone? You have it for a reason, don't you?" she snapped, peeling off her jacket and tossing it to the floor, followed by her hat, which spiraled onto the counter.

"What happened?" Caspar asked, struggling to keep up with her frantic energy.

"Oh, we're in serious trouble." Eliza flipped open a journal and jotting down notes. "The police are on their way here, and we need to get our story straight before they arrive. Understand?"

"Eliza, you're scaring me." He cracked his knuckles as he watched her scribble in her journal.

"Sit down," she ordered without looking up.

Caspar dropped into a chair next to Sedge, gripping the wooden arms as if trying to steady himself.

When Eliza finished writing, she set her pen in the center of her journal and closed it, then leaned against the corner of the table, facing them like a principal about to scold unruly students.

"There's a dead girl on your property." she turned to face him. "And … the police know."

Caspar lunged from his seat in shock, but Sedge held him down.

"How do you know this?" Sedge asked, frowning.

"I always add a local officer onto our payroll whenever Caspar moves to a new town. It helps keep information flowing." Addressing Sedge but keeping her gaze fixed on Caspar, who squirmed in his seat. "It's useful for finding material for Caspar's books, but this time, it was crucial. I think Harper should hear this, too."

"She's not here." Caspar pried Sedge's hand from his arm and leaned back into his chair.

"Where is she?"

"I don't know. A yard sale, I think. She whispered something in my ear just before dawn."

Eliza nodded, her gaze falling to the wooden floor. "That might be a good thing. If we can, we should keep her out of this mess."

"What are we caught up in?"

"I got a call late last night. Moxahala Police Department received a tip that there's a dead woman on your land, near the edge of the forest."

"Who's the girl?" Sedge asked.

Eliza shook her head. "I have no clue. But you can tell me why a girl might end up here." She paused, waiting in silence for an answer. "My job has always been to keep readers from finding out where you're living while you draft your books. Over the years, we've had some close calls. But it's safe to say my role has changed now. Am I wrong?"

"The question is, who called in the tip?"

"The informant didn't say."

Caspar thought of Mara. How he rejected her. When she was angry, she was capable of anything. "Let's find the girl!" Caspar yelled, springing to his feet and darting past Sedge's outstretched arm. Caspar was an anchor, as people often described him. But his usual restraint had vanished, if only for a moment, as he rushed toward the front door, eager to see the body for himself.

He heard Sedge and Eliza's footsteps struggling to keep up, but he ignored their pleas to stay away from what could be a crime scene. The thought of a dead girl and the thrill of discovery pushed him forward until he spotted a figure near the tree line.

She lay on the tall grass and had more in common with a creature brought down by a hunter. But it was the eerie arch of her back in death that sent a chill through him; a pose that belonged on the cover of one of his books, not on the soft earth of his yard.

Sunlight cut THROUGH the branches, casting alternating stripes of light and shadow across the girl's twisted figure.

"Don't touch her!" Eliza caught her breath as she reached Caspar. "She's evidence. If a single eyelash falls on her, you'll be the suspect."

Caspar stared down at the girl, covering his mouth. "She's on my land. I'm already a suspect."

The three of them stood in a semi-circle around the girl's body, like mourners at a graveside, as a gust of wind rustled the leaves above, their thrashing growing louder with each passing second.

"I know her." Sedge drew all eyes to him. "This is Gloria." He crossed himself, looking like a priest in a late-night horror movie.

"Who's Gloria?" Eliza asked, glancing between Sedge and Caspar. "Who is she?"

Caspar reached a hand close to Gloria's cheek. Her skin was smooth, radiating life, even in death. The urge to touch her was overwhelming.

"Don't do it!" Sedge snapped, and Caspar stopped just short of contact. "You'll contaminate the scene."

"How do you know her?" Eliza demanded.

"I confronted her on Caspar's behalf. She said he was involved in something ... evil. That his books were rooted in it."

"She was just a wacko," Caspar said. An urge to touch her returned, even stronger.

Eliza bit her fingernails, stepping back from the body. "A woman accuses Caspar of something dark but then ends up dead at his doorstep. Did she say what he was guilty of?" she asked, not meeting Caspar's gaze.

"I'm right here."

Eliza turned back to Sedge. "Did Caspar know she had something on him?"

"I told him." Sedge examined the grass around Gloria. "Step back a little."

A gentle breeze fluttered Gloria's hair across her face before it died down. "Look around her."

They took cautious steps back, all eyes on the girl. He drew a deep breath at the absurdity of a corpse rising on dead limbs, but the thought crept into Caspar's mind. Years of writing horror novels had blurred the line between reality and imagination.

"Footprints." Sedge pointed and stepped further back. "They circled her."

A heavy silence hung over them as they all stared down. Caspar inspected the tracks surrounding Gloria.

"They don't look human." He met Sedge's eyes.

"You're right. They don't."

"There's something else..."

"Dog tracks," Sedge said. "They're all around her, leading toward the forest."

They turned their attention to the rustling trees and the dark openings in the forest line, each opening like a doorway to something unknown.

"You think the tracks are from Twix?"

Sedge shrugged, while Eliza observed their silent exchange with growing unease.

"A body would attract a dog's attention, sure, but..." Sedge trailed off.

"But what?" Eliza pressed. "You don't think it was Twix? What else could it be?"

They stared at the prints, thoughts swirling, when a loud screech pierced the quiet. Eliza clamped her hands over her ears, and the three turned just in time to see two patrol cars pull into the driveway, their lights flashing against the lawn.

"If they see Caspar here with the body, it'll be in the report, and then in the papers. Get him inside and out of sight," Sedge ordered.

Before Caspar could protest, Eliza grabbed his hand and pulled him back toward Moxie Manor. He was a helium balloon, tugged up and away from Gloria and the strange tracks.

Once inside, Caspar and Eliza positioned themselves behind a large window overlooking the yard. Caspar watched as the officers approached Sedge, who shook each of their hands, a casual gesture that surprised him. Sedge stood over the dead girl, smiling, and gestured to the body as if he were showing them his polished car.

"We need to figure out our next move." Eliza paced behind him.

Caspar pulled his gaze from the scene outside with anxiety etched into every step.

"Relax."

"Relax?" She spun around. "There's a dead girl in your yard. How can I keep this quiet? The secrecy of this location is over."

For years, Eliza's obsession had been to protect his secret locations. Now, with the scene sure to hit social media in hours, she was devastated. He placed his hands on her shoulders to still her.

"We need to pay someone off, make this go away."

"It's too late for that," he mumbled. "You did an amazing job keeping it hidden for years. But this book isn't meant to happen here."

Eliza's shoulders sagged, and she dissolved into tears, her composure crumbling. Her moans were raw, and Caspar was uncertain whether to pull her close or step away.

"I don't want it to end," she sobbed. "Our golden run is over. I should have seen this coming, been prepared."

"There's no way you could have predicted this. This isn't your fault." Caspar's reassurance wouldn't ease her. He drew her into an embrace, feeling her heartbeat slow as her sobs softened.

Eliza stepped back and wiped her face. She looked so vulnerable, her big green eyes misty, her curls disheveled. For years, he'd seen her as a relentless publicist, a pit bull of the industry. Now he saw she'd been more invested in his career than he was in himself.

"This could be a new beginning for us. You're the best publicist out there. Imagine what you could do if you didn't have to worry about hiding me anymore."

A glimmer of relief crossed her face, and Caspar offered a warm smile. For once, he allowed himself to hope that this was a fresh start. Living in his character's crime scenes had defined him for so long. Now, perhaps, the chains were off. They stood in silence until a knock on the door jolted them back to reality.

All of Caspar's anxiety came flooding back as he went to answer it, memories swirling: Twix's nightmares, Harper's growing distance, and now a dead fan lying outside. He found Sedge at the door, his face grave.

"Is everything ... under control?" Caspar asked, wincing at the awkwardness.

Sedge glanced inside, catching sight of Eliza before speaking. "The officers want to talk to you," he whispered.

Eliza approached the door, but Sedge raised a hand. "Let me handle this."

A flicker of irritation crossed her face before he and Sedge stepped outside, closing the door behind them.

Three officers stood near Gloria's body, chatting like friends swapping stories over a car engine. When they noticed Caspar's approach, their expressions shifted, though he couldn't decipher what it meant.

"What should I do?" Caspar murmured.

"Be honest, whatever you do. Don't lie to them," Sedge said as Caspar extended his hand, which hung in the air for an uncomfortable moment before one officer responded. He was shorter than the others, with long sideburns, and his handshake was firm but brief.

"I'm Caspar Finch. Thank you for coming." Caspar was aware of his sweaty palm.

"You didn't call us," the officer with the bushy sideburns said.

"Pardon?"

"Someone else called to report a woman dead on your property." He turned back to Gloria's body.

Caspar attempted a polite smile. "I didn't catch your name."

The officers ignored the question, exchanging looks with each other.

Sedge broke the silence. "This is Detective Winston from the Moxahala Police Department."

Caspar crossed his arms. "Did I offend you, Detective?"

Winston's expression turned ice cold. "Everything about you offends me." Caspar took an involuntary step back as Winston advanced. "You find these tragic locations, come to small towns, dig up their traumas, and leave. Locusts like you thrive on other people's misery."

Sedge started forward, but Caspar raised a hand to stop him.

"I like to think I'm shedding light on history that deserves to be remembered."

"Save that crap for your interviews," Winston snapped.

The accusation cut deep, surprising Caspar. Eliza had crafted that line years ago for challenging interviews, but this local detective saw right through it. His cheeks flushed with heat.

"I think you misunderstand me."

Winston's gaze flicked to Sedge. "You're a horror writer. You dream up grotesque things then buy a church to live in while you do it."

Caspar forced a thin smile. "You don't strike me as the religious type, Detective."

"This isn't about religion. There were horrific things done here at St. Pius. When the original clergy disappeared in 1908, they should've burned this place down back then."

"Who are the dark watchers?" Caspar asked, catching Winston off guard.

Winston only smirked, mischief in his eyes. "You may have bought houses with terrible histories before, Mr. Finch, but this place is different. Have any fans shown up here or tried contacting you since you moved in?" Winston's question threw Caspar off balance.

"No," he lied then avoided eye contact. "Do you know how she died?"

Winston exchanged glances with the other officers before replying. "The cause hasn't been determined. Sedge mentioned you didn't know she was here until your publicist told you. Is that true?"

"Yes."

Caspar could feel Winston scrutinizing his face for any hint of deceit.

"That's all we need for now, Mr. Finch. You can go back inside while we continue the investigation."

Sedge stepped forward. "Mind if I stay and observe?"

Winston nodded, his eyes never leaving Caspar as he turned away.

Sedge put a hand on Caspar's shoulder, guiding him back toward the house.

"I'll head to the station with them tonight. But if I find anything, you'll be the first to know."

Caspar's face twisted with anxiety. "Why do I feel like a suspect?"

Sedge glanced over his shoulder at the officers bustling around the scene. "If a dead person turns up on your land, it makes you suspect number one."

Caspar's eyes widened. "But I'm going to prove you had nothing to do with this, okay?"

Reassured, Caspar steered himself toward the safety of the house, Sedge's supportive arm still on his shoulder.

Chapter Eighteen

BRAND SPANKIN' NEW

*O*n the verge of giving up, Caspar tried Harper's phone one last time and heard her voicemail start again. With the sun sinking fast, the familiar dread of the coming night crept inside the walls.

"She won't answer."

"We'll keep trying," Eliza assured.

By the time the investigation ended, darkness had crept into Moxahala. Even as Eliza tried to coax Caspar away from the window, he remained transfixed by the unsettling scene wrapping up in his backyard. He watched as they measured, took photos, before they hauled off Gloria, carrying her to wherever they took the dead.

Caspar stepped into the chilly night, Eliza trailing behind him. Sedge was still at the police station tying up loose ends, and Harper was gone, as usual. For the night, Eliza was his unwilling companion.

"You sure this can't wait until morning?" she asked, fear lacing her words.

Ignoring her, Caspar clicked on a flashlight. The beam cut through the high grass at their feet as they moved over the uneven ground to where the grass lay flattened. They both stood, gazing at the spot where Gloria had been just hours earlier, as if she was still lying beneath the earth.

"Look at the tracks." He shone the light on the small paw prints. "They go into the woods ... and so will we."

The dense branches formed a doorway. They shuffled inside, and without THE moonlight to guide them, darkness settled over them.

"We should go back," Eliza whispered.

"Just relax. We're fine." Caspar aimed the flashlight along their path. "See? It's just bushes and trees. Same as in the light." He resisted the impulse to shine the light on her face; if he saw true terror there, he might just turn around.

"Let's talk about something to take our minds off this," he suggested, pushing further into the shadows.

"Okay. You know, for all the years I've known you, I know almost nothing about Harper. How did you two meet?"

Caspar stayed quiet, the sound of branches scraping his jacket the only answer for a long time.

"We met in school."

"Really? High school sweethearts?"

"You don't think I'm her type?"

Eliza laughed, and Caspar had to steady the light to keep from dropping it.

"Honestly? No."

Caspar thought of an argument but shrugged it off.

"She was out of my league," he admitted. "We'd been in the same schools since elementary, even shared some classes by junior high. But I never spoke to her. You know her as a woman, but as a girl ... she was an angel. When she looked at you, it was like she could see you for who you were."

"Wow. You really had it bad."

Caspar chuckled despite the gloom surrounding them. He tightened his grip on the flashlight, casting the beam across the dense forest, where no tracks were visible.

"If there are tracks in here, I'm not good enough to find them." He aimed the light over the muddy path winding deeper into the woods.

"How did you get Harper to fall for you?" Eliza asked, her apprehension clear.

"It was after her parents died."

"Both her parents? At the same time?" Caspar nodded before remembering she couldn't see him.

"In a way, I guess I saved her."

"What happened? How did they die?"

Caspar saw Eliza's eyes go wide.

"Wait." Caspar froze; his flashlight trained on a distant tree. He thought of the name Scott Sedge had used for the shadowy figures that watched the church, though he couldn't quite recall it.

"What do you see? I see nothing."

Caspar swept the flashlight over the trees, ragged bark illuminated with each pass.

"Dark watchers," he whispered, just loud enough for Eliza to hear.

"You lost me. Who are the—"

Then they both saw it: a pair of eyes gleaming in the darkness. They didn't reflect light like an animal's eyes, but glowed with an unnatural, battery-powered intensity. At first, Caspar saw only the floating orbs in the mist, with no form attached, until his mind pieced together a figure from the layers of shadows. When the shape emerged in his vision, he stepped back, cracking branches underfoot.

"What is it?" Eliza asked, her voice edged with fear. Was there a risk in saying their name out loud? He moved to the right, and she followed. So did the eyes.

"I see them," she whispered. "What … are they?"

"Dark watchers," Caspar repeated and directing the light toward the silhouette. The eyes glinted before the figure slid behind a tree, disappearing. They stood in the dark, staring at the empty bark for a long time.

"It's gone now." When Caspar turned around, he noticed the moon was high above them, through the trees, illuminating where the watcher had been.

Caspar tilted the flashlight down to the ground, then scanned the trees and Eliza's face, pale as a ghost. She looked like she regretted every step they'd taken.

"I just want to go back." The flashlight cast fearful shadows across her face.

He led the way, pushing down his own doubts. Eliza's footsteps snapped twigs as she went.

As they walked toward the moon, Caspar's thoughts kept returning to the watcher. Had he really seen it? It wasn't the time to wrestle with such questions. He pushed forward, picking up speed, almost tripping over a root protruding from the soil.

"Are you okay?" Eliza asked, her voice trailing behind him, out of breath.

The trees thinned, and the moon grew brighter. They emerged from the woods, stepping into what should have been familiar ground near the church … except snow covered the ground.

Caspar's foot sank into two feet of powder, his shoe disappearing into the icy layer.

"What the hell?" he muttered, as Eliza gasped beside him. Just minutes before, the ground was dry.

"It's not even summer yet." She stared at the snow-covered landscape, where drifts rose past her ankles.

"Let's go." Caspar nodded toward the church.

The moon cast a cold light over the snow, turning the landscape into an alien place. Trees that towered a hundred feet into the sky were smaller than he remembered.

"What's happening?" Eliza asked, pulling her shirt tighter as the wind howled around them.

"We need to get out of this storm. We'll figure it out once we're inside."

They found a path between the snowbanks, taking careful steps over the slippery ground. The mounds of snow around them cast strange shadows, making the drifts come alive and threaten to pull them under.

"I'm scared, Caspar."

"I know." He stopped and turned to face her, forcing a smile. "Me, too. This is just some freak occurrence that we'll laugh about tomorrow, alright?"

Eliza nodded, but no smile touched her lips. The gravity of the moment stretched time to a crawl. With the wind biting at Caspar's face, he resumed his path, only to find a dark shadow blocking the way.

"What is it?" Eliza asked, clutching Caspar's arm. The shadow extended, rising upward into a figure that formed in a drift of snow, then it spoke.

"A character always has a choice, even when they can't see the alternative," a small voice said, soft but familiar, carrying a sing-song quality.

Caspar took a cautious step closer, Eliza's grip tightening as he moved. From this new angle, the mix of dark shades sharpened into the outline of a border collie, standing solid against the snow.

"It's ... your dog, right? And it's ... talking?" Eliza whispered, horrified.

"Where are we?" Caspar asked Twix, his voice trembling.

"Seeking shelter in an ominous place is a tired trope," Twix replied, each word rolling out with a mixture of guttural growls and human inflection.

"Then lead us to the church!"

"As you wish." Twix turned toward Moxie Manor.

They followed Twix through the swirling snow, shadows shifting around them as they stumbled across the uneven ground. The church's stained-glass windows grew larger with each step. Caspar passed the dog, pulled open the heavy doors, and ushered Eliza inside.

ST. PIOUS (1908)

Twix shook his fur, sending droplets of melted snow scattering. They sighed with relief until he spoke again.

"Just because things appear safe doesn't mean they are." Twix eyed the dim space of the church.

The familiar features of Moxie Manor had vanished; the kitchen, bedrooms, and loft were all gone. Instead, rows of wooden pews lined a narrow aisle that led toward an ornate altar. Caspar spun around, taking in the pristine surroundings.

"It's ... brand new."

Eliza, edging around the still-talking dog, looked over the space in awe. High above them, wooden beams stretched across the ceiling, with gas-powered lamps hanging down, casting a warm, fiery glow.

"They're not even done yet." She pointed to tools strewn around unfinished woodwork. "Where are we? How is this even possible?"

"I don't know. The snow, this place ... none of it belongs. They completed the church in 1908. That's all I know."

On shaky legs, Caspar approached the unvarnished trim along the main hall. Pulling his phone from his pocket, he slipped it into a gap between the wood and the wall.

"What are you doing?" Eliza asked, leaning in.

"I have another phone. If this is real—if this is another time—the phone might still be here if we ever get back." He turned to Twix. "Is this a dream?"

"A dreamer is one who can only find his way by moonlight, and his punishment is that he sees the dawn before the rest of the world." Twix sat with a solid thud. A dog-like gesture.

"What is he talking about?" Eliza asked, exasperated.

"It's Oscar Wilde."

"Great, he's well read. But there's no one here, Caspar! Let's go. Now," she pleaded.

Just then, a loud crash echoed from another part of the church. They exchanged glances, then looked toward the sound.

"That came from the living quarters."

"So what? That doesn't mean we have to check it out?" Eliza asked. But Twix had already moved ahead, with Caspar following.

Caspar circled back, hooking an arm through hers. "Safety in numbers." He offered a comforting smile.

Twix led the way down the sloping aisle, like an usher guiding guests to a wedding. Shadows flickered at their backs under the gaslight's glow. The detailed altar loomed above them, marking the end of the aisle, with doorways branching off to the left and right. The noise had come from the doorway on the right. In front of the archway lay what Caspar thought was a discarded shoe.

But as he moved closer, his breath caught. Sticking out from the boot was the lower half of a leg. Blood seeped down to the heel, pooling under the faint light.

Eliza clamped a hand over her mouth, stifling a scream.

"Who ... who does it belong to?"

Caspar inched closer, his gaze fixed on the exposed flesh and bone at the boot's edge, then glanced toward the doorway leading into the church's living quarters.

"Whatever did this is still in here," Eliza said.

A door creaked open, slamming against the wall, breaking the silence of the church. A man tumbled onto the floor, bathed in blood. From his shredded clothes, Caspar guessed he was a construction worker—and the missing leg confirmed he belonged to the dismembered limb lying nearby.

For a long moment, the man lay motionless. With his body soaked in blood, death was inevitable, until a sudden spasm rippled through him.

His arms twitched, followed by his remaining leg, as if he were fighting something from within.

"Holy shit!" Eliza inched closer despite the primal fear prickling her skin.

"That's not the wisest decision," Twix growled, his voice low and guttural, freezing her in place.

Caspar circled the spasming man, inspecting his injuries. Dark, circular wounds marred the man's shoulder and arms.

"These are bite marks."

"From what?"

"Moon howlers. They belong to the watchers," Twix interrupted. "You saw them in the woods?"

Caspar nodded.

"Then they saw you too. And they won't let you go."

"If this is the past, it's already happened..." Caspar muttered, his gaze drifting from Twix to the injured man sprawled near the altar.

A scraping noise echoed through the hall, sending chills down his spine. Caspar's thoughts flitted to Sedge's story of the people dragged into the woods. The injured man squirmed as the scratching sound grew louder, as if something dark within him was awakening.

The source appeared: a creature, tree-like, its body rough and bark-textured, crawling from the shadows, clawing its way across the floor toward them. Each slow slide revealed more of its twisted frame, illuminated by patches of light. The beast sniffed the injured man, moving with eerie precision despite its lack of visible eyes.

"Get!" his voice faltered as another shadow detached itself from the darkness, a towering figure, lean and skeletal, whose features looked carved from shadows themselves.

"You're a watcher." The creature's cold, phosphorescent blue eyes glared out from hollow sockets. The very air around them dropped in temperature, and Caspar saw Eliza shivering from the chill.

The watcher nodded, lifting a spindly arm. The creature responded to its master's silent command, revealing two rows of razor-sharp teeth as it latched onto the worker's remaining leg. The searing pain snapped the man from his dazed state, and he screamed, his voice wet and gurgling.

"Help me." He flailed his hand.

Caspar took it, but before he could hold firm, the creature wrenched the man back, dragging him across the floor.

"Leave him alone!" But the watcher tilted its head, a mocking glint in its ghostly eyes. Caspar had the distinct sense it was smiling, though it had no visible mouth.

Then, in a fluid, balletic motion, the watcher lifted both arms as though conducting an invisible orchestra. Two more creatures slithered into the room, their bark-like skin rippling as they prowled closer.

"Caspar?" Eliza whimpered, her voice trembling with fear.

Caspar reached for her, but one beast lunged, its jaws clamping onto her arm. As he darted to help her, the second creature rammed into him with brutal force, sending him sprawling. He watched in horror as they dragged Eliza away, her final desperate glance searing into his mind.

Scrambling to his feet, Caspar chased after her, his mind racing. But as he took another step, his foot slipped in the blood pooled on the floor. He went down hard, the coppery smelled thick in the air.

The first creature pounced, pinning him with its bark-lined haunches. Through the beast's legs, Caspar saw the watcher standing, its hollow gaze fixated on him, the blue glow of its eyes devoid of any empathy. The beast above him bared its jagged teeth, saliva dripping as it leaned closer, prepared to end him.

A guttural growl cut through the silence, followed by a yelp. Caspar opened his eyes to see Twix locked onto the creature's neck, his teeth sunk deep into its bark-like hide. With a swift, practiced shake, Twix clamped down harder, a low growl reverberating through his body. Blood sprayed as the creature's neck snapped, and it collapsed in a heap.

Twix, his fur matted with blood, met Caspar's gaze, fierce and determined. But the watcher's expression remained passive. It lifted its arms again, and from the shadows, more of its twisted servants emerged, their claws tapping on the floor.

"The woods are calling." Caspar said.

"No, we can't leave Eliza here," Twix protested.

"She's gone. And you will be too if you stay."

Caspar struggled to his feet, his gaze shifting to the approaching creatures. "But what about you?"

"I'll be fine." His mouth formed a grin only a dog could muster. Then, with a last nod, Twix lowered himself into a crouch, poised to defend.

Caspar took one last look at Twix before sprinting up the aisle. He didn't dare look back, not even when the growls turned to agonized howls. He ran, even as the haunting sounds of tearing flesh echoed behind him, until he reached the safety of the woods, the nightmare of the church fading into darkness.

Chapter Nineteen

A Rare Find

Vast and imposing, the church wrapped itself around Harper. What had begun as a spacious, intriguing home, a place for Caspar to finish his next book, had turned into her nightmare. She pictured Riley's face; the anger transforming a child into something demonic.

Panic set in as she pushed the bedspread off and breathed deeper, trying to ward off the claustrophobia that had seeped in since she invited Riley into her home. Caspar wasn't beside her when she woke, and she couldn't remember the last night he'd been there. The days blurred together. How long had he been gone? She had no way of knowing.

A creak of the floor accompanied each of her steps down the hall. The first light of dawn filtered through the stained-glass windows, splashing the WALLS with red, yellow, and green. Harper stared at the prism dancing over her palms, recalling the ghostly girl rising in the spare bedroom and Mara crumbling under her power.

"Mara," she whispered. A chill crept over her when she thought of her sister alone with a ghost. She rushed to the bedroom, forgetting her fear. Even her worry about Caspar faded to background noise.

Harper gripped the handle and swung the door open. Bracing herself, she expected to see Riley perched on her sister's chest, draining her life. She clenched her fists, ready to fight.

The scene was less dramatic than she'd imagined. No demon girl, no life-draining force. Mara sat on the floor in the center of the room, in the very spot where Riley had tried to strangle her. She looked like she'd been sitting there for hours.

"You okay, sis?" Harper asked, though she could see the answer in Mara's vacant stare.

"She did something to me," Mara murmured after a long silence.

"You're safe now," Harper offered, but Mara shook her head, rejecting the comfort.

"You don't understand. She got inside me—crawling around, testing for weaknesses."

"Weaknesses?" Harper echoed.

"We all have flaws, don't we? She was looking for a way in, and we gave it to her." Mara's accusation stung, and Harper took it like a slap.. Losing the baby had set everything in motion. The thought hit her like a flood, and she sank to the floor across from her sister.

"The monitor, the camera ... everything. She used my pain to draw me in. I wanted a child. I thought I could replace mine. That's how she infected me."

"I think we have more things to worry about." Mara crawled closer on her hands and knees and pointed to her scalp. "It hurts."

"Show me."

Mara tilted her head, giving Harper a closer look. Leaning in, Harper squinted, trying to make sense of what she saw.

Jutting out from her sister's scalp were coarse, fibrous strands, blending in color but foreign in texture. They resembled plant fibers, rough and twisted, standing out among her normal hair.

"They showed up after Riley touched me. When my throat stopped hurting, my head tingled. I thought it was just from choking, but..."

Harper touched the strange growth, feeling them squirm under her fingers.

"What the hell?" Mara jerked back, slapping Harper's hand away.

"Holy fuck. It's alive!" They locked eyes, both tearing up. Harper motioned her sister closer. "Hold still." She placed her fingers around the fiber as it wriggled, resisting her grip.

"That burns."

"Stay still," Harper repeated, squeezing harder as the thing squirmed. "Brace yourself."

"What are you going to do?" Mara's voice wavered.

With a firm tug, Harper yanked on the coarse fiber. At first, it resisted, but with a last pull, it finally gave. Four inches of a dark, tube-like creature slid from Mara's scalp. No bigger than a thick pen, the creature writhed, mouths along its sides opening and snapping as if in a frenzy. The fresh air agitated it even more. Harper fought the urge to drop it, fearing it might wriggle away and return.

"That was inside me? Kill it!" Mara begged.

Harper lowered her hand, pressing the creature against the floor under her shoe. She increased the pressure, not releasing her grip until it went still. The creature let out a shrill squeal as she crushed it, ending in silence. Lifting her foot, she looked at the flattened, oozing mass beneath.

"What the hell was that?" Mara's voice shook. Harper leaned forward again, inspecting the spot where she'd removed the creature. A hollow space remained. She grabbed her phone, flicked on the flashlight, and directed it at the wound. Inside, she saw the raw, burrowed flesh where the creature had embedded itself.

"Harper?"

What she saw didn't compute. The hole was over five inches deep, which meant it had dug through solid bone and into brain tissue. But the edge of the brain was dry, like it had cauterized it as it ate away skin.

"This isn't possible."

"What's not possible?" Panic was as alive as ever in Mara's words.

"You'd be dead. You should be dead." She wished she had thought it rather than watch Mara cry. "You're going to be fine," she lied, and saw five or six other rooting creatures along the top of Mara's scalp. "There's more that I have to get."

It took them two hours to remove all the rooting creatures. Harper's patience was unwavering in the face of Mara's terror. She repeated the same procedure as she had with the first extraction repeatedly. Only once did she think she was in real trouble. When she came to the last parasite, it refused to budge. Either it clung to life harder than the rest. As she tugged, the thing embedded deeper into Mara's head.

Harper imagined the hundreds of tiny teeth clamping down all at once in unified protest. The idea of it breaking off inside while she yanked gripped her with fear. And the thought of digging into her head with a tool to retrieve the other half was more than she could bear. Luckily, the burrowing animal relented to ending the adventure. She was glad, because every tug agonized her.

When Harper had surveyed her handiwork, there were seven holes in all. Each was far too deep not to have caused severe brain damage. She thought of the augers that drilled holes in the ground to aerate the soil. No matter how much space her brain was missing, Mara continued to walk and talk as before.

Everything sane was gone. A blackness had crept into their lives and contaminated them. They could feel a change in their lungs, as if it was breathing first, and they got oxygen second hand.

The procedure on Mara had taken a toll. Harper begged her sister to stay home, to rest, but she refused to leave her sister's side. It took a while, but Mara found a seat in the car next to Harper. The springs of the vehicle squeaked like a rusty hinge with every bump, but neither of them said a word for a long time.

"Carol will have the answers. She's been in this area her whole life," Harper said. Mara focused on the view from the passenger window. "I'm going to fix this."

Mara shifted to make eye contact and appeared to ponder something before returning to the scene going by at break-neck speed.

Pressing down further on the gas pedal, she allowed the throttle of the engine to express her anxiety and fear. The vehicle zoomed down the country roads with its fuel and her blood merging into a deadly projectile. When she saw a curve she recognized, one she that made her to slow down, she didn't.

All her apprehension about Mara's situation begged her to step on the gas and watch the car take a spill. The urge to unbuckle and lessen her chances of survival took hold as she imagined the car spiraling after missing the turn. And when she could feel the heat from the fiery crash, she let up on the accelerator to stay on the road.

Was that how quickly death swept down on a person? She thought of giving herself over to the spectacular crash. Was it that easy to accept the urges and take a life, even her own? It wasn't the first moment suicide jumped out as the right answer. The idea had colored her world when she'd lost her daughter and, once more, soon after bringing Twix into her life. But the same part of her that wanted to throw it all away was the same selfish part that fought against her misery.

Her worth was a tide swelling, then receding with each passing second. When she reached the yard bird's house, she stared through the windshield and tried not to think about the sacrifice her sister made so she could bring Riley back.

"You ready?"

"I'm not going in there. Do you see my head? I'm hideous."

An argument whirled in Harper's mind, already coming up with reasons for her not to feel sorry for herself. Instead, she saw the genuine embarrassment in Mara's eyes and let it go.

"Fine. Take a nap. I will talk to Carol and, when I get back, we'll come up with a solution for you."

Mara relented with a smile that had no humor and leaned her damaged head against the passenger window. The urge to gaze back at her sister was so strong that she had to stop several times.

Carol swung open the door as if expecting her visitor. The older woman, dressed in designer clothes from a bygone era, had unmistakable Farrah Fawcett hair, hinting at a decade long ago.

"Hello. Here for more yard bird advice?" she asked.

"Something like that."

"I'm afraid the other ladies aren't around."

"I need your help."

Carol held the aluminum door open wider, the spring creaking under the strain. "Cop a squat." She gestured to a couch sealed in plastic. Harper eyed the airtight furniture before sitting. "Laugh if you want but this couch is twenty years old, and it's like brand new."

"Like Tupperware." Harper smiled.

Carol squinted at her. "What did you do to your hair?"

"I left home in a hurry." Harper fluffed her hair self-consciously. It irked her that a woman stuck in a fashion time warp was judging her, but she bit her tongue.

"So, what can I do for you?"

On the drive over, Harper had debated how much to share, teetering between everything and nothing. In the end, she spilled it all, confessing like she would to a priest. She leaned back, waiting for Carol's reaction.

The older woman stared at her for a long moment, then laughed.

"I should go." Harper rose from the plastic-covered couch.

"Don't. I believe you. Or at least I want to." Carol walked into the kitchen and returned with a glass of iced tea. Harper took it, drinking. "It took courage to tell me all that. I'm a stranger. Where's your sister now?"

"She's in the car. She was too embarrassed to come in."

Carol nodded. "Can I see the camera?"

Harper clutched the white Polaroid, its rainbow stripe bright against the old decor. "I keep it with me all the time now. It's the only way I can see ... the other side."

Carol lifted the viewfinder to her eye. "The other side?"

"I got the monitor from you, but the camera is how I found the other items. Mara thinks I should destroy it, along with everything else, to get rid of the girl."

"And what do you think?" Carol asked, lowering the camera.

A shadow fell over Harper's face, her expression clouding. "My fear is, if I destroy everything and it doesn't work, it'll keep her in our world forever. I'll end up in an asylum."

Carol nodded with a thoughtful gaze.

"But…" Harper continued. "The other part of me thinks that the girl has unfinished business. If I find the rest of the items, it might set her free."

"If she doesn't kill you first." Carol handed back the Polaroid. "What kind of unfinished business?"

"You know this area. If there are answers, you can find them. We need to solve her disappearance. Catch her killer."

"This isn't a TV show."

"No kidding," Harper snapped, then softened. "Sorry."

Carol waved it off. "You have every right to be upset."

"I'm scared," Harper admitted, her voice trembling. "Not for me, for Mara." She dropped her head, her hands clenched in her lap.

In two strides, Carol crossed the room and wrapped her arms around Harper. "We take care of each other around here. There's a big community sale this week. Every yard bird worth their weight will be there, and you might find what you're looking for."

Tears fell as Harper nodded.

"Meanwhile, I'll do some digging of my own." Carol's smile was warm and reassuring. "We'll stop this thing together." Her smile was so bright, Harper couldn't help but smile back.

The clouds overhead drifted above with a sense of menace, blocking out the sunlight as Harper reached her car. Everything around her had a purpose in a way it never had before. Life had once been unrelated moments—moving from breakfast to dinner and to sleep without meaning. Now, it was as if she'd woken from a dream and nothing was random. The early chill of spring, the birds flying in strange patterns, even the cars bustling along the highway were pieces in a larger scheme. Was it all an elaborate performance to distract her, to keep her docile while some unseen evil moved in the shadows?

Harper opened the car door and slid into the driver's seat. She glanced at her sister, motionless and leaning against the passenger door. The thought nagged her that this world encircling them might be nothing more than a prison of illusions. She started the engine and revved it, half-expecting Mara to stir, but she didn't.

"Honey?" Harper asked, her voice gentle, coaxing. Mara's head turned from the window, her gaze still far away.

"Yes?"

"We're on our way home. I'll let you rest."

Back on the road, Harper stole glances at her sister. Although Mara had responded, her expression looked empty, as if something essential inside her had drifted far away. Hoping to bridge the silence, Harper reached for the radio dial, needing something to shatter the stillness. A commercial filled the car, a salesman's voice rattling off prices and addresses in an exaggerated pitch, better than the oppressive quiet. Then, a song began, familiar chords filling the space. *Hotel California,* the same tune that had played through the crackling Walkman. The rhythm beat through the speakers, and with every note, the lyrics took on an ominous weight, reshaping themselves in the light.

A wheezing sound rose around them in the car, drowning out Don Hemley's vocals. The scenery blurred past as Harper glanced over at the passenger seat. Mara's eyes were wide, bulging from their sockets, with red veins straining to their limits. Tears trickled down her cheeks.

"What's wrong?" Harper asked, darting her gaze from the road and Mara's terrified expression. "Talk to me."

Mara's body trembled. The spasms started in her face before taking over her entire frame. For a moment, Harper thought her sister was having a seizure. A gurgling noise escaped Mara's throat, and Harper's eyes caught a movement below her chin. She froze as she noticed fingers curled around Mara's neck.

The hands were small but powerful, wrapped around Mara's throat with just enough force to choke the breath from her. The gurgling turned into a raspy gasp. Harper tore her gaze from the road and followed the small hands to an arm, then to a face peering from the back seat.

Riley was there, sitting behind Mara, her hands squeezing tighter around Mara's neck, her expression twisting into a gleeful smile. The Eagles's harmonies rose all around.

"Leave her alone!"

The child dug nails deeper into Mara's flesh.

"Harper." Mara flailed and kicked at the dashboard, scratching at the small hands blocking the flow of air into her body.

When Harper locked eyes with Riley, there was a flicker of recognition then fear in the little girl.

"It's the song." Harper nodded, more to herself than the girl tearing at her sister's throat. The smile that didn't belong to a rampaging child drifted off her face and, although she never moved, her head appeared to shake.

The radio station, **107.3 WYBZ,** reflected in bold with the song title scrolling across the front. In a sudden jolt, Harper reached for the radio, surprised to find she could move her arm. Behind her, a small, ghostly hand was clutching Mara's neck. The muffled, choking sounds from Mara broke into wheezing gasps as the grip loosened.

The girl shifted her fury from Mara to Harper. The song playing on the car stereo had summoned her from some dark realm, and there was frantic desperation in her movements as she tried to silence the music.

Riley gripped Harper's arm tightly with one hand while forming a claw with the other, reaching toward Harper's eyes. Panic surged as Harper glimpsed both the ghost's extending arm and Mara gasping in the passenger seat. Forgetting about the car hurtling down the highway, she lunged forward, stretching toward the radio like a runner reaching for the finish line.

In her peripheral vision, she caught a flash of the girl's startled expression as the radio sputtered out its final lyrics.

Riley's grip, strong as iron, loosened, and her face twisted before she vanished to wherever she belonged. The thought that Harper might have hurt the ghost was unbearable. Riley's absence was more disturbing than her presence, making the car ride suffocating.

Harper adjusted the steering wheel, exhaled, and glanced at Mara. "Tell me you're okay." The engine whined, its high-pitched drone filling the silence until Harper eased off the gas, letting the car settle to a lower hum on the empty highway. She fought an urge to turn the radio back on, but was the song that summoned Riley lying in wait, ready to strike again?

"You remember Mom and Dad?" Mara's voice was clear and steady, breaking the silence.

"Sometimes." Harper noticed the bright red marks Riley had left on her sister's throat.

"It's funny the way the bad things stick with us. Mom and Dad took us to movies, recitals, all those good things when we were kids. But why does it stay with me—their screams?"

"I didn't hear them, Mara. You did." Harper turned her focus back to the road.

"Exactly." Mara brushed her hair from her face, her gaze drawing Harper's. "Karma, little sis. It's looking for its true target. And it won't stop until it finds me."

"Our parents have been gone a long time, Mara. There's no reason to dig up the past."

But Mara let out a low cackle, as if possessed by some unseen evil. "What's so funny?" Harper shot her a sharp look, unable to hide her irritation.

"Does Caspar know?" Mara taunted. "He's your husband. Don't you share everything?"

"Of course he knows." Harper pressed the accelerator to drown out her sister's words.

"Bullshit. Caspar doesn't know a thing. Keeping secrets, that's what we're best at. Don't you see; you and Caspar are drifting apart."

"How is that your business?" Harper's hand hovered over the radio's power button, wrestling with the impulse to turn it on. Would Riley return? The urge to drown out Mara's incessant taunting was overpowering.

"Why are the objects linked to *her* soul?" Harper asked, changing the subject. Silence stretched before Mara turned to face her.

"What is a soul?" Mara began, as if thinking aloud. "I used to believe it went straight to heaven, but now..."

Harper stayed quiet, watching as Mara turned to stare out the window, her expression unreadable.

"We're drawn to things—to objects—because part of us knows we'll leave pieces of ourselves behind," Mara continued. "When Riley died, her soul shattered, clinging to her belongings like shards of glass. People want to believe we go to some better place, but deep down ... we know the truth is uglier. When we die..."

Harper thought of all the rummage sales and thrift stores, tables covered in once-cherished knick-knacks.

"Are you saying our lives get reduced to a bunch of ... trinkets?" Harper's voice wavered, glancing at the red welts on Mara's neck.

"Doesn't the evidence speak for itself?" Mara gestured to her bruises.

"So, what? If we gathered every single one of Mom and Dad's possessions, we could ... bring them back?" Harper asked in disbelief.

Mara shook her head. "Maybe. Or Riley's trying to make us solve her murder."

Harper's eyes widened, as if the thought had just occurred to her. Collecting Riley's things wasn't just about calling the child back. It was also about reaching into the formless dark where she dwelled.

The world blurred past the windshield as they let their questions dissolve into the hum of the engine and the vibrations of the car ride.

Chapter Twenty

SECOND CHANCE ITEM

*A*mid the eerie stillness, every shadow in the forest reached for Caspar as he pushed through the trees, ignoring the pale moon overhead. The image of the creature dragging Eliza away haunted him with each step, and it might have stayed in his mind forever if the watcher hadn't appeared. Was it the same figure he'd seen in the original church? He didn't think so.

The figure's silhouette blended with the chaotic scenery of the wilderness, barely visible except for its glowing eyes.

As Caspar looked closer at the encroaching woods, one pair of eyes became two, then a dozen, all fixed on him. Hopelessness replaced his fear, yet he pressed on toward the open air. Would they follow? It didn't matter—all that mattered was that the watchers had not only seen but noticed him, and that could mean anything.

Back at Moxie Manor, Caspar stepped through the doors, feeling the old church seized him like a second skin, but worn, tired. Different from the version he'd encountered in the forest. Flicking on the light, he took in the room and saw bright yellow crime-scene tape stretched across furniture and walls like bandages.

"It's been pretty hectic since you left," a voice spoke from behind. "Where have you been?" Sedge asked.

Caspar turned to find Sedge studying him. "It's ... good to see you."

"Really?" Sedge asked, his gaze shifting over Caspar's blood-stained clothes.

"Whose blood is that?"

"It's not mine." Caspar avoided saying Eliza's name.

"Should that make me feel better?"

"I mean, in case you thought I was hurt." Caspar stumbled over his words. "I was gone for less than an hour.

Sedge guided him to a chair, careful not to touch the drying blood. "The police circled back for some questions and didn't find you. You've been missing for days." He looked at Caspar, waiting for a reaction.

"Missing?"

"Where were you? Never mind that. We need to get you out of those—" A heavy pounding on the front door cut Sedge off, making Caspar jump.

"They've been watching the house around the clock. They must have seen you come in."

"Who?" Caspar asked, still in a daze.

"Moxahala police." The pounding grew louder. Worse than the sound was the fear on Sedge's face, something Caspar had never seen before. Was Sedge expecting trouble? Had he called the cops as soon as Caspar arrived?

"Brace yourself." Sedge moved toward the door.

"Wait." But Sedge ignored him, yanking the door open. Two officers stormed in, their footsteps echoing in the large room like the grim march of condemned men. The sound carried a chilling finality, reminding Caspar of death row scenes he'd once watched in old movies.

As the officers approached, Caspar threw Sedge a disgusted look. Sedge returned his stare without apology.

"Please, sit down," Detective Ross Winston commanded. He eyed Caspar with disdain. "We have a lot to discuss."

"Do we?" Caspar looked down at the blood covering his clothes and laughed. "I guess we do."

Winston leaned in, his nose almost touching Caspar's. "Let's start from the begin—"

A phone rang, the sound loud and jarring in the cavernous space, interrupting the detective. Caspar recognized the ringtone, REACHING for his pocket before stopping short. The last time he'd seen that phone was when he'd hidden it in the church wall—on the other side of time.

Winston noticed Caspar's reflexive reach and raised an eyebrow. "Is this a joke?"

The phone's ring echoed louder, drawing all eyes to the wall. Moving from Caspar to the sound, Winston pressed his hand against the plaster, feeling along the woodwork where he lodged the phone. The phone rang again but cut off mid-tone. Winston turned back to Caspar and saw his eyes narrow.

"How are you doing this?"

"I promise you, I'm not doing anything," Caspar lied, his voice steady. They all glanced back at the wall, waiting for another ring. But a chilling howl filled the church. The scream was high-pitched, feminine, and laced with an anguish so profound that Caspar thought only a banshee in a haunted wood—or in the darkest corners of his nightmares—could release such a sound. The shriek tore through the silence, reverberating off the walls, forcing Caspar and the others to clap their hands over their ears, desperate to muffle the dreadful wail.

The shriek continued unabated, though the tone of the cries shifted from high-pitched to a garbled gurgle, as if the source of the sound was underwater or choking on a lungful of bathwater. When Caspar opened his eyes, Sedge and the two officers were gone. He was still in the church, yet somehow, he was in a unique part of the interior.

Following the wailing to its source, he saw Eliza sprawled on the floor. She lay flat against the wooden boards, her head tilted upward, and her wide, terrified eyes locked on him, pleading for help as a bark-covered creature tore into her abdomen.

A cold realization washed over him, chilling him to his core. He had never escaped from the church of the past, never stumbled back into his house; he'd never escaped the watcher. It was all a lie.

The air was thick with the coppery scent of blood and the tang of sweat. Twix, his brave companion from before, lay curled next to his feet. Caspar craned his neck to check the dog for injuries, but as he tried to move forward but an agonizing weight anchored his lower body.

Panic overtook him as he looked down and saw another creature—like the one feasting on Eliza—clamping down on him. Its yellowed, razor-sharp teeth glistened with blood near the puncture wounds in his shoulder, and rose-colored saliva dripped from its mouth. Had he imagined escaping, hallucinating his return home? Was some venom running through his veins, clouding his sense of reality?

A wet, rhythmic slapping echoed through the room—a sound he'd never heard before that night. Devoured flesh. Against his better judgment, he fought the impulse to turn his head, fearing the sight of Eliza in her last moments would be unbearable.

"Let her go!" The words tore from his throat, and the creature stopped chewing. The defiant outburst was foolish. It would only draw its attention to him.

His eyes fixed on Eliza's form, lying still. Blood poured from her stomach and chest into thick pools. Her eyes fluttered from shock or pain. If she was conscious, she was hiding somewhere far away from her bleak reality.

The sudden silence of the room was worse than the sound of tearing flesh. Caspar's gaze drifted to a shadowed corner where something darker coalesced. The dark watcher materialized, its form blending into the shadows. A wide-brimmed hat jutted out from the darkness, and its body, towering over eight feet tall, was thin. Where eyes should have been, only eerie, glowing circles stared back, somehow colder and more terrifying than if they had been empty sockets. Had he been lurking there the whole time, or had he appeared from nowhere? Caspar didn't know, but he suspected the latter.

"We didn't mean any harm. Can you let us go? We'll never come back here," he pleaded. Eliza couldn't survive her wounds, but he was grasping at anything that might save them.

The dark watcher remained silent, as Caspar expected. Then, it lifted a gnarled wooden staff into the light, a staff aged and twisted as though it had crawled from the earth itself.

At this silent command, the two beasts near Eliza lowered their jaws closer to her, their intentions clear. The watcher's skeletal hand gestured toward the door.

Relief and dread fought FOR dominance within Caspar. His captor loosened its hold as he stared at the exit, unguarded yet fraught with danger. The staff swung the door's direction once more, compelling him to make a choice.

"It hurts me to do this, Eliza."

She shook her head as tears fell down her face.

"I have to think of my career, my fans. They are counting on me to fill their lives with stories."

"Don't leave me," Eliza's voice rasped, breaking his focus. Her plea, wet and faint, shattered any illusion of escape without guilt.

"I will keep your name alive with my writing. I promise."

"Please, please don't go."

Caspar's mind whispered that there was nothing he could do that could save her. *I'll immortalize you*. A reasoning that disgusted him even as he clung to it.

Avoiding eye contact with Eliza, Caspar tested the waters, pushing himself to a kneeling position and bracing his body for an attack that, to his relief, never came. The creature's claws withdrew but stayed close, ready in case its master changed his mind.

Sliding his arms under Twix, Caspar lifted the limp dog. As if he had to witness Eliza one last time before escaping, he turned to see her sprawled on the floor, blood pooling from several wounds. Her eyes darted around the room, scanning the watcher and the surrounding creatures before locking onto Caspar, a look of disbelief etched across her face.

"I'll take Twix to safety." Caspar backed away toward the door.

"Caspar?" she gasped as the animals opened their jaws, strings of saliva glistening on rows of sharp teeth.

"I'm leaving."

Eliza shook her head. "You'd leave me here?"

"There's nothing I can do for you."

At that, the watcher raised his staff, and the creatures sprang into action. Teeth sank into her neck and face, ripping into her flesh as her agonized screams filled the air, mingling with the sickening sounds of tearing flesh.

"Sorry." Caspar sensed the watcher's amusement as he slipped from the room.

The church, lit by gas lamps hanging from wooden rafters, looked like a ghost ship ready to sail. Pews stood on either side, silent witnesses to his flight. Twix's heartbeat pounded against his chest, warm and full of life, though the limp weight of the dog in his arms echoed in his mind.

"Stay with me, buddy."

His footsteps echoed in the main hall. A reassuring sound compared to the horror he'd left behind. The last image of Eliza was a blur of motion, her blood spraying in every direction. Even with that haunting memory, it was the watcher's hidden face, its silent malice, which drove him to move faster.

He burst out into the snow-covered landscape, the impossible winter air biting at him as he shuffled toward the woods. Just as he reached the trees, Twix spoke.

"I can't go with you," the dog said. Caspar lowered him, exposing his snout to the cold. "If I cross this boundary, it will break the balance."

"I've already left Eliza behind. I can't abandon you too."

"When the final girl trips over nothing or the hero drops his weapon, you break the reader's trust. But it's unforgivable if the protagonist ignores every warning—it's the mark of a self-centered writer. If I cross the barrier, things will change."

Caspar looked down at Twix, his grip tightening. "Will you survive here? What about the beasts? What will they do to you?"

He held Twix close, feeling the dog's weight—a burden both real and symbolic—as he hesitated at the boundary. Twix whined softly but offered no further protest.

Chapter Twenty-One
EVERYTHING MUST GO

*L*ost in thought, Harper couldn't recall the last time she'd thought of anything but Mara. Her sister's suffering had become the background to her every thought. She froze in the doorway, breath catching as she saw Twix—frail, gaunt, unable to lift his head from the ground. The puppy's skin hung over his ribcage, as though he hadn't eaten in weeks. Which made no sense because Harper prided herself on caring for him. Sure, she sometimes resented his presence, especially with the constant visits from the child, but there was no way she'd forget to feed him.

She rushed to the kitchen, filling Twix's bowl with food. Both his bowls were empty. *It means nothing. He probably just finished it.* The lie stung. No sooner had she poured the food than Twix lunged at the bowl, chomping.

"That's on me." Harper watched the puppy, losing himself in the food and water.

The upcoming sale mentioned by Carol loomed like an anchor. Ready to sink her deeper. This wasn't supposed to be her life. There was an obligation to lay Riley to rest, but with each clue she uncovered, the toll grew. Mara's health was deteriorating, and Caspar became more absent than ever—she couldn't remember the last time they'd slept in the same bed. Had it been a week? The thought drifted out, as it always did, before she could hold on to it.

Since Riley's appearance, her life was a fever dream. On days she didn't contact the girl's spirit, her mind cleared, and she was her old self again. But the days she conjured Riley from thin air, a mist settled over her thoughts, dimming everything's importance—*like feeding the dog.* She shoved the thought away.

It had been a couple of days since Riley had last appeared. Her mind was growing sharper, more alert. She even contemplated abandoning the ghost hunt entirely. She'd pile up all the child's belongings and toss them in the trash. By tomorrow, the garbage men would carry away every tormenting trinket, burying them in the landfill.

The thought circled her mind, lingering as she washed the same glass twice. On her third pass, she set the glass aside and focused on Twix, who was still devouring his food. With a sigh, she made her way to the spare bedroom to check on her sister.

Though she dreaded seeing Riley's belongings, she was even less eager to face Mara that morning. It wasn't just her sister's haggard appearance that twisted her stomach, but the realization that she'd exposed her to a supernatural force. She had begged Mara to leave, but each time, her sister only dug in deeper, vowing to see things through. Harper exhaled her relief to have someone by her side, though her heart still clenched with worry about Mara's safety. *I'll stop it before then,* she promised herself.

Holding her breath. She did that more often these days. She swung open the bedroom door, bracing herself.

"Hey, sis," she greeted her in a cheerful tone. It wouldn't stay that way for long.

Mara sat hunched on the floor with her back pressed against the mattress, knees pulled to her chest. It was the posture of a child seeking comfort or protection, her chin resting on her knees as she stared into the distance.

"Can I talk to you?" Harper asked. Mara dragged her gaze up to meet her sister's eyes. "I have to go to that thing." There was no flicker of understanding. "The sale." Still no response. "I'm not leaving until I know you're okay."

Mara sat on the floor, balancing herself on her arms. A word finally broke through her fog. "I'm scared."

"Of what?" Harper glanced around the room, expecting to see Riley lurking in a shadowed corner or hovering near the ceiling. But there was no sign of the spirit. "You're safe now. What's wrong?"

After a long silence, Mara brought something from behind her back. At first, the bright orange handle of the object made little sense; it looked like a pair of scissors, but the tips were narrow and pointed.

"I can't do this myself." Mara extended a needle-nose plier, the kind an electrician might use to twist wires, or a jeweler to shape delicate metal. But in her sister's palm, the tool was far more sinister.

"What do I need those for?" Harper asked, though she already dreaded the answer.

"Take it." Mara placed the pliers on the carpet. "It's for this." Mara lifted her hands, clenched into fists like a boxer preparing for a fight. They trembled as she held them up.

"What am I looking at?" Harper squinted to see anything unusual. She was about to speak when, just, she noticed the movement.

"When did this start?" The question filled the space between them as she looked from Mara to the pliers on the carpet. In her sister's eyes, she saw a fear that was familiar.

"After Riley choked me in the car. That's when the itching began."

"Itching?" Harper repeated, scrunching her face as though she could feel it herself. Mara nodded, staring at her fingertips.

Mara's nails, unadorned, were clear. She'd always avoided polish, even as a teenager, finding it 'too girly.' Now, Harper saw faint black dots beneath the cuticles. The dots were still most of the time, but every so often, they'd shudder in unison, giving a nauseating sense of life.

"Like I said, it was just an itch at first. A faint prickling, like when you come in from the cold and your fingers warm up. But last night, I saw them all moving at once. We need to get them out." She nodded toward the orange-handled pliers that lay between them.

"They're stuck in there. If we leave them alone, I'm sure they'll die on their own."

"Like the creatures in my head? They would have burrowed all the way through my skull. I want them out. Now!"

Taking the pliers in her hand became more dangerous, like wielding a medieval weapon. The mundane tool transformed in her grip, its weight and cold steel sinister, promising pain.

"Close your eyes," Harper instructed, then positioned the edge of the pliers just under her sister's nail. She hesitated, no actual plan in mind, until the black dots—like the belly of a stingray—spasmed beneath the nail.

With a sudden lurch, Harper dug the tool firmly under the nail, wedging the metal edge between the hard nail and soft skin. The calcified layer lifted higher, and Mara screamed. Driven by her sister's agony, Harper clamped down with the pliers and pulled with all her strength, careful to keep the nail from slipping out of the tool's grip.

Mara's screams grew louder until, at last, the nail tore free from her fingertip. To their astonishment, there was no blood, only the black dots squirming in the open air. Mara stared at her fingertip, transfixed.

"Now pull it out."

Harper made a humming sound, unable to form the words to say no. Her turn to close her eyes, she plunged the tip of the pliers into the gelatinous creature embedded in her sister's flesh. Mara's scream returned, joined by a low hiss that grew into a shriek. The squirming parasite resisted, but with a final yank, the stowaway tore free. The sisters stared at the clear, shapeless intruder as it writhed at the end of the pliers.

"Nine more to go," Mara flashed a trembling smile.

The hum of the tires on the road was the only sound, but it couldn't drown out the anxiety simmering in the air. Leaving Mara home to take care of Twix had been the perfect excuse to go alone. She wasn't by herself, though; she carried the image of peeling back her sister's fingernails, an ugly memory lodged deep in her chest. The sickening sounds of flesh separating were one thing, but the whimpers of her sibling were a whole other cruelty.

Mara had always been a tough one. Good at sports in a way that made the boys uncomfortable. She was the first to fight and the last one to cry. Though she was bigger than the other girls, it wasn't just weight; it was muscle, filling the spaces where others her age had none. She had faced the whispers, but in time she was impervious to their judgment. As the eldest, Mara's duty was always to protect her sister. Harper suspected this role had shaped her more than anything else. Mara refused to let anyone bully her little sister. There was no hesitation when Dad came home drunk and had his little outbursts.

Harper remembered those early years, but Mara had recounted them so many times, they became Harper's memories, too. Whisked to another room whenever their father's breath reeked of alcohol, put to bed early on nights their mother's anger boiled over. Mara endured it all, her guardian angel. And now, years later, Harper couldn't return the favor.

Reflexively, she reached for the radio but drew her hand back as if from a flame, the image of Riley waiting to emerge from the speakers flashing in her mind.

"No, thank you." She glanced at the passenger seat, where a stuffed sack sat as her co-pilot. She'd emptied a beach bag of vacation accessories and filled it with Riley's belongings. Sitting beside the items gave the impression of lounging next to an unexploded bomb. *Better me than Mara.*

The community sale was out past Junction City. She was unfamiliar with the area, except it was known for its railroads and the prison where they'd filmed a movie. She couldn't remember the name but thought Robert Redford starred in it. It had been a big deal when she was a child—locals took off work to watch them film some scenes, a high point in a town where nothing much ever happened. "Nothing much happens," she said with a sardonic laugh. Was this just what it was like in a small town? Private moments of supernatural terror that no one spoke about? She'd seen enough TV to know that locals sometimes gave newcomers cold shoulders, or warnings of strange things to come.

For the past decade, she and Caspar had moved into homes marked by tragedy, murders that had inspired all his books. None of them, though, had cold spots or creaking doors to show a haunting, let alone a ghostly presence. This was uncharted territory. They'd pushed their luck too far.

She pumped the brakes when she saw the community sale sign, steadying the bag so it wouldn't spill onto the floorboards. The car tires crunched over the gravel driveway leading to the Junction City meeting area, drawing glances from other patrons as she pulled into a parking space.

She wasn't sure which item would lead her to the next. The camera had power, but what if another object held the key? She slung the camera strap around her neck and clutched her bag of objects. "Better safe than sorry, wouldn't you agree, demon bag?" she whispered to the sack.

A crowd gathered at the entrance. The yard sale season was winding down, and this was the last hurrah for the yard birds. As Harper entered, her palms turned sweaty, her throat going dry. What if she couldn't find any more items? Panic tightened its grip. Without the last pieces of the puzzle, Riley would never go away—or worse, she'd grow stronger. Harper thought of Mara, trapped with a furious spirit. "I have to find you!" She weaved through the tables with her arms extended, feeling for an unseen force. "Come on. I know you're here."

The musty smell was of garages and attics mixed with mothballs and damp cardboard. Harper breathed it all in, feeling the weight of finality settle in her chest. Riley's belongings were a tragic last stop for her life, scattered here among the relics of strangers.

Drops of sweat dotted Harper's forehead. Beneath the low hum of chatter, she could sense a pulse from the surrounding items, like sonar bouncing back through the room. It was faint, but it was there, then gone before she could latch onto it.

If it took all day, she would cycle through everything in Riley's bag until she found what she needed. With her hand on the Polaroid camera hanging around her neck, a spark jolted through her fingers. The current stung, a shock of clarity in her senses, bringing her focus back.

Instead of lifting the camera to her eyes, she let herself follow the invisible pull guiding her. She held the camera high like an offering, clicked the shutter, and snapped several photos. The instant photos slid from the camera, falling at her feet. When she'd captured enough, she let the camera drop back to her chest.

Bending to pick up the scattered photos, she sorted through them, shuffling like a yard sale poker dealer. She paused, her breath hitching at the sight of a red glow. She raised one photo to eye level, aligning it with the tables in the distance.

A faint red aura highlighted a tiny object on the table. With small, jerky movements, she matched the photo to the distant tables as if piecing together a puzzle.

Using the Polaroid as a dowsing rod, she moved closer. The image acted as a map, leading her toward something far more valuable than a collector's item. She held the picture up, adjusting her stance until the items in front of her aligned with the scene in the photo. Back and forth, she compared the tables to the image, her heart pounding as she drew nearer to her goal.

Deductive reasoning was her new hope as she studied everything around her. The objects sat with no discernible connection. Her intuition screamed there was more to see, but her eyes, kept their secrets.

"Where are you?"She lifted the photo again, losing the alignment she'd glimpsed from afar. Frustrated, she threw the photos to the ground, pulled the camera to her face, and clicked the button once, twice, three times before the camera refused to release more films. With the film spent and her confidence shaken, Harper let the camera swing against her chest, its plastic weight landing against her sternum with a stinging thud.

Something on the ground caught her attention. The photo—the last of the trio—lay on the cement floor, glowing from the center like a neon halo. Letting gravity guide her, she bent her knees and reached for it. A pair of round glasses, the kind a little girl might have worn, making them even larger on a child's face.

It was a whole new game now. The red glow was like a college student's highlighter, marking the answer in a textbook. She knew the red wasn't in the picture but she saw it just the same. A quick swivel of her hips, and Harper spotted the glasses lying between a vintage salt-and-pepper shaker set and a pair of winter galoshes.

"See anything you like?" a voice asked nearby. The question registered. The glasses drew her forward, pulling her hands level, urging her to take them. And she did. A familiar, tingling vibration coursed through her fingertips, tricking her into thinking the metal frames were white hot.

Logic dictated she should drop them, but she lifted them to her face and slid them on.

The burn didn't transfer from her hands, but the tingling remained as the glasses settled on her nose. Though they had a low prescription, her vision pulsed, with a blinding effect. In a flash of light, her surroundings transformed, becoming something feral. The patrons looked like ants in a colony, moving between tables in random directions. But now, every movement had purpose, a purpose Harper alone could see through Riley's glasses.

To her naked eye, there had been no rhyme or reason in the movements. But now, where there had been a single red glow in the Polaroid, the entire yard sale was bathed in a sea of red. Fifty tables, thousands of items, all gleamed with a scarlet light. As if the red glow emitted pheromones, the customers who had wandered moved with a singular purpose. People straightened from their slouches, standing tall as the glowing auras reached out with spiky tendrils, wrapping around them like invisible vines. She watched in horror as each person leaned into the pull of the tendrils, sniffing the air, as if responding to some primal, buried instinct.

What frightened her most wasn't the scene itself, but the unnatural silence that filled the room. Conversations, the chatter of haggling, the hum of people browsing all ceased. Those under the spell, including some vendors, were frozen mid-movement, leaning but silent. The tendrils, as far as she could tell, caused no visible pain, but something stirred beneath the surface. She scanned the room, noting the vendors, who turned in confusion, trying to understand the sudden paralysis gripping their customers.

The silence before the storm. She had heard the phrase countless times, but it had been an empty cliché until now. The crimson tendrils stretched across the room, connecting one person to another, some threads long and taut like umbilical cords, binding multiple people at once. Those multi-tethered connections frightened her the most. Sweat pooled on her forehead, a drop threatening to slide before a sudden shift of movement in the room seized her attention.

With trembling fingers, she slid the glasses down her nose, and the auras disappeared. The crowd's erratic behavior remained, though. Slipping the glasses back on, she saw the red tendrils had pulsed, as if their hosts fed from them. Faces that had been blank now wore clenched jaws and taut muscles, everyone moving with a purpose Harper sensed would soon reveal itself.

Following the red lifelines, some patrons took indirect paths to their objects, winding through the maze of tables. Others jumped over obstacles in their way. A feverish frenzy overtook the crowd. People shoved each other aside, some even trampling bystanders. Parents knocked over strollers or dropped their children, oblivious to anything but their goal. There was no single direction the stampede led, which made the chaos even more frightening as people bashed into one another, each one desperate to reach their object first.

The moment Harper feared arrived. Two treasure hunters, tethered to the same object, stood face-to-face, panting, neither willing to surrender. A large man with a trucker hat, loomed over a smaller, frail-looking man in a suit. Harper braced for the inevitable clash.

But rather than overpowering his opponent, the big man dropped to his knees, opened his mouth, and sank his teeth into the smaller man's leg, tearing through denim and flesh. A scream echoed as the fabric and skin gave way, but the smaller man retaliated like a rabid animal, biting back, coming away with chunks of bloody flesh. Harper waited for the burly man to strike back, but he only collapsed, clutching his mauled leg as blood stained his jeans.

The surreal violence shocked her, paralyzed her. She could only watch, trapped in a nightmare scene of human instinct reduced to savagery.

Blood dripped from the smaller man's lips as he moved toward the table, spitting out a piece of skin lodged between his front teeth. With a trembling hand, he reached for a Victorian Hairbrush. The brush, made of nickel, didn't look valuable to Harper, but to the victor, it was priceless. He squeezed the brush, flashing a triumphant smile at the trucker still rocked below him in pain.

Farther off, another dispute was underway. A woman Harper had pegged as a sweet, elderly lady was digging her bony fingers into the eyes of a woman in a shabby dress. Half the length of the elderly woman's index and middle fingers disappeared into Shabby Dress's eye sockets. The victim might have been able to fend her off, if not for the object clutched desperately in her hands: an old landline phone, the kind mounted on walls in the 80s.

Instead of protecting her vision, she clung to it, unwilling to let go. The older woman pushed her fingers deeper, scooping out Shabby Dress's eyes. With a scream, Shabby Dress let go of the phone, clutching her mutilated face while spewing curses at her attacker.

But what happened next was something Harper never expected. Shabby Dress forgot her ruined eyes, dropping her hands to fumble on the cement floor for the phone, desperate to reclaim it. Her opponent, with the advantage of sight, slid the phone just out of reach, cradling it to her chest like a long-lost grandchild.

Each vendor booth held its own story of conflict, yet the goal was the same: to seize the treasured item that had always eluded them. Harper was certain none of them had cared about these items moments before, but it didn't matter; they became priceless. Some fights ended quickly while others battled to the death.

The red auras flickered above the fighters but solidified as soon as a victor claimed their prize. Harper thought of the original *Tron*, where characters recharged by drinking from energy pools. The victors bristled in the trophies they held above their heads, standing over their defeated opponents.

The mad rush slowed as the losers slumped to the ground or backed away to avoid further injuries. A kind of twisted revelry began among the winners, who looked out over the carnage with quiet satisfaction, exchanging knowing nods or malicious smirks. The once-casual scene in Junction City Hall had morphed into something post-apocalyptic.

Harper's detached fascination ended. Before she could react, the weight of another body slammed her down onto the unforgiving concrete. She gasped, struggling to breathe. Her head filled with a dull hum, as if she were observing through a tunnel.

Above her, a heavy-set woman loomed, older but not by much. Solidly built, with bright red hair and freckles that pulsed with her anger. Her fury made the freckles glow. *How could I have been so stupid?* Harper berated herself. She'd seen a thousand auras streaking through the room but never suspected she was in any danger.

The red-haired woman was frothing, her breath coming in harsh pants. Harper lifted her hand like a traffic cop, a last-ditch effort to stop this enraged woman from attacking her. "Give me a second." Harper struggled to breathe. "You knocked the wind out of me." But the look in the woman's eyes told her she wasn't coming out unscathed. "I can give you these." Harper removed the glasses and held them out as if offering a hundred-dollar bill. A plan formed in Harper's mind.

The woman's aggression masked something else. Was a sense of loss attached to the glasses? It struck Harper then: Riley's objects didn't just connect to each other; they resonated with people's own dark pasts. She had unleashed a virus, awakening the buried histories of each item for these unsuspecting buyers. Would the new owners follow trails of old murders, wicked secrets, or horrors beyond anything Harper could imagine?

Her hand, trembling, extended the child's glasses. The woman looked like a frightened deer, inching closer but ready to jump back at any moment. But then Harper hesitated. If she gave up the glasses, Riley might never leave, and the torment of Mara would never end. *What if they break?* she thought. *They're only made of glass˚.*

The first signs of her opponent's ANGER surfaced, different from the woman's earlier behavior and from what Harper had witnessed in others. It was a modest fire, yet it grew.

Harper laid the frame of the glasses on the cement, but instead of pulling her hand away, she slid them under a nearby table. The bit of misdirection left her opponent confused, like a puppy watching a ball thrown one way but landing in the other. And, like a puppy, the woman ran toward the glasses, driven by instinct.

It was all the time Harper needed. She found her feet and moved behind the distracted woman. Her window of opportunity was finite, and if she didn't act, she would lose the eyeglasses—and Mara.

"You're not giving me a choice."

Stealth wasn't her priority in the chaotic room, but she'd underestimated the other's awareness. Just before the woman reached for the glasses, she swiveled on her heels. Cold eyes fixed on Harper with renewed fury.

"I can't let you have those. I'm sorry," Harper admitted.

If she'd been watching herself from a distance, she'd have admired her bravery. But the question of how to stop this woman loomed.

It turned out her opponent had an answer. As if something had detonated in her mind, the woman's face contorted, teeth bared, hands forming into claws, and she lunged. Harper didn't have time to react before those claws closed around her neck, nails biting into her flesh. The woman wasn't trying to incapacitate her. She wanted to destroy her.

Harper's eyes widened as the nails sank deeper, warm blood trickling down her neck. The woman's eyes possessed something otherworldly. *If only I had the glasses on,* Harper thought. Was she controlled by the red strings, like a marionette?

But that question didn't matter. If she didn't escape, she'd be dead in minutes.

The woman's hands were tired from squeezing and releasing. Her struggle to keep up the force gave Harper hope. *Will she weaken before I pass out?* Desperate, Harper searched her body for anything that might help.

Her hand brushed against the bag of Riley's objects. Plunging her fingers inside, she fumbled through its lining, unsure which item might save her. The world around her blurred as her attacker's face shifted from clear to hazy. She slipped away as a drowsiness overtook her, inviting her into oblivion.

But in one last connection between her brain and hand, Harper's fingers closed around something small. She tightened her grip, letting the object slide until it rested against her knuckles.

Summoning her last ounce of strength, Harper pulled her hand from the bag and jabbed the motel key she'd found straight into the woman's chest. The woman's grip tightened, but then she gasped and staggered back.

The red motel keychain dangled from the key now embedded in her chest. Somehow, Harper had lodged it between two ribs.

The woman stared down, stunned, as if her chest had become a door with a lock and key. Gasping for air, Harper pressed a hand to her own neck, feeling the air rush back into her lungs. The burning sensation was a strange relief.

Watching her enemy struggle to breathe, the dangling keychain swinging with each breath, was surreal. With trembling fingers, Harper reached out and yanked the key from the woman's chest. It made a sickening, slurping sound, and the woman's face shifted back to anger.

In the next instant, she turned and bolted, lunging for the eyeglasses under the table. Harper's mind raced. In a few strides, she caught the woman by the shoulder just as she reached under the table. But the woman retaliated, ramming the back of her head into Harper's face.

There was a nauseating crunch. Harper's mouth filled with blood, and two teeth bounced onto the cement. She prodded the gap with her tongue, feeling the jagged spaces where her top front teeth had been. The sight of her own blood and the sounds she made amused the woman, who laughed a long, sinister laugh.

The laughter was a fuse, sparking a new rage in Harper. The earlier desperation dissolved into a primal urge: *Make her stop laughing.*

Harper seized a handful of the woman's red hair and yanked, cutting her laughter short. She relished the surprise in the woman's eyes, pulling her head back like a dog on a leash.

"Fuck you. You're not taking my glasses." Harper slammed the woman's head against the vendor's table. Her prisoner's head cracked against a plastic object, making a snapping sound. She yanked her up again, and her expression went blank.

As the woman turned, Harper saw a long, golden piece of plastic protruding from her ear canal. A bowling trophy had impaled her skull, the figure broken off inside her. Blood trickled.

Releasing her grip, Harper watched the woman collapse. The redhead's eyes dimmed. Her life ended. Glancing up, Harper caught the horrified gaze of a vendor. She bent down, wondering whether to retrieve her broken teeth. Instead, she scooped up the glasses, tucking them into her bag.

Fights raged around her as she weaved through tables, backtracking and dodging combatants. She burst into the sunlight outside and released a long sigh.

"Harper?" a voice called out behind her. Carol, heading in just as Harper was leaving, stared at her in shock. "What happened?"

"Don't go in there." Harper pressed her hand to her broken mouth, wiping at the blood.

"Who did this to you?"

Harper shook her head. "I have to go home."

"Then I'll take you." Carol guided her away from the sale of the century.

Chapter Twenty-Two

No Returns

Through the haze of his thoughts, a feeling hit Caspar like a wave, overwhelming and disorienting. Living this moment for the second time, down to the smallest detail, took him outside his body. Caspar forced his muscles to relax when he passed through the doorway of Moxie Manor once more.

His last attempt had led him back into the arms of a creature, leaving him without the slightest idea he'd ever escaped. Would this time be any different? Apart from carrying Twix from the church beyond the woods, everything else was the same. He crossed the threshold of the red double doors and flicked on a switch. The lights in the main part of the house illuminated the walls and ceiling.

"Harper?" His voice echoed through the home. As the rooms opened in front of him, Caspar froze in place. Yellow crime scene tape filled the room. The ribbon stretched from one piece of furniture to another, like a bandage on an injured victim. He followed the bright tape as it meandered from one part of the house to the next. A spider's web came to mind—just as it had before.

"It's been pretty hectic since you've been gone," a voice spoke from behind. "Where have you been?"

Caspar turned to find Sedge studying him.

"I'm not sure how to answer that."

"There's blood all over you. And ... snow?" Sedge asked, hiding his confusion. "You've been gone for days."

With all the gentle care of a new parent, Caspar placed the new Twix on the floor.

"The media have been going crazy across the country. Your disappearance has become big news. I wouldn't be surprised if they photographed you coming in here tonight. The press has been camping out around the property, as well as..."

"As well as who?"

"The police."

Caspar nodded and sat in a nearby chair. A patter rose on the hardwood floor, and they both watched as one Twix walked up to the other.

"What's happening? Why are there two?" Sedge asked as the dogs stood in front of each other. Neither reacted as though they were in any danger. The old Twix crept closer to the new one, tilting his head as if peering into a mirror rather than facing a doppelgänger.

"This version saved my life."

"Version?"

Caspar nodded again, hinting there was more to say, though he didn't intend to explain. "I need to get out of these clothes and sleep. We'll talk in the morning."

"You can't just—"

"In the morning." Caspar walked toward another part of the church. Sedge didn't follow, but kept his eyes fixed on the twin dogs that shouldn't have existed in the same space.

Sleep came fast for Caspar, but as he drifted into a dreamscape filled with watchers and malevolent creatures, there was no peace. His night was full of fear, anxiety, and reliving Eliza's last moments.

When he awoke, sweating and terrified, he was more exhausted than when he'd first laid his head on the pillow. The bed he shared with Harper was empty, as usual. He couldn't remember the last time he'd seen her. The worst part was, he hadn't even thought of asking Sedge about her the night before. She hadn't been a concern, slipping from his mind as soon as she'd entered it. As an author, he believed that if a thought or idea was important enough, it would always return.

For every action, there was a consequence, and for an author going missing with his publicist for days, there would be fallout, especially since only one of them had come back. Caspar went through his morning routine in a daze, his movements mechanical, as though on autopilot.

What could he tell the police that would make them believe him? How would he explain himself to the public, to his fans? They were already skeptical. Then there were the conspiracy theorists, not fans of his books but looking for cover-ups wherever they could find them. Ironically, what he needed most was a good publicist.

As he left his bedroom and walked into the rest of the church, the walls pressed in, carrying with them the lingering presence of Eliza's death. The church's hundred-and-fifteen-year-old musk clung to the rafters, the plaster, and even the creaking floorboards. Each step echoed with the memory of his friend's demise.

He'd known about the church's dark history when he bought it. For a writer, it was the perfect backdrop: people had gone missing in his house.

But after witnessing what had happened to Eliza and to the construction workers who'd vanished during the church's early days, he'd never use such a cheap and exploitative detail as Eliza's death. Or at least that's what he told himself.

Caspar had already reached the kitchen when he noticed Sedge sitting there with a cup of coffee in his hands. "Thanks." Caspar brought the cup to his lips before he'd even finished the word.

"Harper isn't here."

Caspar savored the burn of the hot liquid going down, and the mention of Harper jolted him. *Why do I keep forgetting about her?* The urgency of seeing his wife was like a dolphin swimming near a boat—surfacing briefly, only to disappear again.

"Where are my clothes from last night?" Caspar asked.

"I took care of that."

"Okay ... because there was a lot of blood—"

"Meet Matthew," Sedge interrupted, tilting his head toward the kitchen table behind them.

In his morning fog, Caspar hadn't noticed the young man sitting there. "I'd make a terrible detective." He hurried toward the stranger and spilled coffee as he went.

"I'm Matt," the young man introduced himself, not looking up from his laptop.

"Yeah, I heard that part." Caspar raised his voice a bit to compete with the hum of the laptop.

"When you vanished, the press swarmed. Not to mention the public interest—it grew fast. We had several looky-loos creeping onto the property. I dragged them away, but Harper thought it was best to bring in someone to tighten security. Matt's been here since you left."

Matt gave Caspar a tip of an invisible hat. Caspar took him in, noting the thrift-store Led Zeppelin shirt, skinny jeans, slip-on Chelsea boots, and the vaping device never left his hand. On cue, Matt took a puff and blew out a plume of smoke with a sugary scent—vanilla or cotton candy.

"It's for my glaucoma." Matt threw a sarcastic grin.

Caspar had gone down the vaping rabbit hole the year before, researching for his last novel. From what he'd gathered, he wouldn't die from secondhand vape smoke. At least, that's what the public thought. But that's what doctors had said about cigarettes before the fifties. It was no surprise. Even to smokers. It was a shared delusion, a way to keep doing what they wanted.

"I'm Caspar."

"I know you," Matt said.

An idea surfaced again. "Where's Harper?"

"She wasn't here when I got up." Sedge settled into a chair beside the young tech expert. Caspar found a seat across from Sedge, and together, they looked like a pair of adults getting their taxes prepared by a high school student.

"What did you do to the place?"

Matt kept tapping away but shot a knowing smile over his laptop. "With the number of requests Mrs. Finch asked for, I'd say my price is a bargain."

Caspar gave Sedge an are-you-serious-about-this-guy? look°. "Of course, you're a bargain. Tell us how you've come to our rescue."

Matt sat up straighter, discarding his flippant exterior for a moment. Caspar suspected this was a familiar situation in the security business: the wife hires an expensive security specialist, and when the husband finds out, he tries to send them packing—minus the security deposit.

Caspar leaned back in his chair, folding his hands, as if to add a little pressure to the young tech's performance.

"Here's the deal." Already a poor start. Caspar couldn't help but grin. "Wiring a century-old church, especially one made of brick, wasn't easy—kind of like trying to get a boomer to forget their conspiracy theories."

Neither Caspar nor Sedge cracked a smile. Matt pushed on. "Interference in such a solid structure is insurmountable—"

"So, you're telling us you failed?" Sedge interjected, adding a little heat.

"No," Matt replied, surprised by the skepticism. "I installed 360-degree motion sensors around the house exterior and a more sensitive version on each window. That took time, especially with the delicate stained glass." He paused, expecting some praise. None came. "You only had one network monitor. Might as well have had none. I added a two-way monitor outside every exterior door and inside each room, except one."

"Except one?" Caspar asked, and Matt nodded.

"Your wife didn't want a monitor in her spare bedroom. I also connected every light in the house to the intranet, so they *all* work with voice recognition."

"Really? You're serious? It's installed now?" Caspar asked, intrigued.

"Sure. Give it a spin."

Caspar cleared his throat and looked around the room. "Living room lights off," he ordered. The lights went out with a soft electrical snap. It was daytime, so the effect wasn't as dramatic, but it worked. "Living room lights on." The lights responded again. "Nice."

Matt sat a little taller, pleased.

"Everything worked out in the end, but I can't stress enough that Mrs. Finch's unusual requests have raised the estimate quite a bit. It's also why I need to be here full time."

Caspar watched Matt flinch, as if bracing for a blow. "What unusual upgrades?" Caspar asked, turning to Sedge.

"I have no idea. Harper's been out more than she's been in since you've been gone." Sedge said.

Matt cleared his throat, ready for a make-or-break moment. "I installed two full-spectrum recorders. One inside, one at the entrance."

"Recorders?"

"Yep. Night vision. I also set up REM pods at intervals from one end of the church to the other. And I brought one radiation detector—a Geiger counter."

"What the hell kind of stalkers do you think we're dealing with?" Sedge asked.

"And REM pods are what, exactly?" Caspar added, a note of fear in his voice.

"Basically, portable MEL meters," Matt explained. "They detect EMF or temperature fluctuations."

"Wait a minute." Caspar's gears turned in his head. "You're describing ghost hunting equipment."

"Like in *Ghostbusters*?" Sedge asked, but they both ignored him.

"For the price of these high-quality items, I'd call them paranormal equipment."

"What the hell is going on? Are we talking about ghost hunting here?"

"I also have these." Matt pulled two mechanical devices from a bag beside his chair. "This is a frequency scanner, or a spirit box. Good for capturing white noise. And this baby, I got off the dark web. It's a thermal imaging scanner. Chargeable, portable, and perfect for filtering out false positives."

"You piece of—" Caspar's fury boiled over. "You suckered my wife into buying you a ton of expensive ghost-hunting toys." He reached for Matt, but Matt raised his hands.

"Hey, I'll admit I've wanted to use this stuff, but I didn't bring up *any* of these tools. All of it was suggestions from Mrs. Finch."

"Bullshit."

"Listen," Sedge said. "We both know Harper. She's foul-mouthed, hard to fool, and she's not shy about asking for what she wants."

Caspar's face held a look of outrage, words unspoken, before he relented."You're right," he said to Sedge, then turned to Matt. "So ... how does all this stuff work?"

For the first time, Matt grinned. "Gather around, folks, and prepare to be amazed."

He pulled up a screen, where blinking dots moved. "Oh, damn. I didn't have time to test everything, but we've got something heading toward the house right now—and there's more than one of them."

Caspar glanced between Matt and Sedge, his pulse racing. "What's coming for us?"

Detective Winston clamped cuffs onto Caspar's wrists. The steel pressing into his skin was the worst sensation Caspar could imagine. The cold metal, never warming, and the awkward angle forced on his arms were constant reminders of the violation. He heard each click of the mechanism as the cuffs tightened until they dug deep.

A pinch stung as Winston led him out the double doors, only to stop and squeeze the cuffs tighter, forcing two more clicks. *Motherfucker.*

As they dragged him from his house, putting on a show for the neighbors, Winston smiled, steering him to the waiting black-and-white."We'd hate for you to write your way out of this." Caspar twisted back as he walked, spotting Sedge giving a small nod.

The car ride was brief. They could've walked him to the Moxahala police station in the same amount of time, but they wanted to give the press a good show. A dozen photographers had hit the jackpot—or Winston had taken a little something extra to ensure the public humiliation of the talented author's fall from grace. By nightfall, every social media platform would post Caspar's image, followed by every newspaper. The headlines wouldn't even matter. Damage done.

There was nothing more American than a good underdog story, but there was something even sweeter about watching a celebrity taken down a peg, then stew in humble pie for a few years. If this was his reward for packing up to live in a "haunted house" for the sake of the public's entertainment, they could all go to hell.

More indignity awaited him as the police escort stopped in front of the station. Just as he should've guessed, the paparazzi were waiting for his arrival. Moxahala had a post office, a carryout that sold bongs, and a police station, yet somehow big-city reporters were there at the perfect time.

He considered giving them a wide-eyed grin, like Richard Ramirez, or a smirk like Ted Bundy's for the cameras. That would make for some *great* press. They would not hold him long anyway, so why not? But as the cameras—some high-end DSLRs and others just Androids and iPhones—aimed at him, his bravado ebbed, and the chicken in him won out.

The young officer who had the 'honor' of pulling him from the car enjoyed his job a bit too much. *It's your big break, son.* Caught up in his eagerness, he wrenched Caspar's arm. "Take it easy." The officer yanked harder.

The inside of the station was even smaller than it appeared from the outside, if that was possible. Calling it a station was a stretch; it was only a front desk, a couple of offices, bathrooms, and a holding cell in the center of it all.

"What is this, the set of *Night Court*?" Caspar quipped. No one laughed at his joke about the long-forgotten sit-com. "Your loss. That show was ahead of its time." The officers were unmoved. They led him to a large, partitioned cell and tossed him inside, rougher than necessary. The enclosure had three holding cells, all empty except his.

Moxahala was so tiny he wondered how many prisoners it ever saw. Maybe a town drunk needing to sleep off a wild night or a domestic dispute that spilled out onto the lawn, he supposed.

Detective Winston Ross strode into a smattering of applause, as if he'd single-handedly captured Jeffrey Dahmer. "I don't belong here."

Winston turned and pointed at him. "Take him to the back."

No sooner had they thrown him into his cell than they were jerking him back out, testing the limits of police brutality with each tug and pull. They took him to the conference room, which was even shabbier than the front of the station. The room looked older than the rest of the building, not designed for interrogations.

An officer swept books and files off a small table in the center and shoved Caspar into a chair. It was a storage closet, or a breakroom, anything but an interrogation room. Inside were two chairs and a table, with no two-way mirror like in the movies. *I'll spring for the mirror when I get out.*

"What's the matter? Don't like our place?" a voice said behind him.

Caspar stiffened, counting each step echoing in the cramped room as Winston collapsed into the seat across from him. "We meet again. That didn't take long." Winston adjusted his suit jacket. Though youthful, the detective's face showed a trail of wrinkles, especially around the eyes, that hinted his best days were behind him.

"What did you do with Eliza?" Winston's words shot out like a drunken sailor.

"She isn't with you?" Caspar asked. "How would I know where she is?"

Winston eyed an officer left behind and, with a tilt of his head, signaled for the two of them to be alone.

"Caspar Finch," he announced like a teacher calling roll. "Let's be honest with one another. You're not a hot-headed asshole, and you're not a showboat. So why the pretense?"

The words cut Caspar, but instead of answering, he retreated further into himself.

"If we're being honest about who we are, I'll start first." Winston leaned forward. "I know everything about you, and it's not just because I'm a diligent detective—though I am. You're a nerd who likes video games, vintage consoles, and arcade machines. You love the original *Star Wars but* hate the sequels. Your favorite books are fantasy-driven, even though you've made your living writing horror. Because you hit it big with your first novel, and if I had to guess, you'd rather it hadn't been horror so you could be free to write whatever you want."

Hypnotized by Winston's cadence and unnerved by someone speaking about him, Caspar watched the detective's mouth open and close as he continued.

"You married your high school sweetheart, Harper, right out of school. I've seen interviews with you two—she's smart, beautiful, and way out of your league. Yet you've stayed together."

"This is impressive." Caspar escaped from his stupor. "But I could throw a rock and find a dozen stalk—fans who could recite my life back to me."

"Fair enough. I call you out, you call me out." Winston paused, letting his words sink in. "When people meet their favorite author, there's a question that burns in them. It floats in their minds when they read the books, at signings, and even while watching A&E specials. And I have one for you."

"Go ahead. Ask it." Caspar braced himself for the worst.

"How do you pick the houses?"

Caspar leaned back, avoiding Winston's intense stare, and fixed his eyes on the ceiling.

"Isn't that what it's all about?" Winston pressed. "The rest is just fore-play, right? The books, the fanfare, the movie based on your book coming out next summer. Everything about you comes down to one question: *How do you pick the houses for your novels?* You're the Willy Wonka of horror novels, and I want to know your recipe, your secret sauce."

"I just get lucky."

"Bullshit," Winston let his frustration loose. "No one gets that lucky with the details of unsolved murders or missing persons cases. I'm speaking as a fan here: you know more about how the victims died than the families who lived through it or the officers who worked the cases. How does that happen?"

"I have a good team around me. Sedge has been vital." A smile crept over Winston's face. "Thanks for bringing it back around for me, Caspar. Your long-time, faithful publicist, Eliza Jenkins. *Where is she?*"

Caspar folded his arms, realizing he'd underestimated the detective and walked right into his trap.

"I don't think I need a lawyer," Caspar lied, "but since I already pay for one, it'd be stupid not to have him sit in on this conversation."

Winston's grin returned, though a flash of anger flickered beneath it. He pounded his fist on the table, and Caspar tensed at this first show of aggression. He exhaled when an officer entered a moment later.

"Take our guest back to his cell," Winston ordered. "It's going to be a long night for you." It was Caspar's turn to smile.

The police station, small, outdated by modern standards, had over ten officers bustling around inside. No matter how busy they were, Caspar noted their frantic movements as their eyes kept drifting back to the cells. He was the main attraction. King Kong captured and on display. An author, called a celebrity in most circles, but in the tiny blip on the map called Moxahala, he was an absolute supernova.

His arrival had already caused a divide within the community, but after his arrest, the frenzy reached fever pitch. So many locals had visited the station that day, they were forced to lock the door and post an officer to keep the curious public away. Some people made up excuses—lost dogs, suspicious smells of natural gas—anything for a glimpse of Caspar Finch sitting in his pen.

One brazen resident shoved his way through the station's front door, camera raised, hoping to snap a photo of the author in his compromised position. Allowing press photos outside was one thing, but having pictures of the station's interior floating online was a lawsuit waiting to happen. With the door secured, the stream of visitors ceased.

Caspar spent hours with nothing to do but watch Detective Winston's head as he bobbed over paperwork. This was his day, and he suspected it was a tactic by his fanboy-turned-captor, to wear him down until he couldn't take it anymore. But Caspar had a lot more left in the tank than they gave him credit for. What was the alternative? Describe Eliza's brutal end at the hands of animals no one had ever seen before? Orchestrated by a faceless figure fit for a YouTube urban legend?

Darkness descended upon the precinct, and a few officers switched on desk lamps to continue working. A large ticking clock, the kind found in school gyms, hung high on the wall and marked each excruciating second. The relentless cadence was worse than the boredom itself. Just as the ticking filled his head like an unwelcome guest, the front door opened.

When Sedge stepped through, Winston met him immediately. They were too far away for Caspar to hear, but he would have given anything to eavesdrop. Instead, he watched their silent exchange. They shook heads and pointed fingers at center stage in the station's foyer. The officers stopped their work, captivated by the unfolding drama.

Whether it was a staring contest, a game of chicken, or one of them won the argument, Winston flinched first. His head shifted from a defiant horizontal shake to a reluctant nod, as if conceding to whatever Sedge had said. Butterflies stirred in Caspar's gut as Winston stepped aside, allowing Sedge to walk toward him without an escort.

Sedge's expression was grim, and Caspar's excitement at seeing the cavalry shrank as he registered the tension in Sedge's face.

"You okay?" Sedge asked, not waiting for an answer. "The prick won't give me long, so just listen. Your lawyer was surprised; he's on vacation." Again, he didn't wait for a response. "But don't worry. One of his colleagues will be here in a few hours to spring you."

Caspar exhaled a long breath.

"That's great news."

"Is it?"

"What's wrong? I didn't kill anyone. I swear."

Sedge gripped the iron bars of the cell, his face hardening.

"Did you know how Harper's parents died?"

"What are you—"

"Shut up, Caspar." Sedge's voice was low, strained. "I've been working for you a long time, and I thought you were a friend." He held up a hand before Caspar could respond. "This isn't the time or place to get into it, but we're going to talk about why you kept something like that from me."

"Listen—"

Piercing screams echoed from outside, filling the station with an eerie dread. The officers exchanged glances, confirming they had all heard the same agonized cries. Frozen in place like players in a game of red-light-green-light, they waited, wondering if they'd imagined it.

Then louder screams erupted, accompanied by the sound of something heavy slamming into the locked door. Officers drew their revolvers, checked the chambers, and tightened their grips as a second, bone-jarring crash struck the door. The next impact resonated through the station like an elephant charging at a thin wall of wood.

Like an army sergeant, Winston directed a line of men ten feet in front of the door. He shuffled back to Caspar, Sedge, and the cell, all without breaking eye contact with the front of the station, which reverberated under the constant onslaught.

"Get your asses up!" Winston hollered at several officers behind desks who, Caspar was sure, were more adept at pushing paper than dealing with a spontaneous assault on the station. They obeyed, forming a second line behind the first, drawing their weapons with shaky hands.

"What's behind the door?" Winston asked Caspar, still focused on the entrance taking a beating.

"The watchers. You wanted to know what happened to Eliza? You're about to find out."

Winston turned toward him with disbelief etched across his face. Caspar nodded to confirm. The pounding on the door wasn't the same as when the initial impact had rung through the cramped police office. Like a musician tuning his instrument, the sound had shifted from a heavy thud to a hollow smack as cracks appeared in the wood. Light veins ran along the door until its surface looked like stretched silly putty.

"It's not going to last," Sedge voiced everyone's fear. With that, Winston pulled out his own gun. "You're safe in there. I'm the only one with a key." Caspar noted the thick key dangling from the detective's hand, like a piece of carved jewelry.

One officer in the front line, closest to the door, mumbled something Caspar couldn't catch, but the effect was clear—their frames straightened, shoulders tensed, and they braced themselves.

"They're coming through." Caspar took a step back inside the cell as if it were any safer.

The banging, which had been growing louder and stronger, stopped. The officers exchanged anxious glances, each gauging the reactions of the others. Silence descended, somehow more terrifying than the incessant pounding. No one dared to move; the quiet was so profound that the raspy breathing of anxious officers became audible.

"They gave up," someone from the second line—a paper-pusher said.

The entryway crashed open. Wood splintered inward, and large shards of material scattered across the room. For a moment, there was only darkness beyond the ruined door. Then, writhing limbs poured through the threshold like something from a fairy tale nightmare. Knowing what awaited them didn't make Caspar feel any safer. As the creatures with eyeless faces invaded the precinct, the first line of defense fired at the advancing monsters. Smoke wafted above the weapons, and the creatures jerked as bullets impacted their bark-covered skin. But, aside from a brief pause in their movements, they continued forward, unaffected by what would have incapacitated a human.

The officers kept firing, but the creatures kept advancing, closing in until the two groups occupied the same space. The horror began with one lunge, then another. These creatures—with thick, muscled bodies on all fours, long, had lean torsos like a human's but with the hindquarters of a giant cat—were the twisted result of some nightmarish evolution.

From within the cell, Caspar got the fleeting impression that the officers were winning. The bullets were hitting their marks, and the men fought in what looked like a strategic embrace. But then the first hints of blood appeared. The struggling figures in the front line, at first resembling boxers locked in a clinch, devolved into a horrifying struggle.

One creature gripped an officer's head with two hand-like paws, tearing into the flesh of his cheeks and gobbling it. It snapped back to rip off an ear, and similar scenes began unfolding with every officer up front.

The second, smaller line took a step back, clutching weapons that did nothing.

"What do we do?" a voice called out, breaking through the grim silence.

Another gunshot rang out as a creature clamped its jaws onto the arm holding the weapon. Teeth sank into flesh. Blood seeped then gushed from around the creature's mouth as its powerful jaws crushed flesh and bone, biting off a section of the arm, which fell to the floor as the creature chewed.

The officers faltered, pushed down by injuries or by the sheer weight of their adversaries. The balance of power shifted in the creatures' favor, and screams of pain replaced the gunfire. The front desk—a hub for greeting locals and processing paperwork—obscured most of the scene, but the gruesome struggle was visible above it.

One officer hiding behind the desk flung himself onto its surface, clawing his way up like a sailor clambering onto a life raft. Curled into a ball, he pulled his knees to his chest, hugging them to make himself as small as possible. But hiding in plain sight wasn't an option. One creature, as if assigned to him, planted its mouth on the desk office. Razor-sharp teeth hovered in the air before piercing the officer's leg.

"No, stop!" the man cried, clutching the side of the front desk, his grip desperate. The creature thrust its claws into his other leg, the one not already in its mouth, and pulled its panicked prey closer. Caspar hadn't expected the man's death grip on the countertop to last forever, and it didn't. As the man's frame descended behind the desk, his cries grew louder.

For a long time, nothing stirred, just the sickening lapping sounds of the creatures feeding. Was the beast now full? Or were the others next on the menu?

These questions hung in the air, increasing the dread among the last line of defense. The awful lapping, coupled with the ticking clock, built a mounting tension. The mechanical click of the second hand added urgency, pressing on the officers waiting in line.

In a blur of movement, a creature leaped onto the front desk. It landed with graceful precision, more like a bird landing than a massive four-legged predator. It moved with an eerie nimbleness for its size, and Caspar thought its agility was a gift from the rugged, uneven terrain of the woods that were its home.

"It has no eyes." Winston turned to Sedge for confirmation.

"It must use some other sense to find us."

"They smell us." Caspar watched as the creature lifted its head. Its stance was lean and powerful, like a lion with bark-like skin. "It smells everything—the walls, the furniture in its path, and definitely our scent."

"How do you know that?" Winston asked, but his question faded as another creature lunged onto the counter beside the first, followed by a third, which knocked chairs aside as it landed. They all tilted their heads upward in unison, then trained their eyeless faces on the row of pencil-pushers holding guns.

"What do we do?" one officer asked, glancing at Winston, hoping for guidance.

The tree-beasts took the question as a signal of threat. They tensed, then leaped down from the desk, jostling each other to reach their next meal.

"Fall back!" Winston ordered. They obeyed, but the creature's unnatural speed made the humans appear slow. The only woman among the group abandoned the attempt at a tactical retreat and broke into an all-out sprint toward Winston. Those left behind had no choice but to squeeze their triggers and hope for the best.

Even at close range, the bullets did little to slow the beasts. Heads snapped back with each shot, pausing them, but they resumed their prowl.

Breaking from the pack, two larger ones headed toward the cells. Caspar pointed as they approached, but everyone was already aware.

By the time the female officer reached Winston, the men she'd left behind were being torn apart. There was no pretense of sport in this second assault. The creatures went straight for vulnerable spots—some lunged at their stomachs, others at their necks.

"Get in here!" Caspar yelled above the sickening sounds of snapping bone and tearing flesh. The advancing beasts paused, reacting to Caspar's call. The swarm then redirected toward the cell, leaving behind the carnage they'd wrought on the second line of defense.

"Winston?" Sedge barked at the detective, transfixed as the creatures advanced. Whatever thoughts had distracted Winston seconds earlier, reality slammed back into him. He reached into his pocket for the key. "Hurry!"

He pulled the key out as if by magic, keeping the suspense high. With the creatures moving, he had no room for error. He slid the key into its slot and turned it as if he'd done it countless times before. The door swung open.

The female officer rushed inside, followed by Sedge. Caspar saw Winston hesitate, considering his options as the creatures drew closer.

"Now!" Caspar urged, pushing Winston to decide. The detective obeyed, sliding into the cell in one fluid motion and slamming the door shut behind him. To Caspar's horror, the cell didn't lock. Winston reached his hand through the bars to turn the key just as a creature's jaws closed around his arm. The beast yanked him back, smashing Winston's face into the iron bars.

"Let go!" Caspar shouted.

The group inside the cell rallied around Winston, grabbing hold of his body to pull him back. What would happen if the creature tore off his arm while they held his body? Fortunately, the beast's grip slackened, allowing them to pull Winston free, but not before it left deep, vicious bite marks around his wrist. Any longer, and the creature would have taken the hand off.

The female officer emptied a pillowcase, using it to wrap around the bleeding wound. She tied a makeshift tourniquet, pulling it tight. Winston's eerie stillness terrified Caspar more than any outward display of pain.

"Thank you, Susan." Winston gave a polite nod.

The creatures that had followed the group to the cell returned to finish their meal, while a few others paced around the bars. The one that had attacked Winston's hand prowled back and forth, its body language seething with frustration. Lacking faces, their anger and agitation were conveyed through their movements. With no apparent vocalizations or signals, the creatures launched a coordinated assault on the iron bars.

Their heads slammed into the cell, each impact shaking the enclosure and ringing it like a bell. But, unlike the front door, the bars didn't bend. Caspar took a wobbly step back.

The creatures kept moving. With renewed desperation, they extended their sharp claws through the bars. Sedge, standing closest, fell back just in time to avoid certain death.

Frustrated, the creatures froze in place, their movements synchronized. Caspar's gaze drifted beyond them, landing on an unknown figure entering the station. The silhouette bent to avoid hitting the door frame. As it straightened up inside, Caspar estimated its height at eight feet. The overhead lights, sufficient for normal tasks, recoiled from the figure, creating an effect as if the light itself couldn't survive.

"It's a watcher," Winston said.

Susan, hearing the word, lost control. Her body writhed as though in pain, retreating further into the cell. The sight of the immense silhouette, coupled with its name, triggered something instinctual and terrifying within her. Caspar watched her head shake as though answering an unspoken command from the watcher.

The creatures near the watcher parted to let it pass, then fell in line beside it. Their ferocity dimmed. From inside the cell, Caspar saw faint pinpoints of light where the watcher's eyes should be, illuminating the slightest suggestion of a human form.

Surrounding the cell, the frenzied creatures turned to regard their exalted leader as he strolled into the center of the station. The watcher slid a staff from a hidden recess—the same staff Caspar had seen him use in the church—and struck it against the floor. The movement had an otherworldly quality, reminiscent of Tolkien's writings. But this was no Gandalf the White standing before them, and no elegant display could convince Caspar that the revenant in front of him was anything but pure evil.

With the creatures now subdued, the wounded officers clinging to life released pitiful moans as they teetered on the edge of oblivion. Lives vanished as easily as a candle's flame extinguished under a snuffer.

Susan, pressed against the back of the cell with nowhere to retreat, crossed herself. Caspar made his own version of the sign.

"What does he want?" Sedge whispered to himself. But one creature cocked its head in response, and Sedge fell silent, his gaze fixed on his shoes.

The watcher raised his gnarled wooden staff with a steady grip, showing no sign of wavering under its weight. The staff's tip pointed to each person in the cell, finishing with Caspar. The watcher stood motionless, his arm outstretched and defying gravity as he held the staff aloft, like a living statue. The group shifted their gaze to Caspar, each taking a step back without a word, making space for whatever was about to happen.

The watcher's rigid stance loosened, and he swung the staff's tip from Caspar to the open door, an invitation that made Caspar's heart sink.

"Don't believe him," Susan snapped.

"He's trying to get us out in the open so he can pick us off," Sedge said with desperation.

Caspar thought he saw a smile flicker across the watcher's face, and his mind flashed back to his last encounter. The watcher offered him an escape into the night, just as he had before. And like last time, others might pay the price. Memories of Eliza's desperate plea for help and the pain in her eyes when he abandoned her flooded his mind. Caspar took a step closer to the bars, feeling torn.

"I wouldn't do that," Winston warned, struggling to stand as he clutched his injured wrist. "Do you think he'll spare your life after what he's done to everyone else?"

There would be no mercy, but he couldn't admit aloud that the watcher had already offered him that choice. "You're right." He turned back to the watcher. "You can go back to hell!" he shouted at the silhouette. The watcher nodded, or so Caspar thought, though he couldn't be sure he hadn't imagined it.

The staff lowered and struck the floor with a resounding crack that echoed off the cement walls. The creatures, which had been as docile as house pets, charged the holding cells, their bodies slamming against the iron bars. As several attacked at once, the structure shook, revealing that their sense of safety had been an illusion. Each impact brought the bars closer to bending, and a chill ran down Caspar's spine. If the creatures broke through, there would be nowhere to hide; they would have all the time they needed to finish the job.

"Stop!" Caspar screamed. But the creatures continued to hurl themselves against the bars, oblivious to the harm they might cause themselves. The watcher raised his staff, and a hush fell over the station once again. Pointing toward the broken front door, he directed the creatures out. One by one, they scurried past him, through the door, and into the night.

"He listened to you," Susan said with astonishment.

The watcher, now alone in the center of the police station, tilted his head and tipped his wide-brimmed hat. The hat merged into his shadowed form; Caspar couldn't tell where it ended, and he began. The watcher turned and strolled back into the darkness from which he came.

Long after the station was empty of anything supernatural, no one spoke. They stood there in stunned silence, surrounded by the dying officers whose faint breaths were slipping away. The thought crossed Caspar's mind to get out and help the fallen, but he'd seen their injuries. Nothing would save them. Trying to comfort them in their last moments would only add to their indignity as they passed from this world to the next.

How long would they stand here in the jail cell, frozen by fear? If Caspar had a choice, he thought he would stay there forever.

"What do we do now?" Susan asked between long sobs.

"There's a place where we'll be safe. My church isn't far from here. You're welcome to stay with me until all this blows over." The words came out hollow to Caspar.

Chapter Twenty-Three

MEMORIES INCLUDED

*I*ndifferent to the world around her, Harper still tasted blood in her mouth as she walked into her church. The lingering scent of Caspar's aftershave hung in the air. For a moment, she considered calling out for him, if not for Carol playing nursemaid.

"Not sure Caspar's home." She tried to hide her embarrassment at not knowing the last time she'd seen him.

"I heard about your husband. Isn't he missing?" Carol asked.

"Oh, yeah." All at once, Harper remembered the officers rummaging through every nook and cranny, searching for clues to his disappearance. "It's been hard." The lie slipped out.

"This place is incredible." Carol's gaze roamed upward, her neck arched as if she might catch sight of Jesus himself perched on a rafter, swinging his legs. "I've never been inside, but I have relatives who were married here. When it was a church, mind you."

Carol's words faded as Harper's mind drifted back to the objects. Did the scene at Corning Hall happen? She was sure she had walked away with the glasses. But the rest? Customers attacking customers, a red line leading shoppers to their obsessions like a laser pointer to a cat? If it wasn't just mania or lack of sleep, then the bowling trophy wedged in the ear of that heavy-set woman was real too. She tried to separate the horrific memory from the items but found no sensible conclusion.

"I need a little more of your help."

Carol paused her examination of the church's grand interior and turned to Harper.

"That sounds ominous."

"You know the area's history, and you said you'd look into Riley's death, right?"

"I did."

"I don't have all the pieces to find Riley—the real Riley—but I'm going to try. My sister is by my side when I need her, but she's not doing well. I can't do this shit alone."

When Carol looked back at her, compassion radiated from her eyes, dark and cavernous with understanding—and fear.

"Right now, I'm on the outside, an observer. If everything you've said is true, then whatever power these objects hold and whatever they've un-earthed will pull me into their spell along with you and your sister. I'm too damn old for this supernatural mumbo jumbo. I guess what I'm saying is, I've had a long life, and if I'm going to die, I'd rather it be for a good reason."

"What about righting a wrong? Seeing justice done for a child who never asked for this?"

Carol's gaze returned to the church interior. Her eyes flitted across each stained-glass window as if seeking an answer there.

"I've stumbled into something bigger than I ever imagined. I'm not a religious person. I switch the channel or radio when anything holy comes on. But if this is my chance to sneak behind the curtain and see something my human eyes weren't meant to witness, then what's the point of living in this skin if not to take it?"

"You'll help?" Harper asked.

"Stains cling to objects, sure. But they cling to people, too. There are things you can't unsee."

Harper thought about pulling the creatures from Mara's skull. "I don't think it'll be that bad," she lied.

"What do we do?" Carol asked, tucking a strand of gray hair behind her ear. Harper gave a toothless smile. Her gums were raw and swollen where her top teeth once sat. She caught the flicker of Carol's reaction and shut her mouth.

From the bag slung around her neck, Harper placed Riley's items on the dining room table, one by one. She made sure not to let any of them touch, spacing them: the camera, cassette player, key, glasses. Then, the once-living items—hair, teeth, and fingernails. They all found their place in the strange grid that traced Riley's last moments.

"Feels like we're grave robbers." Harper had the same thought as Carol but couldn't give up her mission.

As Carol took in the arranged collection, the floor creaked, and she grabbed Harper's arm. A tall, thin man emerged, each step pressing the boards harder as he entered their space, looming over them.

"What do we have here?" Matt asked, his face breaking into a grin.

Harper pressed a hand to her chest. "You scared the shit out of us." Matt stood there in his Led Zeppelin T-shirt with a cocky smile plastered across his face. "This is Matt. My head of security." Saying she had a staff member was ostentatious, but she savored having someone on her own payroll. Caspar had always had employees—now she had one, too.

"These." She pointed to the items. "Are going to help us tonight. Grab your hunting gear."

"Hunting?" Carol's face went pale.

"Ghosts, not animals," Harper assured her, though the words sounded worse out loud than they had in her head. Matt disappeared into the other room.

"What now?" Carol asked.

"Now we use these to find Riley."

"Or just another clue," Carol offered with a wry smile.

"Maybe." Harper picked up the small, round glasses meant for a child, stopping a few inches from her face. Carol gave a slight nod of approval, and Harper slid the glasses over the bridge of her nose.

Once on, the red lines streamed all around her. Unlike her first attempt at the sale earlier, a buzzing sound now accompanied the red streaks. The high, screeching blast burrowed into her ears, and though she pressed her hands over them, the sound came from within. Turning around to explore the inside of the church, she scrunched her face at the red streaks radiating in every direction.

Exploding red, coupled with the high-frequency pitch, overloaded her senses. Her first impulse was to rip the glasses from her face and let them shatter on the hardwood floor. She resisted. And that's when the sound grew to a roar, and more lines bounced off objects that came with the sale of the house. An old mirror on one wall glowed with an aura as bright as the sun, appearing like a doorway to another world. Red tendrils wrapped around the rafters above, like ghostly nooses. Remnants of a haunting past.

Spinning around, the great hall revealed even more lines, and she sensed a century of history had left its secrets there. A hundred mysteries never solved. With a quick movement, Harper pulled off the eyeglasses, blinking at the sight of Carol standing in front of her, staring in awe.

"What did you see? What was in here?" Carol asked. "I could see your eyes through the lenses, but it was like you weren't in this world anymore."

Harper took a deep breath, feeling her pulse pounding in her throat.

"Riley's glasses work like a black light, but they reveal stains of past deeds. They're showing me how each object connects to another. The problem is this church has too much history and too many sins. Most of it has nothing to do with Riley."

"Then we need to start at the beginning. We have to go to Riley's home." Carol pointed to the house framed in the window.

Matt arrived with his equipment strapped to his vest.

"All set. Are we ready?"

Harper didn't answer but shrugged, making sure Carol saw. "Yeah. We're ready."

She would have smiled if not for the breeze that tickled her gums.

Crossing Route 13 was dancing on the edge of a knife, one slip away from oncoming traffic. The highway stretched out on either side of the group. On a normal night, the cadence of cars passing between the church and the abandoned house was regular enough to serve as a timer. But this evening was different; they hadn't seen a single car since reaching the edge of the road.

Carol wrung her hands and expected otherworldly experiences, while Matt held out a device resembling a radar gun with a small LCD screen on top. Carol looked on with curiosity.

"It's a thermal imaging gun," Matt explained, holding the business end of the device over his hand. The LCD screen, filled with swirls of dark blues and greens, burst into flames of red and orange when his hand moved to the center. The warmth of his palm glowed brightest, with the tips of his fingers and areas beyond his hand fading to a dark, fuzzy hue.

"You can see ghosts with that thing?" Carol asked.

Matt tilted his head. "We're gonna find out, aren't we?" He slid a pair of headphones (not unlike those a DJ might wear) over his ears. Adjusting a knob on an electronic device clipped to his belt, he added, "EVP." Noting Carol's blank look, he continued, "Electronic Voice Phenomena recorder. It can capture sounds and movement that human ears can't detect." He turned back on his gear, forgetting she was there.

Harper was the first to cross the street, with the others tagging along—Matt still fiddled with his equipment while Carol wore a faraway look, as if she might flee at any moment. Like kids who'd dared each other to summon Bloody Mary but soon regretted it.

As they stepped off the asphalt and onto the grass leading to the dark, silent house, Harper stopped.

"Do you hear that?"

They all stood motionless. Holding their breath, listening to the night. Carol nodded first.

"What is that?" she asked.

"It's screaming," Matt said. "But where's it coming from?"

The moaning and intermittent screams were distant, but steady.

"There's not much in Moxahala," Harper said. "The police station is down the road, but I haven't heard a peep from them since we moved in. Might be farm animals. Cows sometimes sound freaky from a distance."

They exchanged skeptical glances and continued up the steep embankment toward the old house. "We should be far enough from the church now." She pulled Riley's glasses from her bag and taking a deep breath before sliding them onto her face.

She braced for the high hum she'd experienced in Moxie Manor but was relieved to feel only a faint whisper. It tickled her ears, like a spider's legs brushing against the walls of her ear canal. She rubbed the outside of her ears, but the sensation remained.

Angling her head toward the house, she saw shades of red—not from the wood porch or roof, but from a window, glowing bright scarlet, like a ghost watching their approach.

"There's something inside with us."

"What's inside?" Carol asked, apprehension tightening her voice. "I didn't know Riley's parents, but I'm acquaintances with a woman who did." They moved onto the porch, the boards creaking under their weight.

Matt adjusted the recorder volume. "Riley told her parents, months before she disappeared, she thought someone was in her room at night," he explained. "The parents shrugged it off as a child's imagination—an eerie feeling from living in an old farmhouse full of creaks and groans. But they believed her when she said she'd seen someone sitting beside her while she slept. She claimed they whispered they'd be back for her."

Harper turned the doorknob and led them inside.

A bold red light appeared, leading from her glasses, through the living room, and around a corner.

"Something is leading us to the kitchen," Harper whispered.

"I think I'm hearing something." Matt squinted as he pressed the headphones tighter against his ears. "Footsteps, I think." Carol nodded but held back from asking aloud who might make footsteps in an empty home.

Harper moved through the living room, following the floating red streaks. *Corners are not your friends,* she thought, her heart racing as she edged around the corner, expecting to see Riley herself and praying she wouldn't.

In the small kitchen, Harper saw the red trail end in the center of the room.

"The footsteps are continuing somewhere. But I can't tell where."

Harper rummaged through her bag and found the Walkman. With shaky hands, she clipped it to her waistband and adjusted the headphones over her ears. Carol and Matt stood ready, waiting for her to start the show.

It took more effort than she expected to press **PLAY**. She'd yet to have a pleasant experience with Riley's song, and standing in a lightless, decaying house in a forgotten Ohio town didn't help her confidence. But what else could she do but push forward with the tools she had? Although Riley's objects had been devastating to Mara, they'd always revealed another clue in the mystery.

In the darkness, Harper's fingers walked their way to the button, pressing down until she heard the robotic click and the squeak of the cassette wheels. For a moment, she questioned if it was even working, but then Jagger's bluesy voice pulsed through her.

The song, combined with Riley's glasses, stretched the red aura across the room to an unassuming black door in a shadowed corner of the kitchen.

"Could the footsteps be coming from here?" Harper asked Matt. He listened through his headphones and gave a thumbs up. Harper moved closer to the farmhouse door and rubbed the paint with her knuckles until flakes fell away, revealing red beneath. "It's a red door." Which meant little to them but everything to her. "This is the way."

A realization sparked in her mind, a fire she couldn't believe hadn't ignited sooner. Confirming the glasses were in place, she rummaged through her bag, where a bright glow met her gaze.

"You idiot, Harper." She watched the others peek inside the bag, though their expressions revealed nothing of what she saw. The motel key, that she thought was now useless, glowed at the bottom of the former beach bag. "These objects interact with each other," she murmured, diving her hand in to grab the latest supernatural marker. Warmth spread across her palm as she lifted the key into the air. Even through her clenched hand, the glow seeped through like light cupped in her fingers. "Isn't it beautiful?"

They watched her hoist her hand skyward but remained silent until she unfurled her fingers.

"A key?" Matt asked.

The key pulsed even brighter in her open palm, vibrating. She raised it, noticing how the key and glasses fed each other. Holding it up, she saw a faint red line stretching from its tip to the door's knob.

Caspar was the gamer in the family, not her, but she'd seen enough games to know when an object "activated" something. It reminded her of how Caspar's video games brought elements of the background to life. One moment, the door's knob was inert like everything else; the next, it beckoned, waiting.

She slid the key into the lock, feeling an electric charge as they met, a reaction as visceral as touch. She twisted, hearing a click, and the key's light dimmed as the door swung open.

Harper couldn't help but think of her first time watching *Willy Wonka* and the awe of seeing a door open into a land of wonders. This transition wasn't as beautiful, but it was just as jarring. She glanced back at the others' awestruck faces and smirked, giving them an I-told-you-so look.

Beyond the door should have been the basement, it was the only logical direction for a door off the side of a kitchen. Instead, they were looking into a bedroom. Riley's bedroom. Frilly and lace-laden fabric adorned the room, evidence of a mother's touch, Harper thought.

Posters of pop stars lined the walls. Harper didn't keep up with the newest faces, but she was sure these were the latest idols Riley admired. She thought of the Walkman with the Eagles cassette tucked inside that she'd found in the motel. *A gift from her father*, she imagined.

She nodded for the others to follow, though they hesitated, unsure. She repeated the gesture until they stepped into the room. Darkness swallowed them until the moonlight, and their adjusting eyes, revealed details.

They moved toward the bed and froze mid-step. Riley sat rigid, her posture straight. Duct tape covered her mouth, wrapped several times around her head to keep her silent. Tear streaks glistened down her cheeks, dampening the tape beneath her nose and above her chin. *How long has she been here?*

Then Harper saw him crouching in front of Riley. He had been there all along, lurking by her bed, shrouded in shadow. The realization that he'd been watching the entire time sent a chill down Harper's spine, locking her in place as she stared into the outline of his presence.

The scene was a glimpse into Riley's history, but the past had a way of intruding on the present. Could they prevent what was about to happen? Matt edged closer with his recorder, holding the thermal imagining device near the bed. Riley's form appeared alone on the screen, with no trace of the stranger.

A gruff voice cut through the silence. "If you stay quiet, you may live through this night."

Riley gave a slight nod, acknowledging the stranger's false promise. The figure began pulling her from the center of the bed to the floor below. As if it were the simplest thing in the world, a knife glinted in the moonlight before its tip entered the girl's abdomen. Blood pooled on the floor, spreading around her. "That was a warning for what will happen if you resist," the voice whispered. Riley's tears streamed harder, dampening the duct tape over her mouth.

The intruder continued. Arms slid under Riley's armpits and began dragging her.

"Let go of the girl!" Harper shouted, startling Matt and Carol. But the figure ignored her, backing out of the room and down the stairs. Harper darted toward the door, only to face the basement stairs, rickety and narrow, plunging downward.

Matt aimed his device down the stairs, his hand trembling. "Look at that," he said. Harper leaned over his shoulder, peering at the LCD screen. A red shape, outlined, appeared at the bottom of the stairs.

Carol clutched her mouth. "What is that? Was that the figure we saw in the bedroom?"

"I can't tell."

They edged closer to the screen as the face on it pulled away, retreating deeper into the cellar.

"Well, that's not creepy at all," Matt said, still holding the imager in place.

"We're not really going down there, are we?" Carol asked, her voice wavering.

"Just because something appeared on Matt's equipment doesn't mean it's as real as we are," Harper assured her, though her voice was less than convincing. She turned to Matt. "Right?"

"These devices don't come with instructions for the paranormal. They play by their own rules."

"We go down." Harper decided. "Oh fuck, oh shit. You can do this."

Carol looked ready to argue, but Harper had already started her descent, giving her no chance to protest. The acrid smell of wet soil and decaying wood filled their lungs as they crept down. The stairs groaned and bowed under their weight. Harper pulled the glasses back onto her face and lit her cell phone, casting a narrow beam that pierced the darkness. With each step, the old wood protested.

The phone's light created a vignette effect, casting the center in brightness while shadows swallowed the edges of the space. Forgotten mason jars filled with ancient preserves lined the shelves, and rusty farm tools, including scythes and rakes, hung from ceiling beams. Harper noted their positions in case she needed a weapon.

As they distanced themselves from the staircase, a sense of dread settled over her. The stairs were her only escape, and moving deeper into the house's dark belly made her feel trapped.

"Stop moving. Listen," Matt whispered. Harper dimmed her light, watching as Matt closed his eyes, focusing on something only he could hear. "It's coming."

"What's coming?" Carol asked, her voice above a whisper.

"Footsteps. And something else ... dragging."

Harper heard another noise close by and saw that the cassette player around her neck was still playing The eagles sang about living it up in the hotel. The faint dragging sound Matt mentioned filled the room, amplified for everyone to hear. They huddled together as heavy footfalls echoed toward them from above. The girl hovered inches off the stairs in a lying position. The girl was being dragged, her heels banging on each step. Harper removed her glasses and saw the girl without them.

"She's being dragged down here," Harper whispered.

"It's Riley, isn't it?" Carol asked, dread lining her voice.

There was no visible figure pulling the child. Riley was alone, yet her body floated in mid-air, descending in the grip of an unseen force. When her heels struck the dirt floor, the invisible captor turned toward them, leaving two deep tracks in the soil.

Riley whimpered from her injury. Matt kept recording, and his thermal imaging device tracked the movement.

As they passed, Riley looked up, meeting Harper's gaze with wide, terrified eyes.

"She can see us!" Harper cried.

"That's impossible," Matt said.

Unable to hold back, Harper shone her light on Riley, sprinting toward her. But just as she got close, the captor picked up speed, dragging Riley into a dark tunnel carved into the farmhouse basement. Wooden beams lined the tunnel's walls and ceiling, holding back the earth.

"These are coal mine tunnels," Carol said, trailing after Harper and Matt. "But I've never seen them extend under homes."

To Harper's horror, Riley had already disappeared into the tunnel's shadows. Clutching her phone, she focused on the drag marks. Harper sprinted after the sound of the girl's heels scraping the dirt floor.

"Where do these tunnels lead?" Matt shouted over his shoulder.

"I don't know!"

Harper kept running, her heart pounding in her chest and her legs burning. She collided with something massive and solid. The impact knocked her backward, and she fell to the ground.

Dazed but determined, Harper raised her light to reveal a wall of dirt blocking the way forward. The trail of Riley's dragged heels vanished into the solid earth.

Fueled by rage and desperation, Harper pounded her fists against the barrier, her anger echoing in the hollow silence of the tunnel.

Chapter Twenty-Four

MOVING SALE

Nestled in the heart of nowhere, Moxahala was a rural town, wild by nature, full of wildlife city folk had never seen. Coyotes roamed the area and locals spun yarns about wild boar that would trample unsuspected hikers.

Caspar thought the stories were to scare newcomers. When he first heard about missing children, he assumed it was an exaggeration. In a small town, two drunk drivers were an epidemic. Why would disappearances be any different?

Whether they were grandmothers, schoolteachers, or meth heads, it didn't matter. They all disappeared. For an author, these stories were the icing on the cake. In America, few things were more enticing to readers than crime thrillers, especially if you could slap "based on a true story" on the cover.

But Riley Spears's disappearance wasn't like the rest. Caspar's problem was that there wasn't a body. How could he give readers a satisfying ending without a discovery? Sedge was a skilled investigator, but plot twists weren't his strength. It was Eliza who convinced Caspar to focus on Riley. "Remember *Lovely Bones*?" she'd said. "There was no body in that novel."

"I thought they found an elbow."

"A talented writer doesn't need a body—or even a murder weapon—to make a great story."

Eliza's challenge pulled him to Moxie Manor. The problem was that the story became less about Riley and more about the hundreds of missing people in Moxahala. Sedge was right all along. People torn from the world without a trace was the story he wanted to tell.

Out in the country, far from the city's light pollution, the stars were pinpricks against blackness. It was a reminder of how small humans were, their lives flickering out in the blink of an eye in the vast universe. After the vicious attack at the police station, walking out into the open was lunacy. Caspar eyed his little group of survivors and shook his head at their chances.

Winston's groans broke the stillness, amplifying Caspar's fear that one creature still lurked in the dark. Winston's bite wound was deep, and while Caspar averted his eyes, self-preservation taking over as he thought about leaving the group behind more than once.

"We have to move faster," he urged.

"If they were out here, they would've attacked already." Winston clutched his forearm.

A guttural shriek echoed from the woods, followed by a second scream.

"They're communicating." Susan glanced toward the trees.

"They're coordinating," Sedge added.

"It's only a quarter mile to the church. Pick up the pace," Caspar pressed.

Branches snapped near the tree line.

"They're watching us," Susan whispered.

Caspar dismissed it as ridiculous but couldn't ignore the truth for long. When he started running, they all followed, even Winston, who forgot his pain, spurred on by the fear of teeth sinking into him again.

"I can hear them." Susan fell behind with her shorter strides.

Twigs and branches cracked along the woods, matching their pace, then went silent.

"Keep going," Caspar managed, though a sharp pain in his side begged him to stop.

"Wait!" Susan's voice trembled as three of the creatures darted out, cutting her off from the others. The way they positioned themselves around her reminded Caspar of wolves.

The group stopped just in time to see the creatures encircle her, their bark-like skin glistening under the moonlight.

"We have to help her."

"We have no fucking chance against them," Caspar argued. "You saw what they did back there."

"I have a gun. So does Winston," Sedge shot back, already moving toward her. Caspar swore under his breath, took a reluctant step toward the church, then turned back.

As the three men approached, the creatures retreated, moving behind Susan, who huddled on the ground, trying to make herself as small as possible. Sedge raised his revolver, while Winston struggled to steady his weapon in his uninjured hand.

Caspar dashed forward, pushing past Sedge and Winston to reach Susan. Wrapping his arms around her, he shielded her as best he could. Eliza's last moments flashed through his mind.

The creatures froze, some even taking a step back.

"Get back!" Sedge commanded, extending his gun, but Caspar sensed the creatures weren't reacting to the guns, they were reacting to him. Standing tall over Susan, he scanned the line of trees, expecting to see the watcher orchestrating the attack. Steeling himself, he helped Susan to her feet and guided her toward the church, away from the menacing creatures.

"Stay close together. Huddle around me," Caspar urged, though he continued to shuffle further away. The watcher's servants stayed back, except one creature, unwilling to give up. It followed them at a steady pace, waiting for a moment to strike.

Caspar heard the beast sniffing the air, picking up their scent. It kept pace behind them like a shark that smelled blood in the water, poised to lunge at any sign of weakness.

As they huddled together, a living mass of arms and legs clinging in fear, Caspar caught the sharp trace of sweat in the air. Sedge's voice broke the silence. "There's ONLY one now. If we work together, we can take it down."

But Caspar had already decided. Just a hundred feet from the church, he chose a different path.

"Run!" he yelled, breaking away from the group and sprinting toward the safety of his home.

The others followed suit, but Caspar's worst fear became a reality. The beast sprang to life, energized by the sudden movement of its fleeing prey. Its enormous strides closed the gap with terrifying speed. "We won't make it," Susan gasped as Caspar flung open the church doors, just as the creature°prepared to strike.

Chapter Twenty-Five

Lost Reels

Everything around her felt unreal, standing in the center of Moxie Manor with a shovel in her hand. Reality stopped making sense to Harper—if it ever had. Losing her parents so young tore away a part of her soul. She'd sworn never to forgive Mara, and she often questioned if, deep down, she ever had.

Harper couldn't bear any more loss. That's where it had all begun, she decided—the void that had grown in her chest, swallowing everything beautifully. And from that emptiness, the yearning for a child of her own was born. Only a child, she believed, could fill that loneliness, and ease the loss.

She watched life grow instead of withering, clinging to the hope that she might find the child she had lost so many years ago. They called pregnancy a "life event" for a reason; it had also opened the door to Mara. Though Mara was no longer the same girl she'd once shared a bedroom with, Harper could still see a spark in her sister that years of therapy and antipsychotics had failed to extinguish. After all these years and countless tears, it had been Mara who comforted her when she'd lost her precious child, a cruel irony Harper didn't miss.

"I could not care less," Matt grumbled, "but there's no way I'm setting foot in that house again. I thought I'd be cool with trying my hand at paranormal investigation..."

"But you didn't believe any of it?" Carol asked, raising an eyebrow. Matt nodded.

Harper tightened her grip on the shovel, a reminder of the abductor as she leaned over Matt's shoulder. He played with his laptop like a musician, headphones blocking out the world while sound waves danced across the screen. The audio stayed flat and steady for a while before spiking, something breaking through.

"Listen to this." He unplugged the headphones so everyone could hear. The faint voice of a girl whispered, *"Help me ... don't do this. I want my mom."*

Disbelief passed between them in silent glances.

"I heard nothing when she passed us," Carol said.

"She didn't speak; she couldn't," Harper added. "Her mouth was covered with duct tape—*we saw it.*"

"There's the proof." Matt replayed it.

"We have to dig out that tunnel." Harper's fingers trailed over the handle of the spade.

Matt shook his head. "Do you think that little girl is still alive? If that scene in her bedroom wasn't a hallucination, I saw her get stabbed. No way would an intruder take her to a hospital to stitch her up. She's ... gone."

Harper gripped the shovel tighter; Matt caught the intent.

"Where could the tunnels lead?" She turned to Carol. "You've lived here. You must have a hunch."

Carol sank into a nearby chair, deflating. "Coal mines used to be everything in this area. Every family had connections to the coal mining industry back in the 1800s. But the Moxahala furnace was miles from here—I can't imagine why a tunnel would be under Riley's farmhouse."

"Finding the end of that passage might bring peace for Riley and stop Mara's suffering. Who's going with me?"

Harper's gaze moved between them. Matt looked down, but Carol met her eyes.

"I want to help," Carol whispered. "Losing a child's light is the worst thing I can imagine. But ... that basement..." She paused, a shudder passing over her. "There was something evil with her when Riley passed us. Like it wanted me to interfere, just so it could attach itself to me, like a parasite."

Harper slapped the flat of the shovel; the metal rang. "Fine. I'll go alone."

"You don't have to go at all," Carol said.

As she turned to leave, a thought spiraled within her. No matter how many people are in your circle, friends, family, even a spouse, you always end up alone.

She regulated her breathing, tossing aside fear and doubt, and moved closer to the exit. Both doors flew open, slamming hard against the walls. Caspar rushed in, his hand swathed in so much gauze it looked like a pillow, and behind him, Scott Sedge charged in, followed by a shorter woman in uniform.

"Get in here so I can shut the door!" Caspar yelled.

The woman scrambled forward, tripping, as something heavy struck the door, knocking it back out of Caspar's grip. A creature, otherworldly and grotesque, shoved its way into the foyer. Harper's mind scrambled for a word to describe it; a *thing* was all she could manage. Its legs were long, muscular like a man's, with clawed, stubby hands where paws should be. Its face was a blank expanse of leathery skin, with only two small holes that might be nostrils. But it was the bark-like texture of its skin that sent chills down her spine.

Caspar locked eyes with her, a flash of recognition there, and he pulled the shovel from her hands. A cold sweat pooled as she watched her husband charge the creature, weapon in hand.

"Get me something to tie it up!" he shouted. Harper blinked, stunned, before realizing he was speaking to her. She stumbled to the back of the church, her legs shaky, and grabbed a length of rope.

When she returned, the newcomers had piled on top of the creature, struggling to hold it down. Caspar yanked the rope from her and began binding the creature, starting with its mouth. The beast thrashed, its sharp teeth snapping just inches from a female officer's arm. Harper watched, horrified, as Caspar cinched the rope tighter, the bark-like skin giving way under the force.

He stepped back, satisfied with his knots, while the others slid off the creature, catching their breath. Caspar turned to her, pulling her into a long hug.

"Are you okay?" he asked. She nodded, but as she pulled back, he caught sight of her bruised face and missing teeth.

"What happened to you?"

She pressed her lips together, smoothing her hair self-consciously. "Long story."

Carol and Matt, their faces still drawn with shock, drifted toward the living room. They exchanged glances with each other, casting nervous looks back at the foyer as if expecting the creature to break free any second, making the night even stranger than it already was.

The strangers sat in a strange church, gathered around a coffee table, eyeing unfamiliar faces while the creature in the other room struggled against its bindings. Whenever the thrashing grew louder, Caspar couldn't resist checking on their prisoner, each time returning to the circle of tense silence.

"The rope's holding," Caspar announced, rubbing a dark bruise on his forearm, a reminder of his encounter with their uninvited guest.

"I guess the first question is, where have you been?" Harper asked, running a hand through her hair. She watched Caspar shift in his seat, as if weighing a lie.

"I've been here. Inside this church the whole time."

She studied his face, catching no hint of deception. He'd always been a terrible liar, despite his aptitude as an author. His stories might be convincing, but for real-life lying, he was hopeless. Her gaze swept across the group, who watched their exchange with interest.

"Well, this gentleman turned everything upside down looking for you." She gestured to a man with a gauze-wrapped hand.

"I'm Winston," he introduced himself.

Ignoring the introductions, Harper continued. "I would have noticed you." Riley's disappearance had clouded her attention. Caspar lifted a hand, left the room, and returned carrying a dog, settling the canine on his lap. "Here's my proof."

"Our dog is your proof?" she asked, but before he could respond, the sound of claws tapping against the wood floor announced another arrival. A dog stood in the doorway. A gaunt, identical version of the one on Caspar's lap.

"What the hell is going on?" Harper whispered, bewildered.

Caspar glanced at the dog in his lap. "Why was I gone for days?" he asked the dog. Silence filled the room, the others watching the dog, wide-eyed, until Matt laughed. A few others joined in—except for Sedge, who watched Caspar and the dog.

"It wasn't days for you," the dog said. Matt's grin faded, Carol shot to her feet, and Susan, who had been sitting closest to Caspar, stood, and backed away.

"Conversion of time," the dog continued, "depends on the energy it takes to pass through the barrier. That's *your* time."

"This is a gag, right?" Matt asked, lowering himself to inspect the dog as if it were a prank.

Caspar stroked the dog's head. "Since I already have a dog named Twix, I thought it fitting to call him Snickers."

"Snickers?" Winston asked with a laugh. "You named your talking dog after a candy bar?"

Caspar shrugged. "He saved my life," Caspar said. "Eliza and I followed the moon through the woods and found this church—but it was 1908."

Carol shifted in her chair, and Susan, keeping her distance, looked ready to bolt.

"What happened to Eliza?" Winston asked, slipping into his detective tone.

"She's dead." Caspar flinched as pain flashed across his face. "Creatures attacked us. Like the one tied up in the entryway." The group glanced toward the doorway. "A tall man controlled them—"

"Dark watchers." Snickers rested his head on Caspar's knee with what looked like sadness.

Caspar turned to Winston. "You know about them, don't you? The night I went to the other side, before we saw anything, you mentioned them."

"Anyone raised in this area knows about dark watchers." Winston turned his attention to Snickers. "We grew up hearing the folklore."

"I've seen them, too," Susan said. "In the woods near here."

"What do they look like? What do they want?" Harper asked.

"Mostly shadow," Winston explained. "They appear at dusk when light and shadow blend and confuse the senses. They say they'll leave you alone if you don't interact with them."

"And if we do?"

"Then they take an interest in you." Carol drew everyone's gaze. "My mother always warned me never to stare at a dark watcher if I ever saw one in the woods."

"Is that what you did?" Harper asked Caspar.

"I don't know ... I don't think so."

"They've taken an interest in us?" Matt clutched his knees.

Caspar nodded. "Those creatures attacked the station tonight." Winston looked at Harper before turning back to Caspar. "They killed a lot of outstanding officers. If they're serving the dark watchers, they'll come back for their servant, and for us too."

"What's our alternative?" Harper asked, her tone sharp. "Let it loose and hope it returns to its master instead of attacking someone in the neighborhood? What if it finds a child playing outside in the morning?"

Winston threw up his hands, forgetting his injured one, and winced in pain. "Let's ask the dog. It's from their time—it might know."

The group turned to Snickers, who sat in Caspar's lap. The dog sniffed the air, scratched behind his ear, then tilted his head toward Matt.

"The early settlers called them the dark watchers, and their servants the moon howlers. Dark watchers existed long before humans walked the Earth, when nature was in balance. The early people learned from the watchers and respected them. But then, progress..." Snickers trailed off, his gaze distant.

"I saw them here when the church was first built."

"Why are they back?" Winston asked. "What did we do?"

"The town had promise," Snickers said, "but it never grew enough to thrive."

"They've been reducing the population," Matt said with fear. "They've done it before, haven't they? Used these creatures to wipe us out."

"Cleansed the town," Winston said.

"Brought balance," Snickers corrected.

"We have to stop them," Susan said.

"Is there a way?" Matt asked. The dog glanced around, saying nothing, his silence unsettling.

Sedge looked around. "It's the church itself. Every local I've talked to about this place has awful stories about it. It's like their families have passed down warnings for generations."

"I'm the fiction writer here," Caspar joked, though his expression was grim.

"Think about all the lives this church has taken," Sedge interrupted. "The suicides, the disappearances—not all of them from dark watchers. This place is a lightning rod for misery."

"I've seen *Ghostbusters*," Matt added. "Houses don't channel spirits." He tried to grin, but it fell flat.

"That's not funny," Sedge snapped.

"I don't want to be here anymore," Carol said.

"Me neither," Susan added.

Winston rose and pointed at the creature bound near the entrance. "You're free to leave. But after what we saw tonight, those creatures ... they tore armed men apart like they were cardboard."

Carol cried, and Harper held her close.

"What can we do?" Carol sobbed.

Susan spoke up, her voice steady. "We can use this place. I've been in church every week as an adult, Sunday school before that."

"And?" Matt asked, skeptical.

"The faith of countless worshippers consecrated this building. We can use that against the watchers," Susan said with conviction.

Caspar shook his head. "I've seen them walk these halls without an ounce of fear of God."

"Then it's the dog," Susan stood as though she'd only just noticed its presence. She pressed a forefinger against the smooth gold cross lying against her chest. "The dog came from them, right? We must destroy it. It's evil." She looked around the circle, rallying the others, and squeezed her cross as if to activate its power.

"Fuck you," Caspar snapped, his tone blazing. "When I was at the mercy of those animals, he saved me. If you don't approve of him, you can get the hell outside. I'll put you there myself."

Harper had never heard Caspar speak so passionately and pondered what had changed. She watched Susan's defiance crumble as she considered facing her fate alone in the woods of Moxahala.

After a long, tense silence, Sedge asked his own question. "Then why didn't Snickers save Eliza?" Harper turned her gaze to the dog, half-expecting it to answer, but it remained silent.

"He chose me, I guess," Caspar admitted, biting his lip. Harper recognized the reaction; she'd seen it many times before. Guilt was eating at him from the inside. *What did you do?*

"I'm just lucky to be alive. And you're all welcome to stay here as long as you need," he added, then gave Susan a side eye.

"Of course." Harper saw Caspar's look of guilt, She let it slip from her mind as her sense of hospitality took over. "We have plenty of space."

Winston pointed to his injured arm. "We need to think about that monster we tied up. If it gets loose while we're sleeping, it'll tear us to shreds before we even open our eyes." Heads around the room nodded.

"It's my house. I'll take the first shift," Caspar promised. He had never been the brave type, and Harper stared at this new version of the man who had always shown courage only in his writing.

"I'll help everyone get settled," Harper said to Caspar, throwing him a surprised look, which he caught.

As Harper moved to prepare the house, her mind returned to the tunnel beneath Riley's home. The pull to finish what she'd started became an obsession or an inevitability. She *had* to uncover the truth of the tortured spirit of the little girl.

What puzzled her most was the strange power these objects wielded within the church. Sedge's description of Moxie Manor as a "lightning rod" resonated. There was a heightened reality within the walls, something that amplified her emotions, including her love and concern for Mara. Carol was too scared to go back into the tunnels and Matt checked out of the entire supernatural adventure. Whatever was coming, she needed her sister by her side.

Chapter Twenty-Six

Buried in a Bin

Matt expected a certain comfort when he slammed his laptop lid down. Even as he closed himself into the back bedroom of the church, listening to the creaks of the house settling and the wind rattling against its walls, he imagined it might be one of those creatures testing the place's resolve.

When Harper offered him a security job, it was a simple decision. She'd agreed to his price without even trying to negotiate—a red flag he'd ignored. And then there was Caspar Finch, the real blind spot. Having a famous author on his client list was worth more than money; the name would look great on his resume and open new opportunities. He even dreamed of writing a book about paranormal investigations, with Caspar at its center. Harper insisted on a non-disclosure agreement, but he figured they wouldn't take him to court if he mentioned it years down the line.

He'd watched his fair share of paranormal shows on YouTube, and adding "ghost hunter" was a natural extension of his work. A couple of extra electronic devices, a dust particle in the lens, and he'd be set to rake in cash.

He hadn't expected to find an actual haunting.

Ghost shows, with their over-the-top hosts reacting to a door opening an inch over four hours, were tame compared to what he stumbled into that night. If he were honest, the experience scared the hell out of him. When Harper's "objects," as she called them, transported him to the scene of an abduction, it was like ice filling his veins. He'd tried virtual reality and even tested high-tech equipment with haptic suits, but nothing compared to standing next to a child as some bastard snatched her from her room.

It was visceral, heartbreaking, and he'd carry that memory forever. He hadn't even had time to research whether there ever was a real life, Riley. But standing in her bedroom, experiencing the moment firsthand, without a visor or filter, was as real as anything in Matt's memory banks.

What disturbed him most wasn't the grotesque details of what he assumed was Riley's inevitable fate, though that was chilling enough. Even the old lady, dressed in 80s clothing, looked like she was about to collapse in terror. But Harper? Her expression suggested she'd expected the whole thing, as if she'd seen this before, like a rerun waiting for its dramatic beats.

By the time the experience was over, Matt was ready to list his ghost-hunting devices on eBay. The last few hours had turned his stomach, and he couldn't imagine doing this kind of investigation ever again.

Lying in bed with all his gadgets scattered around him, only one thought spun through his head: *I want to go home.* He would have bailed if not for what he owed Harper, a sum he couldn't repay. And with the creatures prowling outside, his better judgment told him to stay put and wait for the storm to pass.

Just as he drifted off, a low, dull beeping echoed from his laptop speakers. Groaning, he slid the laptop onto his stomach and saw an alert screen he'd buried under other windows. It was his proximity hub for the REM pods, showing an alarm triggered by a temperature fluctuation in the back of the house.

"The sensitivity's way too low," he muttered, studying the readout. But his REM pods were the cheaper model, and there was no remote change setting. "Damn it," he cursed, realizing he'd have to adjust it manually.

Tossing the covers aside, he hopped out of bed and onto the cold floor, cursing himself for not buying the better model. The church was quiet and darker than it had been the past few days. Nothing was different, he told himself, trying to shake the internal argument. *It's just you, Matt.*

Matt had stationed the REM pods in the farthest room of the church—the laundry area, overlooking the road and with a door leading down to the cellar. He was sure it was the perfect spot for a spirit to trip the alarm. Now, late at night and alone, he regretted his choice.

As he entered the laundry room, a blast of frigid air hit him in the face, chilling him. He looked down at the laptop, the screen illuminating his startled expression.

"Thirty degrees? That's impossible." He tried to ignore the inexplicable cold seeping into his skin and what it meant.

The REM pod looked like a thick hockey puck with LED lights sprouting from its top. White, yellow, and red bulbs pulsed in repetitive intervals as Matt lifted it, turning it over like a turtle. He spun the grooved dial with his finger, but instead of shutting it off, another alarm blared from his laptop.

He balanced the computer on his forearm, staring at the proximity sensors as they erupted into chaotic noise. Glancing at the nearby window, he saw no signs of a break-in; vibrations alone set them off. Standing in the cold laundry room, the temperature dropping with every second, he watched the sensors flash on his screen. He tried to convince himself it was a malfunction until he noticed a shadow sliding down the wall.

He thought it must be a passing car casting a funny shadow. But when he turned to look out the window, he saw only darkness. The shadow on the wall didn't fade, and instead took solid form, which was all he needed to see.

He slammed his laptop shut, whipped around, and bolted from the laundry room; the shadow stretched toward him. The cold followed him, seeping into his skin with every step. A rattling sound began overhead, growing louder in front of him and bringing him to a stop. As he squinted down the dark library hallway, his pulse pounded against the silence while books along the shelves shimmied in place.

Then, something heavy hit the back of his head. His ears rang, and when he looked down, he saw a leather-bound Bible lying open at his feet. He touched his skull, expecting blood, but his fingers came away clean. Peering up, he saw the other books on the shelves trembling, as if an invisible earthquake had struck the small hallway.

In a wave, books toppled down from the shelves. Matt raised his laptop above his head, using it as a shield against the falling avalanche of hardcovers and paperbacks. The first few struck hard, bouncing off his laptop and slamming into his abdomen, knocking him to the ground. Realizing that escape was his only option, Matt dropped the laptop and sprinted toward the safety of his bedroom, with only the library hallway standing between him and sanctuary.

Books fell with a force that defied gravity. Out of the corner of his eye, he saw volumes hurtling toward him, rather than dropping from the shelves. Books battered his shoulder, chest, and neck, the last one striking his collarbone with a painful snap.

Clutching his broken bone, he pushed forward, knowing that stopping now would be as dangerous as sinking into quicksand. As he ran, he saw more books ahead lining up to fall, anticipating his arrival. Another wave of books crashed down on him with the weight of concrete. Something cracked in his ribs this time.

Thrashing under the pile of books, he shifted the weight off his back until he freed his arms. Shaking and bloody, Matt dragged himself to his feet, stumbling over the scattered books as he staggered toward his bedroom. Once inside, he dove onto the bed, yanked the blanket over his head, and called out to his security system.

"Bedroom lights off," he whispered. Through his fabric shield, he saw the lights respond, plunging the room into darkness. He lay there, listening to his ragged breaths and licking the salty taste of blood from his upper lip, until he heard the faint creak of floorboards outside his door.

"I don't understand the request," the system replied in a robotic tone. "I'm sorry, I don't recognize the voice."

Matt's stomach twisted. The blanket over his face shifted as the security system continued its strange conversation, as though someone else spoke.

"Voice approved," it spoke.

Pain throbbed through his broken ribs as he adjusted his position, breathing as he listened for movement on the other side of the door. The anticipation was worse than the pain from his injuries.

"To answer your question," the system began in its electronic voice, "we are not sure if ghosts feel pain. There is no physical proof that spirits exist."

Matt had had enough. "System, turn off," he hissed, sitting in the tense silence that followed, wishing he'd run straight to his car after the farmhouse incident. *Why didn't I leave?*

"Actually, yes," the system replied. "I can see you. You have my permission to come in."

"What?" His hand moved to pull the blanket off his face, but he stopped, clutching it to his chest.

The bed Harper had provided was more like a daybed, with a wooden headboard attached to the side against the wall. The scratching started then, somewhere above him. It sounded like tiny feet scuttling in the walls—a mouse or even a rat. That would have been creepy enough, but in the depths of Moxie Manor, he prayed that was all it was.

But the sound grew, turning from a faint scurry to a louder, heavier scrape, like something much larger trying to claw its way through. He heard something trapped behind the wall, scratching, as though something solid blocked its way. The noise intensified, reverberating with a disturbing fury. The intruder was determined to reach him.

The system's voice chimed again. "Ready or not."

Matt reached outside his blanket fort, groping for anything within reach. The scraping on the walls slowed, becoming more deliberate and ominous. His hand brushed against the thermal imaging gun, and he grabbed it, pulling it under the blanket. Turning it on, he pointed it toward the source of the noise, praying it would work through the fabric.

In shades of blue and black, the room materialized on the screen, lifeless until he saw a flash of red in the direction of the sound. The blurry blob materialized into a shape, humanoid but grotesque, like something from a nightmare. It slid down the wall toward him.

"Go away," he whispered, his voice trembling as his mother's face flickered in his mind, her voice comforting and warm. He'd taken her for granted. *Why didn't I call her more?*

The plaster above his head cracked, releasing dust and particles onto the bed frame. He remembered old builders used hair in the plaster, and the thought of it—a blend of human hair and lime—made whatever was headed toward him even more grotesque.

"Ready or not," the system's voice chanted again.

Matt froze as the wall went quiet. Then, with an unnatural stillness, a hand reached down, glowing red on his thermal screen, ripping the blanket from his face and exposing him to the icy air. His eyes widened, seeing the creature as screams tore from his throat, uncontrollable and raw.

As everyone went their separate ways, Caspar couldn't help but feel like he was living out a bad Scooby-Doo episode. *Let's split up, gang!* His life had become a series of horror tropes, each one more absurd than the last.

He met Harper's gaze, spinning his gold band around his finger. When their eyes locked, their feet led them to each other.

"Hey beautiful," Caspar said. A moment passed while they stood eye to eye before Harper threw her arms around her husband. With his arms joining the moment, their bodies pressed hard enough for Caspar to feel the strain of his muscles. Harper finally let go and stared into his eyes.

"I have so much that I have to say to you," she said. "I'm just not sure I won't come off as crazy."

Caspar looked around the interior of the manor. "Something tells me I'll believe you," he said with a smile. "Where's Mara?"

"She's still here … I reached for my sister when I should have asked you for help."

"Same. There are some things I need to say to you. There are secrets I kept because I thought I needed to protect you."

Harper nodded. "When this is all over, we lay everything out on the table?"

"I love you, Harper."

"I know you do. And I love you back."

He watched as she led the guests in the opposite direction, but something unspoken lingered in her eyes, a hint of condemnation or a confession about something that happened while she was gone. It wasn't clear.

Setting up base camp was his next task. He dragged a chair across the floor, tipping it back on two legs as he settled five feet away from the creature bound in ropes. Snickers trotted over and collapsed beside him. Twix might have been Harper's dog, but Snickers was his now, for better or worse.

The creature's body undulated in the dim light. Without eyes, it was impossible to tell if it was lying in wait or asleep. Caspar matched his breathing to its steady rhythm, letting himself drift, shutting out everything else.

"Can we talk?" came a voice from behind. Caspar turned halfway to find Sedge looming over him. Snickers raised his head, sniffing the air, his attention fixed solely on his master.

"I know what you're going to say. I kept you in the dark, but it wasn't about you."

"You're right. It wasn't about me. I thought we were friends." Sedge stepped in front of Caspar, just a few feet from the bound creature.

"Sedge. You shouldn't—"

"I was just a tool to you, a forward-facing weapon. You never had faith in me." Sedge edged closer to the creature, which lifted its head and sniffed the air. "Why didn't you tell me Harper's parents were murdered?"

Caspar looked through Sedge, unblinking. "Because it was horrible. And because it wasn't my story to tell."

"Eliza and I were there to find your stories, to guard your secrets. You could have given us some clue about something so dark."

"You're right. I should have told you."

"Don't placate me, Caspar. I'm not one of your reporters or TV hosts. Someone wealthy had the details of their deaths sealed—was that someone you?" Caspar shook his head, but Sedge took another step toward the creature. "I checked around your hometown. People whisper that one sister might have been involved, that one—or both—ended up in an asylum. Did that just slip your mind?"

"That's news to me," Caspar lied. "I swear it's the first I've heard of any such rumor."

"What really happened to Eliza?"

"One of these creatures. Just like I said."

Sedge stared off into space, weighing his options, his calf brushing against the beast's mouth. Caspar tensed, watching the creature strain against its ropes, its jaws struggling to open.

"I'll take your word. But if I find out you've lied to me." Sedge paused, "you'll never see me again." He took a step back, away from both the creature and Caspar.

Caspar exchanged a glance with Snickers, their silent communication loaded with understanding.

"There are too many stories that rely on the *parents-die-at-an-early-age* trope," the dog said. "Dead parents can highlight a character's devastation, making their choices plausible. But unless you handle it well, it'll never ring true."

Susan took the couch, and that suited her fine. The thought of following Caspar's wife deeper into the church sounded like the worst idea ever. When Harper assigned rooms, Susan raised her hand high and asked if the couch was an option. Harper glanced her way, lost in her own head. No doubt, the discovery of a snarling, murderous creature in her foyer had stolen her focus—and Susan didn't blame her one bit.

Sleeping inside *Blood Manor* was strange enough. Susan heard of Caspar Finch's background, how he dragged his wife from one haunted house to another, tempting fate. She'd tried one of his books right after high school. His style was decent, but his stories were too graphic, and he took the

Lord's name in vain on every page. What could blasphemous words add to a plot, anyway? It made no sense.

But it wasn't his writing that bothered her. You could wrap garbage in a box, and if you had good marketing, someone would buy it. What got under her skin was how Caspar chased tragedies like an ambulance-chasing lawyer, profiting from the grief of survivors, from atrocities that affected children. She had no way of knowing his true intentions, but she doubted he'd tell her if she asked. And she was certain there was something darker beneath his surface.

Reading the Bible as many times as she had, she could see the temptation in others. You didn't move your family into a place that tasted blood. You didn't open the windows and let history blow out into the world. And if she was smart enough to know that, so was Caspar Finch.

Her first moments in Moxie Manor were as if the walls and ceiling were breathing, as though she were inside a diseased lung, expanding and contracting. In the beast's belly, devoured by her own choice to enter.

Her mother had married there back when it was still a Catholic church, as had many from neighboring towns. By the time Susan was born, the place had fallen into local hands. It was sacrilegious to strip a holy site of its sanctity, only for some couple to move in, tainting it with their sins.

Despite watching her coworkers meet horrible ends, it was the talking dog that haunted her mind. She had spent countless hours with the guys at the station—working, eating, and enduring their dirty jokes. They didn't think she noticed their glances, sizing her up. They were there to serve and protect, but they were sinners like everyone else, more so. They wore uniforms that read "trust us" but that meant nothing. They invited her to the pub every night, yet none of them ever showed up at church on Sundays.

When the moon howlers attacked, killing the officers, it appalled her. But watching the massacre taught her more about herself than any other experience in her life. She had always believed in God, always sat in a pew every week, listened to her pastor's words, hoping to feel a spark of divine connection. Yet the spark never came. Not until that night.

What the others in the station hadn't seen was that God's hand was in everything. He allowed her to escape into the holding cell while his dark watchers delivered justice. *These creatures were instruments of His will.* God was not just a voice in scripture or a line in a hymn. He was here, now, active in her life. And for the first time, her fears melted away. She no longer had to fear judgment for her choices or confusion over her fascination with other women. She gave all her worries to Him. He held them now.

But the dog—*that* was different. Just as she found her place in the world, a serpent entered the garden. The moment the creature sat on Caspar's lap, she saw it was a deceiver. When it spoke, she couldn't breathe. And the others? They were rapt, smiling in astonishment at the unnatural act. It stunned her how easily Satan's spell took hold, how willingly they fell under it.

They wouldn't take her without a fight. After a lifetime of confusion and guilt, she was awake and had no intention of going back to sleep. Lying there on the couch, she watched as headlights from Route 13 swept into the room, casting shadows across the furniture, the walls, and the ceiling, spreading like contamination before vanishing with the rumble of each passing car.

Susan waited until she was certain no one else was awake. She hadn't heard a sound in hours. The wood floor was cold beneath her bare feet, shooting a chill up her spine as she walked. Was Moxie Manor evil? Or was it meant to draw out evil? Could it be St. Pius's legacy, working as an undercover agent for a heavenly purpose? The questions lingered, too vast to answer, as divine intervention often was.

She remembered her pastor's sermons on *Intelligent Design*—what nonsense. Suggesting that God set evolution in motion just to appease modern science was just a way to water down faith. If you needed to see proof in dinosaurs or physics, you weren't believing; you were just finding excuses.

Moving with care, she headed toward the foyer. She remembered the kitchen was just past the entrance. She slipped into the small country kitchenette with its wraparound countertops, hanging pots and pans, and empty jars labeled with cliché ingredients. She noticed the mason jars, locked tight from the top—pretenders. Caspar and his wife thought matching the decor to the era would enhance their status. As if using *authentic* containers from the 1800s would secure their roots in their rural town. *Pathetic.*

Spotting a titanium knife block, she pulled out a butcher knife. Another car passed, illuminating the blade in a sharp gleam before the light faded. The foyer was only a few steps away, but her thoughts collided as she moved, her body on autopilot while she tagged along, watching her choices unfold. She planned every action, but things were different now. God was here, in everything.

Through the foyer's threshold, Susan saw the chair, empty and unattended. The beast that had taken four adults to subdue and tie down was gone, along with Caspar. Only the dog remained beside the vacant dining room chair. Caspar must have dragged the watcher's pet somewhere more secure. His absence was the reprieve she'd needed.

Lowering herself on the wooden floor, Susan crossed her legs, scooting forward until she was inches from the magical canine. The dog awoke, watching her. Susan pulled the golden cross out from under her shirt—her Uncle Terry's gift when she was sixteen—and placed it against her chest.

"Is this the part where you try to discover yourself through me?" Snickers asked.

She waved the knife in the air, forgetting she held it until its gleam caught her eye. As she leaned in, she noticed the dog's collar shining back. Around his neck was an aged leather band with a brass buckle, and on the front, a small brass plate bore an inscription: ***BE VIGILANT OF HOUNDS, THOSE EVILDOERS, THE MANGLERS OF THE FLESH – PHILIPPIANS 3:2.***

She twisted the knife's hilt in her hand, the tip angled toward his neck. Snickers didn't flinch as she slid the blade between his collar and fur. In seconds, she'd sliced through it, and the collar dropped into her palm. She weighed its heft, scrutinizing it before lifting it to her eyes.

"I know this verse. But why is it on you?"

"A gift from my master."

"Caspar Finch?" she asked.

"No. The parish priest. I think it was his joke."

"How so?"

Snickers tilted his head in a doglike gesture. "The verse is about evildoers. It suggests that those focused on the flesh are no better than dogs. He figured some sinners couldn't resist reading it—and by reciting it, they'd be calling themselves out."

"Are you an evildoer?" she asked, observing him.

"I'm a dog," he replied, without a hint of sarcasm.

"No, you're much more than that. This is our time of tribulation, isn't it?"

"For you, it is, Susan Walker," he breathed.

"You know my name," she murmured, eyes narrowing. "Are you a prophet?"

"Do you want to know your fate?" he asked, meeting her gaze. "You don't have to be afraid."

"I think we should all be afraid."

"Come closer," the dog whispered. "I want to tell you a secret."

Light flickered along the walls, fading as a car passed outside. She leaned forward, tense with uncertainty.

"A little closer," he coaxed.

Bridging the gap between them, she inched nearer. Snickers jerked his snout forward, mouth open, and bathed her face in a wet, eager lick. She stifled a giggle, surprised, then let him continue his slobbery kisses.

Although Moxie Manor was many things to many people, for Caspar, it was a reflection—casting back the image he brought with him. He'd seen the consecrated ground change the moment the moon howler and the dark watchers entered his house. Like inviting a vampire into one's home, these creatures altered the DNA of the church, forever shifting its fate. Once meant to embrace the townspeople of Moxahala, it now harbored something darker. Whether it was the atrocities committed there, the blood spilled on holy ground, or the voiceless missing, their stories would go untold.

Since his first night beneath the Manor's roof, sleep had eluded Caspar. The church resisted peaceful rest, as though slumber was an act it refused to grant anyone within its walls. Over the few weeks he'd spent there, he could count on one hand the hours of restful sleep. Yet, as he positioned a chair beside the deadliest creature he'd ever encountered, he drifted into a deep sleep.

There was no gradual fade to darkness, no dreams tugging him one way or another—just an abrupt plunge into nothingness. Then a high-pitched bray shattered his unconsciousness, yanking him awake. Caspar sat up, heart pounding as his senses reeled back to life. The creature remained a few feet away, ropes still secure. Relief washed over him as he glanced at Snickers, curled up nearby.

But the braying resumed, sharp and insistent. He pulled his phone from his pocket, its screen illuminating his hand: **CALLER ID: CASPAR FINCH**.

The sight of his own name as the caller made his blood run cold. A voicemail intervened, cutting the ring short, but the call came through again immediately. He hesitated, then tapped **Accept Video Call**. The static screen flickered before a face filled the display. Eliza's face.

Caspar dropped the phone, his stomach plummeting. Snickers raised his head, and even the creature stirred at the thud on the wooden floor. The phone's screen glowed like a portal to another dimension, Eliza's damaged face staring up at him. Her nose was a hollow divot, her cheekbone exposed through torn skin, and her ear gone. The creature had gnawed at her face.

Despite knowing it was only a video, the sight shook him. Then Eliza spoke, her mouth twisted from a missing upper lip. "Welcome home." The effect was ghastly, like a dog baring its teeth in an attempted smile.

Caspar shut the phone off, his breathing ragged as he turned to Snickers. "Do you think that's the last we'll hear from—"

The screen lit up again, casting a vibrant glow over the room, reflecting off the dog's fur and the creature's slick, bark-like skin. He ended the call, waiting, his gaze fixed on the screen.

Nothing.

He exhaled in relief, his breath escaping in one long, shaky sigh. Then a faint ringing began again.

"What the hell is going on?"

"It's not this phone," Snickers warned.

Caspar's gaze dropped to the phone on the floor. It was silent. The ringing persisted, but softer, distant.

"It's in the walls!" He bolted to the main hall, hands skimming along the trim as he tried to recall where he'd buried his original phone. The ring grew louder as he ran his fingers along the wood, tracking the sound.

He found the spot. Pressing his ear to the wall, he heard it, a familiar ringtone, muffled but insistent. Sliding his fingers into a crack at the top of the trim, he dug in, feeling for a gap.

Years of paint layers held the trim in place, resisting his efforts. He tugged harder, ignoring the need for a pry bar in his impatience, pulling down with all his weight. The trim held for several seconds, then creaked and tore free from the wall with a loud snap.

Behind him, he heard the click of claws on the floor as Snickers settled down, watching his every move with keen interest.

The ringtone blared from the hidden space, lighting up the dark crevice in the wall. Ignoring what might share the space with the century-old phone, Caspar plunged his hand in and pulled it out. A layer of black dust or soot coated the device, and he wiped it clean, as if rubbing a magic lamp.

"Impossible. The battery wouldn't last a month, let alone since 1908."

Yet the phone rang on, clear as the day it rolled off the assembly line. With shaking hands, he accepted the call, and a video of a girl's face appeared. The camera zoomed in, revealing Riley Spears, her face expressionless and empty-eyed. She wasn't alive. The shot panned down to her torso, showing a deep incision between her upper body from her lower.

The video glitched, revealing a younger girl, Shelly Pritchard, the character in his novel *Forever Midnight*. Her black hair and eyebrows were unmistakable, and her body was covered in saw-marks. Another shift, and Veronica West appeared, a character from his second novel. She still wore a plastic bag over her face, and parts of her arms were missing. Caspar remembered how much he'd sympathized with her story while writing her; now, seeing her like this was brutal.

The images played like a grotesque slideshow, one after another. As Caspar stared, a figure appeared in his peripheral vision; a shadowy woman, hovering in the doorway to the library hall. No features were visible in the moonless night, but he could tell she was waiting.

He moved toward the library, checking to make sure Snickers was beside him. The dog kept pace, bringing a measure of comfort. As he drew closer, the shadowed woman drifted toward his writing room, a room that had yet to see a single story unfold.

"Who are you?" he asked. She didn't respond, slipping into his office. He followed, one hand on the doorknob, giving Snickers a last, uncertain look. Chasing a stranger was one thing but cornering them in a room was another.

He remembered the woman with the sharp teeth from his first night at the Manor. Was that a dream? He wasn't sure anymore. Reality blurred.

"Well, fuck it," he said, yanking the door open. The force sent it rebounding off the wall and into his back. Snickers slipped through the opening ahead of him, and Caspar stepped in after, his gaze fixed on his computer's soft glow.

The room was empty, save for the faint light from his monitor. Shadows twisted around him, and he glanced around the room, every curve and corner a potential threat. But he was alone.

"You're losing it." He looked down at Snickers. The dog's muscles were taut, his body poised for action, eyes locked on a hidden threat.

A low growl rumbled from Snickers' throat, a sound that cut through the stillness. Caspar kneeled beside him, following his snout. Snickers let out a bark that echoed off the walls, the sound painful in its intensity. Caspar lifted his gaze, following the dog's focus upward.

In the highest corner of the room, a woman clung to where the walls met, her hands and feet pressed against opposite surfaces like an insect poised to strike. Caspar froze, feeling like prey caught in the gaze of a predator.

Snickers barked again, a fearful, high-pitched yelp. Caspar considered bolting for the door, or diving under his desk. But he couldn't move. He watched as the woman detached from the wall, dropping onto him. Her legs drove his shoulders to the floor, and he hit the ground with a force that knocked the air from his lungs. Desperate for breath, he lay gasping as she loomed over him.

"Hello, Caspar." She leaned closer.

He recognized her brutalized face, the surrounding flesh exposed rib bones, her missing top lip. It was Eliza, or what remained of her. She smiled, and the effect was monstrous, her bare teeth stark against the torn skin.

Snickers, who'd fought against the creatures before, whimpered, backing into the door. Eliza turned her head, her right eye dangling from its socket, and Snickers pressed himself flat against the wall, nowhere left to escape.

"I'm sorry, Eliza," Caspar caught his breath. She faced him again, her lipless grin stretching wider.

"Where I am now, they're *still* eating me." Blood seeped from a fresh wound on her cheek, as though an invisible mouth had taken another bite. "And I feel it. Every bit. Thanks to your bravery!"

"What—who has you?" he stammered.

Her body jerked, as if something invisible were pulling her apart. "You're not getting away with this, Caspar. They're coming for you."

"Who's coming for me?" he yelled, his voice breaking.

"These houses you picked weren't random. Your stories were a lie. You deceived me."

"That's insane."

Blood spilled from a gaping wound in her neck, but she kept advancing. "Little girls, stolen from their families. She toyed with them. And when she killed them, she gave you all the details you needed for research."

"That's not true!"

Her body convulsed, and her left arm tore free, vanishing before it hit the ground. Tears welled in her one remaining eye, but her expression stayed cruel.

"When your tongue is in your stomach, maybe that'll be the last time I hear you talk." She paused, nodding with satisfaction. "It won't be long now, Caspar."

A smirk spread across her face, then her jaw peeled away, bone and muscle exposed, before she vanished.

Drenched in sweat, Caspar staggered to his feet, stepping around Snickers, who cowered in a puddle of his own urine. Every step away from the office was an attempt to wash the memory of Eliza's final moments from his mind. But the images clung to him, like a stain he couldn't remove.

He stumbled into the main hall, intending to check on the creature they'd tied up. The sound of licking—wet and relentless—echoed through the foyer.

When he arrived, his stomach twisted. Susan, the officer, was on all fours before the creature, her head inside its mouth. Blood pooled beneath them, seeping between its teeth as it gnawed at her head. A kitchen knife lay beside her, but she hadn't had time to use it.

Caspar's mind went blank, the shock blotting out all rational thought. He opened his mouth, and a scream tore free, echoing through the Manor until his lungs burned.

Sedge was deep in a dream with Sarah Deville when the screams began. She wore a wedding ring with an emerald as green as her eyes. In his dream, he asked if she was still alive when Nathaniel Deville placed her in the wall, a question he would never dare ask in real life. But that was the strange freedom of dreams: they let you say things you never would otherwise.

The dream shifted, and he was back at the bar with Gloria Mazel, sipping Coca-Cola as they had the night they met.

"Who killed you, Gloria?" he asked.

She smiled, tilting the glass bottle to her lips and draining it. "You know who killed me." She shot a sly smile.

"Was it Caspar Finch?" he pressed, feeling as if he'd had a breakthrough. Caspar's name kept coming up with Gloria's death—and Eliza's disappearance. "Has he been playing me for a fool?" he muttered, as though Gloria hid the answers. "The clues are there, but I can't figure out the connection."

She raised her bottle for another sip, her charm bracelet jingling against the glass and ringing out like a tiny chime. Sedge's focus shifted to that bracelet, and all other thoughts faded away.

Just then, he heard her screaming. He looked up, expecting to see Gloria's open mouth, but she remained silent. The scream continued, piercing and distant, until it cut through the fog of his dream. By the time he stirred himself awake, he stared up at the ceiling with the last remnants of sleep evaporating.

A surge of panic drove him from his bed. He threw off the covers and bolted into the dark hallway. Another door opened across the hall, and he saw Winston's alarmed face before they both sprinted toward the sound. An older woman—he thought her name might be Cheryl or Carol—joined them as they rushed to the main hall, where the scream still echoed.

They found Caspar standing alone in the foyer, his back to them, screaming at the rafters. Sedge gripped his shoulder and turned him around. Behind him, the creature still lay bound—but beside it was the headless body of the female officer.

"Susan!" Winston cried, pulling her body from the creature's jaws. Her torso hit the floor with a sickening thud as he dragged her free.

"What happened?" Carol asked, stepping back from the grisly scene.

"I was only gone a few minutes," Caspar said. "I came back and found her like this."

"She cut the ropes." Sedge pointed to the frayed ends dangling from the creature and the knife lying beside her. "Why would she do that?"

"Maybe she didn't mean to," Winston offered.

"Or maybe the church did it," Sedge said. Silence fell over the group.

The blood pooling around Susan's body was too gruesome to look at, but none of them looked away. Whether it had been an accident or suicide no longer mattered, the church had claimed another soul.

A loud clack echoed through the room, then another. Sedge glanced at the metal roof, uncertain of where the sound was coming from.

"What now?" Winston asked, sounding defeated. A third, even louder noise shook the church. Carol covered her ears as the entire building trembled.

"It's the roof," Winston gestured upward. But the ceiling remained intact.

Sedge turned to Winston. "You still got your gun?"

Winston nodded.

"Stay here and watch that thing," Sedge ordered, nodding toward the creature. "We're going to check out the noise."

Caspar joined him, and they moved toward the library. Carol hesitated, casting nervous glances between the hallway and the creature in the foyer. She followed, choosing the unknown over the bloodthirsty beast.

Opening the library door was like opening a dam after a flood. Books covered the floor in a three-foot pile, having toppled from the two-story shelves lining the hall.

"What caused this?" Caspar asked, but no one had an answer.

Caspar tried to scramble over the mounds of books, slipping and sliding back with each step. Sedge took a different approach, wading as if navigating through deep water, pushing books aside to clear a path.

With a steady hand, Sedge helped Carol up the incline. She hesitated, then opted to crawl on her hands and knees, with Sedge doing the same. Caspar, still determined, tried a third time, sidestepping his way up the slope like a skier, just staying upright.

Carol reached the other side first, standing at the door to Matt's room as Sedge and Caspar stumbled their way through. Caspar caught his breath. "Next time, I'm taking a window."

Sedge approached Matt's door, feeling the cool metal of the antique doorknob beneath his hand. He paused, then pushed it open.

The room was empty, with no sign of Matt. Sedge scanned the room, not noticing anything amiss until he heard Carol's sharp intake of breath behind him. He turned just in time to see movement above the bed.

Three feet above the floor, a pair of legs flailed, kicking. Matt's legs, dangling from the wall. The sight reminded Sedge of the fish he'd caught as a boy, flopping and writhing in a desperate bid for freedom.

"We have to help him!" Sedge rushed forward.

Carol backed away, pressing herself against the far wall, staring at the legs kicking through the plaster.

Sedge and Caspar grabbed hold of Matt's legs, struggling to get a firm grip. They could hear his muffled screams through the wall, sending a jolt of claustrophobic terror through Sedge. His mind flashed back to the shadowy figure of Sarah Deville, jumping from rafter to rafter, in his nightmares.

"She's got me!" Matt's voice came through the wall, muffled and desperate.

Sedge froze, his mind reeling with the memory of Sarah's eerie presence. Caspar's shout jolted him back into action, and they pulled harder. They stopped Matt's descent, his legs now locked in place. It was like a game of tug-of-war, neither side gaining ground.

Sweat beaded on Sedge's forehead as he shouted encouragement, desperate to keep the house from swallowing the young man.

"One, two, three—pull!" Sedge shouted, and they synchronized their efforts, hauling Matt another foot out of the wall. Relief spread across Sedge's face in a relieved smile.

"One, two, thr—"

A sudden, forceful yank from within—the strength far beyond that of the petite Mrs. Deville—undid all their progress, dragging Matt deeper into the wall than before.

"Carol, we need you!" Caspar called, wrapping his arms around Matt's legs and digging his heels in. "Hurry. He can't breathe in there!"

Many seconds passed before Carol edged her way over to join them, her face contorted with fear.

"I don't want to die," Matt whimpered through the thick mortar. "I just want to go home."

With Carol's added strength and Sedge timing each pull, more of Matt began emerging into the light. The sight of him seeping out of the wall, inch by inch, recalled a tube of toothpaste squeezed out, a disturbing transformation from flesh to soot-covered limbs.

"One, two, three!"

With one last, unified tug, Matt's head broke free from the wall's grip. He gasped, coughing up dust and spitting out bits of soot, his arms still buried in the wall as he fought to draw in air.

Carol was the first to notice the hands. Sedge saw her expression shift to raw horror; her nostrils flared, her cheeks lifted in shock, and her eyes widened as she backed away, clapping a hand over her mouth.

Gray, desiccated hands clung to Matt's arms, their skin shredded down to bone from struggling within the walls. Sedge and Caspar pulled again, and this time, a woman's half-decayed body emerged along with Matt. Her black hair, thick with dust, hung limp and pale, turned a sickly shade of gray. She wore a tattered white dress, stained with age and grime, and as she raised her head, her cracked lips revealed yellow teeth.

Her eyes were as black as midnight.

"He is coming for you, Caspar," she rasped, fixing him with her dead gaze. Caspar released his grip on Matt instantly, recoiling as her empty eyes shifted to Sedge.

"Give him to me, or I will come back for *you*," she warned, her voice laced with debris and decay.

"Grab him again!" Sedge shouted, but it was too late.

With inhuman speed, she yanked Matt back into the wall. One moment, he was dangling before them, the next, he had vanished into the wall's depths like a magic trick gone wrong.

Sedge plunged his arm into the cavity, groping through the darkness for any trace of Matt. His fingers scraped against something solid, and he clenched down, his hand closing around a shoe. Panic surged as he saw Matt's foot was no longer inside it. As he pulled his arm back, holding only Matt's shoe, his mind reeled with the horror of what he'd let slip away. The scraping within the walls intensified, reverberating as she dragged him further up toward the ceiling.

Following the sounds, they traced the noise to where the wall met the ceiling above them.

"What was that thing?" Carol's voice trembled as she spoke, her hand still covering her mouth.

"We have to go after him!" Sedge looked to Caspar with urgency.

Caspar shook his head, glancing around. "Where? Look at this place! The church is enormous. He could be anywhere inside these walls. I need to find Harper—make sure she's safe."

Sedge stepped closer, his voice a low, sharp edge. "You didn't answer me! Are we abandoning Matt?"

Sedge turned, seeking an answer in Caspar's face, then in Carol's. But their silence told him everything.

Chapter Twenty-Seven

STRAY FINDS

When Harper escorted her new guests to their rooms, she became the caretaker in an old black-and-white horror film, the kind she'd seen as a child, where the manager of a spooky hotel guided lodgers to their rooms by candlelight. Sleep would not come for any of them.

Experience had taught her there was no solace inside Moxie Manor, not for her or any living creature under its roof. The night always brought something bad. Even the return of Caspar after a day's absence hadn't affected her the way it should have. What did that say about her? She couldn't believe the creatures existed, even after seeing one herself.

Harper checked her phone for any reports of disturbances, but no alerts came back. Whatever had happened that evening was confined to their small neck of the woods. The local legends and haunted history of the area became all too real, yet none of it mattered to Harper. All she cared about was the tunnel—and finding the last clue to Riley Spears. She had started this journey with her sister, and Mara needed to be by her side when she unearthed the answers.

A pang of guilt tightened in her stomach as she saw it had been hours since she'd last checked on her sister. She slipped into Mara's room, an uneasy feeling churning in her gut.

The baby monitor glowed on the nightstand, casting enough light to chase away some shadows. Mara lay curled up on the floor, near the foot of the bed. The bedspread and pillows lay untouched; Mara had chosen the cold floor over the guest bed. Harper's eyes fell on the objects she'd arranged on the floor: the baby monitor, Riley's belongings, and all the Polaroid photos she'd taken since finding the camera, including the first one of Mara and Twix. She gathered everything into her beach bag.

"Mara," she whispered. Harper grew tired of always waking her sister. Mara's eyes blinked open first, followed by a faint, toothless smile that made Harper's heart sink. She dropped to her knees beside her.

"Mara?"

Mara's smile faltered as she tried to hide the pain, but it was too late—Harper had already seen the wreckage in her mouth. "I know what I look like."

"The insects?" Harper asked. Mara's sad nod confirmed it.

"I'm so sorry." Harper held back tears to keep her sister steady. "But it ends tonight. Help me stop this. Let's send Riley back to wherever she came from."

Mara's response was a quick, earnest nod, her chin moving in determined jerks. Harper had seen her so vulnerable. Riley's visits had stripped her down to her most raw, exposed self—a side she seldom showed to anyone, even Harper.

As Mara rose to her feet, Harper noticed for the first time that she'd been wearing the same clothes for days. That detail wouldn't have caught her attention, it wasn't something Mara ever concerned herself with either. But since Riley had come into the picture, everything had changed; Mara wasn't herself anymore, and neither was Harper.

"There's a house full of people. We need to leave with no one noticing." Harper looked toward the door.

"People?"

Mara's tone carried a mix of confusion and fear, but Harper didn't explain about the strange guests, the creatures lurking outside, Caspar's unsettling story, or the tunnel they'd be digging in before dawn. Instead, she nodded, a broken smile spread across her face—another thing they now shared.

Traversing the highway was easier than Harper had expected, though the shadows came alive, twisting into shapes of creatures lurking along every path to Riley's farmhouse. Her anxiety ratcheted up with each step, heartbeat thrumming at the thought of encountering a beast. She clutched the shovel like a spear, ready for anything. But they made it to the porch without a single glimpse of movement.

The silence was eerie—a hollow, unnatural quiet. Moxahala was alive with the calls of coyotes, barking dogs, and night creatures. But now, only the wind whispered around them, as if even the animals had fled. Mara stayed close, her presence a comforting shadow, though Harper could tell her sister was a shell of her former self. She took some comfort knowing that night would end their misery.

As they stepped onto the porch, the front door swung inward with a slow creak. Harper exchanged a wary glance with Mara.

"A welcome wagon?" Mara murmured.

Harper tried to remember if they'd shut the door on their last visit, but the memory was elusive. Instead of dwelling on it, she stepped forward, compelled by an invisible force drawing her inside.

She thought about grabbing one of Riley's items from the bag, THEN changed her mind. She needed to be light on her feet as she ventured into the house.

The darkness swallowed them, carrying a thick scent of mold and decay that clung to their skin. The scent was unbearable, a suffocating presence that filled the room and tickled the back of her throat. The walls groaned under the weight of the seasons. The wood expanding and contracting with each temperature swing, giving the place an air of slow decay. The scent reminded her of the rotten earth from an old novel, a dark tomb keeping secrets from the light.

That's what Riley's farmhouse had become—a legacy of death. Riley's parents had abandoned it, leaving a haunted monument to the life they'd lost. Harper thought of her own child, lost too soon, and she experienced the depths of a mother's emptiness. A heart, once full of promise, became a sieve, unable to hold anything but sorrow.

They moved through the home in silence, their steps guided by memory, brushing past furniture that stood as silent witnesses to a forgotten horror. Harper sensed Mara close behind, as familiar as her own shadow.

In the kitchen, the smell of rotting food clung to the air, overpowering everything. It was as if the house itself was decomposing, waiting for someone to release its final, terrible secret.

"God, that's awful." Harper covering her nose as she hurried to the basement door, eager to escape the nauseating stench. She swung the door open, and a jolt of fear ran through her as she recalled the eerie face they'd seen on the thermal device. Though nothing stirred on the staircase below, she descended anyway, Mara at her back.

They huddled together at the bottom of the stairs. Harper fumbled through her bag until her fingers closed around a road flare, striking it to life with a satisfying hiss. A red glow bathed the cellar, casting sinister shadows along the walls. She held the flare like a torch, feeling a grim satisfaction at the crackling flame.

Moving further into the tunnel, the red light stretched, distorting the support beams. Shadows leaped at them, twisting into shapes before fading into harmless curves in the soil. The path took longer than before. Fear stretched each step as the darkness thickened around them. She followed the faint drag marks left from Riley's abduction, small signs she might have missed had she not been looking.

At last, Harper's head bumped against an obstruction. The tunnel ended, a mound of earth blocking their path. She laid the flare on the ground, casting a semicircle of light over the dirt, and spat on her hands, rubbing them together before gripping the shovel. She was pissed at herself for not packing gloves. Mara watched her, a strange intensity in her gaze as Harper drove the shovel into the soil.

"Why did you—" Harper's voice faltered. "Why did you burn our parents?" she asked, not daring to stop her digging.

"You never asked me that before. I wonder why." Mara's voice was soft, thoughtful. "Every night our parents tucked us in, there was always another visit later. He'd creep in, quiet as a shadow, and make me promise to be just as quiet."

Harper's heart hammered, but she kept digging, afraid her sister's confession might dry up if she stopped.

"He was always the same—never changed. I didn't question it. He was our father."

"I didn't know."

"No, but that's not why I burned them."

Harper paused, glancing back.

"I had a boyfriend once." Mara stared past her sister. "He loved me and wanted to take me away. When I told him what was happening, he promised we'd leave. But our father found out and beat me. That night, something in me broke." Mara's voice turned bitter. "So, I waited. I waited until deep into the night. I poured gasoline over their bed, struck a match..." Her voice wavered but didn't break. "I watched them burn."

Harper didn't respond. The horror of Mara's admission settled over her as she continued shoveling, only silence accompanying the rhythmic push of dirt. After an hour of hard digging, she broke through to an opening, revealing an archway beneath the mounds of soil.

A shiver ran through her as she dropped the shovel and began clawing at the dirt, widening the gap until it was large enough for her to slip through. Mara followed close behind.

They found themselves beneath a vast structure, the beams and floor joists forming a shadowed ceiling overhead.

"Oh, my God!" It finally made sense. "We're under Moxie Manor."

"We should leave this alone."

Harper shook her head, defiant. "We're so close. We can end this." She began laying out Riley's belongings in a careful circle, hoping they'd reveal some last clue to the girl's fate. She lifted the camera, aiming it at the foundation and snapping a photo.

Hum.

She fanned the film, watching as the image of Riley's face took form. A face with sunken eyes and a sickly smile. She dropped the photo, chilled by the cruel expression on the child's ghostly face.

"To hell with that." Harper slipped on Riley's glasses for another view.

The glasses revealed a faint, red line in the air, tracing a path toward a floorboard at the far end of the cellar.

"This way," she whispered, urging Mara forward. The trail grew narrow as they moved until she saw a section of the ceiling blocked by a nailed plywood board.

"We shouldn't."

Harper ignored the warning, slid her fingers on the edge of the plywood, and used her weight to pull the board away. The length of the plywood tore away, some carpenter nails stuck to the wood while others remain as jagged spikes hanging from the supports.

The wood didn't react as she thought it would probably because she never thought ahead. Along with the plywood, Riley's body crashed to the dirt floor in front of her.

The body of the little girl wasn't a skeleton, but a shrunken form with skin holding everything together. When Riley's body tumbled to the ground, it behaved like a marionette.

The event shocked Harper, dug into empathy, and tore into her realization that there were no happy endings left in the world. Seeing a child treated with such disrespect deflated her hope for humanity. If she took the time to reflect on how it was going to end when she found the missing girl, this was the way it was always going to finish. As painful as it was, Harper forced her eyes over the girl's body, taking in every detail. Making sure she missed nothing with her mental inventory.

Still dressed in pajamas, she saw her in the vision. A wound on her side, where the abductor punctured her, was visible. The blood she was sure was once bright red and had dried to an ugly brown. Duct tape that she saw wrapped around her head and mouth remained, but it sat loose on her now that her skin lost its plumpness.

When she spilled on the surface, an item bounced from atop her chest to the ground next to Harper's feet. A pocketknife. A solid-looking kind that most grandfathers kept for slicing an apple or opening an envelope peered at her from below. Harper reached for it.

"What are you doing?" Mara asked.

She didn't get an answer. Instead, Harper tucked her hand to the sleeve of her shirt and carefully clasped the knife.

"In case the murderer's fingerprints are still on it." She slipped it into the front pocket of her jeans. With the weapon in a safe spot, she resumed her survey of the dead girl. The knife struck a chord. The abdomen wound stuck out like a sore thumb but as she examined her further, there was no other evidence that the knife was ever used again.

"But how did you die?" she whispered to the girl.

Tracing the form of Riley from her bare feet to the top of her head she saw something out of place. A discoloration of the skin around her neck.

"She didn't die from a stabbing." Harper pointed. "Her throat. Right there. Riley was strangled." Mara never looked her way. "And her eye. It's completely blood-red. Her capillaries collapsed. Even her—" Harper went quiet. She studied Riley's hand, clenched into a fist long after death.

Dangling from tiny fingers was a silver bracelet.

"That's yours. How is your bracelet between her fingers?" Harper asked but couldn't bring herself to make eye contact. "All the girls in Caspar's books ended with strangulation, but no authorities found the bodies. You killed them. Every single one. And the woman found on our property. What'd you fuckin' do, Mara?" Harper turned to find Mara, who no longer stood beside her. She scanned the cellar, doused in red light, and saw her sister was gone.

Chapter Twenty-Eight

HIDDEN TREASURE

Caspar sprinted for the hall library, avoiding a twisted ankle as he stumbled over the scattered pile of books he'd already forgotten about. Sedge was close behind, while Carol trailed at a safer distance.

The scraping sounds that had vanished in Matt's room now echoed from behind the library shelves, drawing their attention in unison. From another part of the church, Winston's voice cut through the silence. "What was that?"

"Quiet," Caspar hissed back.

They clambered over the blockade of fallen books, and Caspar pressed a finger to his lips, signaling the others to listen as he leaned closer to the wall. The rustling continued, growing louder as it moved through the walls toward the main hall.

Caspar swallowed; his long-standing fear of vermin was trivial when replaced by the terror of watching Matt disappear into the spaces between the walls.

Winston appeared from the kitchen, pausing. "The demon creature is out like a light. I think—" Caspar raised a hand, silencing him. The others gathered around him in the center of the room, their eyes following the scraping sounds that crept up the right side of the church, ascending toward the ceiling.

"What is that?" Winston asked, gnawing his nail, his gaze darting from side to side.

Sedge said what they all feared, "It's Sarah Deville."

"Bullshit," Winston scoffed.

"Stop moving," Caspar warned. The sound stopped, and all eyes lifted to the rafters, where the shadows obscured everything above.

Sedge edged closer, whispering into Caspar's ear. "Do you see her?"

Caspar squinted, searching for any trace of movement. "Right there." Sedge pointed toward a shadowed face high above Winston. Caspar beckoned Winston forward with a subtle wave.

"Get over here."

"What the hell are you talking about?" Winston remained in his spot.

But before he could react further, a dark shape plummeted from the rafters, landing above Winston. As the officer looked up, his eyes went wide in horror. Sarah Deville's ghostly form lunged, yanking him into the air, his limbs flailing and dragging him into the shadows. A scream reverberated through the hall.

They couldn't see him, but Sarah's pale, menacing face appeared, flickering like a ghastly apparition as she thrashed against him in the dark.

Caspar whipped out his phone, turning on its flashlight with the speed of a cop drawing a weapon. He aimed the beam upward, catching the struggle in its dim glow.

Carol gasped, her hand flying to her mouth as the light illuminated Sarah, her lips stretched into a hideous snarl as she bit into Winston's throat.

"Hit the lights!" Caspar shouted, pointing to the switch nearby.

Carol lunged forward, flipping it and flooding the hall with bright light. In an instant, Sarah vanished, but Winston, suspended in her grasp, fell.

He plummeted two stories, hitting the wooden floor with a sickening thud. The sound was brutal, like a bag of cement slamming onto concrete. Blood pooled, darkening the floorboards. Winston lay motionless.

They rushed to his side, glancing at the now-empty rafters, half-expecting Sarah to reappear. Winston's body convulsed, broken limbs twisted, his clothes stretched tight over fractured bones. The gash on his neck bore a gruesome mark where Sarah's teeth had torn into him.

They stood in stunned silence, watching as Winston's body spasmed in grotesque, involuntary twitches. Carol turned away. Her face contorted in revulsion as she buried herself in Sedge's chest. "I can't look at this anymore," she whimpered.

Caspar met Sedge's eyes, his expression weary and resigned. "I'll drag him outside," he said.

Chapter Twenty-Nine

BASEMENT RESCUE

The manor swayed, struck by something so immense that Harper couldn't even guess what it was. If Moxie Manor was a slumbering, breathing creature before, it was now wide awake and gasping for air.

On shaky legs, she climbed up from the underground, never expecting she'd be coming from her own cellar. The thought that Mara could come out of the asylum as a "refurbished" human being—a person who could live as if nothing had happened—made Harper feel sick.

It was foolish optimism to think that someone who had killed their own parents would just buy a condo and carry on. Yet she had clung to that hope, allowing the thought of having her last remaining family member cloud her instincts.

The ghastly discovery chilled her, but her concern for Mara outweighed her fear.

Then a more chilling thought crept in; what if Caspar had something to do with these girls' deaths, too?

Caspar and Mara had once been close, but she'd noticed him avoiding her. She had dismissed it as growing apart. Shaking her head, she'd have to unravel these questions later.

She rushed through the back half of the church toward the library and stopped short, her jaw dropping. Scattered across her path lay every book. She wracked her brain, trying to understand how an avalanche of books even happened.

Sedge and Carol, clutching each other in the main hall, turned around as she approached.

"Where's Caspar?" she asked.

"He went outside," Sedge stammered, then added, "He took the body…"

"Come with me." Harper tugged them both along, snapping their attention back as they scrambled to keep up.

"Where are we going?" Carol asked, quickening her pace.

"I need you to tell me I'm not going crazy."

When they reached the sea of fallen books, she could tell by their lack of surprise that they'd already crossed it. To their credit, they didn't complain as they stumbled over the scattered volumes again.

At the cellar door, Harper swung it open. Carol's face paled, no doubt recalling her last harrowing descent. "Don't worry," Harper reassured. "Nothing down there will hurt you."

Carol wasn't convinced, but she and Sedge followed her down the creaking stairs. At the bottom, Harper flicked on the light, flooding the cellar with a brightness that WAS a welcome change from the flare's red glow.

"See this." She led them deeper. But before she could continue, Carol caught her hand, bringing her fingers into the light.

"Wait. What happened here?" she asked, staring at her fingertips, which were red and nail-less. The mud caked on some of them couldn't cover the damage. Sedge as he noticed her missing patches of hair and cracked teeth.

"Harper…" Sedge whispered. "Your teeth. They're all broken."

The memory of Mara wielding a hammer flashed in Harper's mind, distant and unreal. She shook it off. "Don't worry about that right now. There's something I need to show you."

She led them further, watching them stumble forward like zombies, every step hesitant. Finally, she pointed at a spot in the cellar. "There."

Carol clutched her mouth in horror. "Riley was under your roof the whole time?"

"Riley? The missing girl from Caspar's novel?" Sedge asked, stepping back from the gruesome sight at his feet.

"I know who did this."

"You do?" Sedge looked at her, his face a mix of confusion and horror.

"It was Mara. My sister."

"That can't be possible. She didn't even own this church when it happened."

Harper pointed to the tunnel's entrance. "I followed the tunnel from Riley's home, and it led here."

Sedge was processing her words, but Carol already connected the dots. "When was the last time you saw Mara?"

"Tonight. Just minutes ago."

"But she's been staying here for weeks, and I haven't seen her once," Sedge said.

Harper's voice softened. "We all had dinner together when she first arrived. When you told us those stories about the church ... and Sarah Deville."

Sedge's brow furrowed. "I remember the night, but Mara wasn't there. I've yet to meet her."

Harper's face fell, her mind racing through fragmented memories. "She even mentioned how you ignored her." she laughed.

"I missed that. What did you say?" Sedge asked, but before she could answer, a voice interrupted.

"I think we've heard enough."

Harper froze. Mara stood between her and Carol. As Harper opened her mouth to speak, she noticed the pocketknife in Mara's hand. The same one Harper had found with Riley. When she checked her pocket, it was gone.

"How did you get that from me?" Harper asked, her voice tight with fear.

"A woman has her ways." A sly smile spreading across Mara's face. "Stay calm."

Out of the corner of her eye, Harper saw Mara move. She registered what was happening before a small red spot bloomed on Carol's chest, expanding into a dark, spreading stain.

Carol's face twisted with shock and horror, her mouth falling open as she accepted her fate. She slumped into Sedge's arms, sliding to the floor.

"Why did you do that?" Harper screamed, her voice cracking as she looked at Mara.

"Look in your hand," Sedge pleaded.

Harper glanced down at her right hand, and horror flooded her. The knife, once in her sister's hand, was visible in her own, its blade stained red, drops of blood pooling on her fist. She raised her eyes to where Mara had been standing, only to find the spot empty.

"I ... I don't understand." Harper's mind reeled.

"There is no Mara," Sedge turned his attention to Carol. He removed his shirt and pressed it against the wound in her chest, trying to stem the bleeding.

"That's not true," Harper said. She couldn't take her eyes off the knife. It was unnatural in her grip, like it could somehow leap into someone else's hand if she dared look away.

Her thoughts blurred, as though a shadow had passed over her mind. She took a hesitant step back toward the staircase.

"Wait," Sedge said with desperation. "Help me get her upstairs." But Harper moved on, his words fading into the background until all that remained was silence.

Chapter Thirty

High Price to Pay

Caspar watched the church sway, like a ghost ship adrift. The rafters creaked like timber on a ship's deck, forming a haunting symphony, a discordant melody of wood and metal that filled the air with unease. With each lurch and dip, the floor tilted at precarious angles, forcing Caspar to steady himself in the main hall.

In a surreal haze, he watched as Sedge entered, dragging someone with him. Under normal circumstances, this would have terrified him, but absorbed in the church's rocking, he observed it with detached curiosity. Suspended light fixtures swung on their chains, casting hypnotic shadows.

His vision blurred into trails, reminding him of his first time getting high as a teenager—an out-of-body experience.

He refocused, pulling himself back to reality as Sedge's urgent voice pierced the fog.

Carol lay in Sedge's lap, her gaze fixed on the ceiling. "It was her. She did this," she said.

Caspar crouched beside her, his focus sharpening. "What happened?"

"Harper happened. She thinks her sister is here. She was talking to air. There was nothing there."

"Mara was never in an asylum, was she?"

Caspar closed his eyes, then sank down beside them. "No. It was Harper who lived in the asylum after their parents died. I met her there."

Sedge's face twisted with confusion and horror.

"I loved Mara,' he said a lifted his head toward the swinging light. "We were going to get married."

"Why didn't you?"

"The night she planned to tell her parents, Mara set their room on fire. That's when Harper stabbed her sister to death."

Sedge's eyes widened. "Is that true?"

"According to the authorities," Caspar said.

"You went to the asylum to visit Harper and what ... fell in love with her?"

Caspar looked down, ashamed. "I went there looking for answers, but it was Mara speaking. Not Harper. I can't explain it. I'd visited as often as I could, desperate for those moments when Mara would shine through. Over time, I even tried to make Harper trust and love me, hoping to keep Mara alive."

Sedge's expression soured. "You manipulated Harper—made her fall for you, just to be near Mara?

"No."

"And the murders? All those children killed for your novels—those were Mara, weren't they?"

"At first, I thought it was someone else or maybe Harper. I received an anonymous tip about a child's abduction with details that weren't public. I assumed it was someone on the inside, a detective. But Mara ... she confessed to the murder. And the stories wrote themselves."

"She confessed about killing children, and you let it go on?" Sedge's voice trembled with anger. "Another girl, another book—over and over?"

Caspar broke down, a sob racking his chest. "I had Mara ... and I had the writing career I'd always dreamed of. But—"

"Something changed."

"Harper and I ... *we* fell in love. Mara showed up less and less, only reappearing to tell me what my next book was about."

"And Eliza and I researched those murders for you, thinking they were cases you stumbled upon."

Caspar nodded, unable to meet his gaze.

Sedge looked down at Carol, clinging to life. "I don't give a damn how sorry you are!"

Snickers trotted over, his claws tapping on the floor. "Are you ready to complete your journey?" Snickers asked, a strange glint in his eye.

"What are you talking about?"

The dog lifted his snout, then unleashed a bark that echoed through the hall. A soft pounding sounded from the front doors, then a crash something massive smashed against them.

"It's the police station all over again." Sedge pulled Carol closer. "I guess this is it."

The pounding intensified, with more creatures slamming against the doors in a relentless rhythm.

"A hero's sacrifice. Nothing is more rewarding," Snickers said. "This is your moment—when a character shows their true nature."

"Who's making the sacrifice?" Sedge asked, panic creeping into his voice.

With a splintering crack, the doors burst open, and moon howlers flooded the room—massive, snarling creatures with jaws powerful enough to shatter bones. Paralyzed by the intruders, the pack surrounded them.

"The master has arrived," Snickers said. The beasts went still, as if awaiting a command.

Caspar's stomach twisted. "You think I'm going with them?"

"It's an honor to serve the dark watcher," Snickers replied.

"It wasn't me. It was my writing. I just went along with everything for my art. You can't hold that against me. I didn't have a choice."

Snickers nodded, as though humoring him. The watcher lifted his staff, and two of the largest moon howlers seized Caspar's legs, yanking him to the ground. He pressed his hands together, praying.

"Wait, wait! Just hold on for a second. I can make things right," he begged.

"You will make an obedient moon howler." A twisted smile spread across the dog's face. The beasts dragged Caspar across the floor, his fingers scraping against the wood as he struggled in vain.

Sedge looked down at Carol, her body limp. The dark watcher made a small motion with his staff, and the remaining moon howlers moved back, releasing their snarling jaws from her body.

"We have our prize." Snickers locked eyes with Sedge.

"Why me?" Caspar asked with terror filling his expression.

"Because you have the perfect temperament. selfish, fearful, and blood-thirsty."

The pack, the watcher, and even Snickers moved to the exit. Caspar, helpless in the creatures' jaws, screamed for Sedge, for Harper—for anyone who could save him. But no one came to his aid. They pulled him through the door and out into the night.

Chapter Thirty-One

DEVIL'S DEAL

Harper's gaze remained fixed on the knife—and the hand holding it—all the way to her spare bedroom. Blood from the blade, Carol's blood, left a twisted trail of crimson breadcrumbs behind her, as if inviting the darkness to follow.

Questions flooded her mind, each one harder than the last: *Where was Mara? Had she ever been here? Was Caspar involved in the killings?* And the worst question of all: *Had Mara used her body like a puppet to carry out these horrors?* She thought of Riley°, of all the others, then of Caspar—how he'd discussed the deaths as if they were mere plot points. The thought made her stomach churn.

And if he had known Mara was there all along, why had he stayed? The notion that he might have found some thrill in dining with or even making love to her while Mara hid inside was revolting. Or worse, she was the prisoner as they ... she didn't want to think of it anymore.

When she entered the guest bedroom, she found Mara lying on the floor, asleep as always.

Harper moved to the bed Mara never slept in and emptied the beach bag, spreading the contents across the bed with her palm. The Polaroids caught her attention first, the one of Mara and Twix. She remembered Mara's irritation when she'd taken it. She held the picture up.

Mara was missing from the photo. Only Twix appeared. Her stomach lurched and as the it all came flooding in, she let the photo drop.

Harper replayed every memory of her sister. Was she there? At least since her release from the asylum. But doubt gnawed at her. *Sedge is trying to make you feel crazy. This picture proves nothing,* she tried to tell herself, yet she couldn't deny the truth of Riley's corpse.

Clutching Riley's last possessions, Harper walked past her sister's sleeping form. *Or was she really sleeping?* The unsettling thought clawed at her. Watching her sister's stillness, she noticed with horror, that Mara's chest didn't rise or fall. She leaned closer—no sign of breath. A realization took hold. *Had she murdered those children herself? Was she responsible for everything described in Caspar's novels?*

Harper steadied herself. If she was the one who always "woke" Mara, that meant she gave her the power to use *her* and she wasn't about to do it again. She set the baby monitor in the middle of the room, plugged it in, and powered it on. She gathered Riley's objects, balancing them in her arms, and placed the Walkman at her hip, slung the camera around her neck, and slipped the motel key into her pocket. With everything arranged in a circle around the monitor, she rewound the tape, listening to the whining of the cassette's wheels. Just as she prepared to put on the glasses, a chilling realization struck her—the knife was missing.

She spun around, searching the room, but it was nowhere in sight. Her gaze landed on Mara, now standing by the door, holding the knife against Twix's throat.

"I'll kill him." Mara pressed the blade against the dog's fur.

"Why would you do that?"

"Because you killed me," Mara said. She held out the knife, its edge catching the light. "You used this very blade. I was trying to set us free, and you rewarded me with a knife to the throat."

"No, that's not true. They took you to the hospital, to help you get better," her voice trembled.

"That's where *they* sent *you*. They believed you killed our parents, right along with me."

Harper staggered back, her world fracturing. "Then you're ... not alive. You're ... a ghost?"

"I'm as alive as you are." Mara smirked, a strange gleam in her eye. "When I see through your eyes, move your limbs, even touch *my* husband—what difference does it make?"

"Your husband?" Harper repeated, a fresh horror dawning.

"Did you ever wonder why I set the fire that killed our parents? Our father's 'visits' were bad enough, but when he found out about my boyfriend, he threatened to hurt him."

"Caspar?" Harper whispered, feeling herself unraveling.

Mara's smirk deepened. "Caspar was mine. He only married you to be with me. I killed those girls to give him the career he deserved. What have *you* ever done for him?"

"I'll go to the police—I'll tell them everything!" Harper threatened.

"And tell them what? That your dead sister possessed you to kill children?" Mara taunted. "Your fingerprints are at every crime scene. They'll laugh you straight into a prison cell."

"Then why help me track down Riley's killer? Why help me hunt for a murderer if we were both involved?" Harper demanded.

"I needed a way back."

"A way back to what?"

"To Caspar. Over time, he fell for *you.*" Mara's bitterness shone through. "So sometimes I pretended to be you—just to keep him interested. But then he started wanting you, and only you. That's when I had to kill again, just to get him to notice me. When he told me you were pregnant, that's when everything changed."

"What are you saying?" Harper demanded, dread pooling in her stomach.

"I took care of it. I would not let *us* have an awful life."

Harper's mind spun, memories fragmenting. She was sure Caspar consoled her after the miscarriage ... or had he? Had Mara?

"Why didn't you talk to me?"

"What was I supposed to say? Oh, by the way," Mara paused, "your dead sister killed your baby?" she added with a laugh, a cruel, hollow sound that cut through her soul.

A surge of fury, grief, and guilt overwhelmed Harper. She'd lived her life as a vessel, keeping her sister's spirit alive. But as the truth settled over her, she wanted control.

Her hand found the knife, and she saw the shock on Mara's face, her fingers now empty. She opened the door, letting Twix escape, then turned back to face her sister.

Holding steady, Harper walked to the center of the room and plugged the speaker cable from her laptop into the Walkman, pressing play. She placed the glasses on her face, and through the lenses, Mara's true form emerged.

Gone were her angelic features. Her eyes sank into hollow, blackened sockets; her skin stretched tight over her bones, resembling a twisted corpse. The Eagles' Hotel California played as a pale light flickered in the baby monitor—Riley's face solidifying on the screen.

The ghostly outline grew with her form building in the room like a figure returning from the dead. Harper could feel her rage, her vengeance. The song's urgency matched the beat of Harper's pulse as Riley, in her spectral form, turned to face Mara.

Mara recoiled, her voice quivering. "Don't let her do this, Harper. You need me. Together, we can make everything right. You can even have Caspar back."

But Harper said nothing, meeting Riley's determined gaze as the spirit advanced on a sister that was never in her picture°.

"It's okay. I don't want him."

Riley bent down to Mara's level, lifting her hands to cradle her sister's face. Harper flinched, expecting the girl to squeeze the life out of her as she had tried before. But Riley cupped Mara's cheeks like a mother showing affection to a child.

Mara's eyes welled with tears, and Riley's gaze mirrored the sorrow. As Riley pressed her palms more firmly against Mara's skin, a tremor coursed through Mara's body, beginning in her shoulders, and spreading downward. Her frail frame shrank, diminishing even further as the song reached its crescendo.

Memories that were never hers, slipped through the cracks and she saw herself carry out the death of the children. Tears fell from her eyes as she watched herself being led by Mara into the clinic that took her child from her. With wetness streaming down her cheeks, she watched her sister become a mere shadow.

Just before the end, Mara looked back at Harper, her expression a mixture of regret and pleading. And then, as Harper watched, she saw her sister fade away. The presence inside her slipped free, like a taut rubber band snapping and releasing all tension. Mara was gone.

Riley remained in her place; her hands still poised in the air, as if holding onto Mara's neck. After a moment, she stood, crossing the room to face Harper.

"I'm sorry," Harper's voice broke. She couldn't think of anything else to say. Riley's expression softened, and she mouthed the words, "It's okay."

Gathering the objects together, Riley gave a faint smile before turning away. She moved toward the wall and, without hesitation, passed through the bricks as though they were never solid. Harper rushed to the window, watching the small, solitary figure emerge on the other side. Riley's form drifted across the front of the church property, crossed the highway, and made her way up the hill toward the house where she had once lived with her family.

As Riley's slipped out of sight, Harper closed her eyes, hoping that she—and the other children—found peace. She was FREE.

Chapter Thirty-Two

LEFTOVERS

Sedge concentrated on his breath as he stood next to Harper. They stared up at the Reclamation Mental Health facility. The former prison towered over them, daring them to step inside.

"Is Mara gone. I mean, really gone?"

Harper stared at the massive facility and shrugged. "You're guess is as good as mine. If she's still with me, we'll have an eternity to work it out." Harper smiled.

"You never got to say goodbye to Caspar."

"I didn't have to. He left his cologne on Mara's ghost. That was more than enough closure."

"Most women would just slash the tires. You, uh... let your dead sister take the wheel."

"Technically, she took the whole car. I was just in the trunk. Spiritually speaking."

"What made you buy the items that brought Riley back?"

"I didn't buy her things. Not really. They found me. She followed me home, Sedge. She showed me things I was never supposed to see—people's sins, their pasts, their deaths."

"Why would you let her suck you into her world?"

"At first, I thought I was helping her. Helping her find peace. But she didn't want peace. She wanted company. So, I gave her company."

"I meant Mara."

"Well, it wasn't *me*. It was *her*. I just provided the ambiance. Think of me as the haunted Airbnb." Harper went quiet. "I didn't kill. I just watched. I saw everything and made myself forget. I didn't even know it was possible. But it is," Harper said, with tears in her eyes.

"You're going to be okay here." Sedge watched the officers escort her into the facility.

"Good. Maybe I can finally get some sleep without my sister hijacking my body." Harper took one last look before Sedge led her inside her new home.

Officers took Harper into custody as a reporter moved closer to Sedge, shifting from one foot to the other, a subtle twitch that Sedge thought betrayed her nerves. Or, more precisely, the reporter was eager to make the most of a rare chance to speak with someone involved in the Moxahala Massacre.

Sedge watched as guards from the mental facility prepared Harper for entry. One condition of her surrender for evaluation had been that he could escort her. The other condition was sitting in his arms: Twix, the young border collie. Though not yet grown, the puppy was getting heavier by the minute, and Sedge set him down.

"You stay put," he ordered. He kept a firm grip on the leash. His eyes found Harper again as the guards searched through her belongings.

"Scott Sedge, right?" The reporter's voice brought him back.

"Yes."

"Do you know the location of author Caspar Finch?"

Straight to the point—no small talk, no warm-up. She must have thought she'd get only a few questions in, so she wasn't holding back. Sedge kept his eyes on the orderlies while they cataloged Harper's things.

"I don't." He replied he had a good idea Caspar was deep in the Ohio woods. Poor bastard. The reporter pressed on, unfazed by his answer.

"You worked for Caspar," she said in an accusing tone. "How did you not know he was orchestrating these murders for his novels? Some in the media believe that his publicist, Eliza, heard the authorities were closing in, and that's why she went into hiding."

Sedge held back a laugh. Even if things continued as they had for another ten years, the authorities would know as much as they did. Nothing.

"Eliza was always a kind and generous person," he replied. "She had no reason to run, and that she's missing now only gives me more reason to worry. My thoughts are with her and her family until we get some answers."

The reporter fumbled with her notes, unprepared for his composed response. This interview wasn't going as she'd hoped.

"Some believe that Moxie Manor itself—the former church—caused these deaths. What do you say to that?"

Sedge's gaze drifted to Harper, who was nodding at the guards. After a moment, as if sensing his thoughts, she glanced his way. Harper—about to enter an asylum for the second time in her life—smiled and nodded to him. Sedge returned the gesture, then turned back to the reporter. For the first time during the interview, he was about to give her what she wanted.

"In my career, I've come across plenty of bad people," he said. "And I've seen enough to know there are things we can't explain." The reporter's eyes widened, hanging on his words. "But I have never stepped foot in a place as evil as Moxie Manor. I only got a glimpse of what that church is capable of, but this won't be the last time you hear about it. As terrible as the allegations are against Caspar—and they are terrible—they're nothing compared to the souls lost in that unholy place."

A sudden yelp from Twix made them both turn.

"Impatient, are you?" Sedge asked, looking down at the dog, who returned his gaze with a tilt of his head.

"What breed is he?" the reporter asked. "He's so expressive."

Sedge bent down and stroked Twix's fur. "He's a border collie."

"It's like he wants to say something."

Sedge chuckled, leaning closer to the dog. "Is that true, Twix? Do you have something to say?"

Twix glanced from the reporter to Sedge. Then he opened his mouth.

Acknowledgements

I'd first like to first mention my family—the unsung heroes who endured countless hours of me vanishing behind a closed door, lost in another world for far too long and far too often. Your patience and support mean everything.

A heartfelt thanks to the incredible folks of Appalachia, Perry County, and Southeast Ohio. Though my church stands proudly in the town of Moxahala, it's the neighboring communities—Corning, New Lexington, Crooksville, Shawnee, Roseville, and Zanesville—have always wrapped my family in a warm sense of belonging. Your kindness doesn't go unnoticed. And I hope you will please respect the privacy of Moxie Manor and any future owners.

Shoutout to my brilliant editors, Elle Turpitt and Ellie Killiam, who weren't afraid to drag my missteps out so I could mercilessly cut them. And to my gifted cover designer, Matt Seff Barnes—you breathed life into my vision and gave it a face that spoke before a single word was read.

And to my loyal readers—you champions of curiosity—thank you. You've endured my relentless pursuit to make every book an experience, not just a story. Sometimes I stick the landing; sometimes I go down in flames. Either way, you ride shotgun, and I'm eternally grateful.

About the Author

Jerry Roth's work spans both traditional and indie publishing. He has written for Ohio newspapers and sports articles for the *Disc Golf Pro Tour*. After reading *The Stand* by Stephen King, he became passionate about creating his own work of fiction. He currently lives in Ohio with his wife Tricia and his two children, Jesse and Lea.

About the dog

Snickers is a pure breed Border Collie born in Ohio to an Amish family. At the time of writing this novel, Snickers was a active puppy that sniffed the church to let us know of visitors, regular or supernatural. There's nothing more sobering than a dog barking at the air itself.

St. Pious church (Moxie Manor) built in 1908.

More about the Author